PAGAN KING

Gods and Kings Book II

M J Porter

M J Publishing

Copyright © 2016,2022 M J Porter

Porter, M J Pagan King (previously published as Maserfeld: A Novel of 641)
Copyright ©2016, 2022 Porter, M.J,
All characters and events in this publication, other than those clearly in the public domain, are fictitious and any resemblance to actual persons, living or dead, is purely coincidental.

ALL RIGHTS RESERVED. No part of this publication may be reproduced, stored in a retrieval system or transmitted in any form or by any means without the prior written permission of the author, nor be otherwise circulated in any form of binding or cover other than that in which it is published and without a similar condition being imposed on the subsequent buyer.

ISBN: 9781914332197 (ebook)
ISBN: 9781976952852 (paperback - Amazon)
ISBN: 9781914332210 (paperback)
ISBN: 9781914332159 (hardback)

Cover design by Shaun at Flintlock Covers

CONTENTS

Title Page
Copyright
Place names and where they are (roughly)   1
⌘ Prologue ⌘   3
⌘ Chapter 1 ⌘   9
Chapter 2   16
✢Chapter 3✢   23
✢Chapter 4✢   29
✢Chapter 5✢   37
⌘ Chapter 6 ⌘   43
⌘ Chapter 7 ⌘   47
Chapter 8   58
✢Chapter 9✢   73
✢Chapter 10✢   76
✢Chapter 11✢   79
⌘ Chapter 12 ⌘   83
⌘ Chapter 13 ⌘   87
Chapter 14   92
⌘ Chapter 15 ⌘   102
✢Chapter 16✢   107
✢Chapter 17✢   112

⌘ Chapter 18 ⌘	115
⌘ Chapter 19 ⌘	118
Chapter 20	130
✤Chapter 21✤	133
⌘ Chapter 22 ⌘	138
✤Chapter 23✤	147
Chapter 24	152
✤Chapter 25✤	159
⌘ Chapter 26 ⌘	164
⌘ Chapter 27 ⌘	173
✤Chapter 28✤	179
⌘ Chapter 29 ⌘	186
✤Chapter 30✤	193
⌘ Chapter 31 ⌘	198
⌘ Chapter 32 ⌘	207
✤Chapter 33✤	215
⌘ Chapter 34 ⌘	230
✤Chapter 35✤	244
⌘ Chapter 36 ⌘	248
Anglo-Saxon Chronicle	255
Cast of Characters	257
Historical Notes	260
Meet The Author	263

PLACE NAMES AND WHERE THEY ARE (ROUGHLY)

It's extremely difficult to assign firm borders to any of the very early kingdoms. This is how I interpret the many maps/details that are available. It's more than likely far too simplistic but hopefully not 'wrong'.

Gwynedd – North Wales
Powys – North East Wales
Ceredigion – Between Gwynedd and Deheubarth
Deheubarth – (Dyfed) – South East Wales
Dumnonia – Cornwall
Alt Clut – (Strathclyde) North east Scotland
Northumbria – The North of England – including Yorkshire, Northumberland and Cumbria
Deira – Part of Northumbria – Yorkshire
Bernicia – Part of Northumbria – Modern day Northumberland and into the borders with Scotland
Mercia – the Midlands of England
Hwicce – a tribal name for an area of Mercia – roughly the area around Gloucester
Magonsaete – a tribal name for an area of Mercia
Elmet – Ancient Anglo-Saxon kingdom – below Northumbria

Lindsey – Ancient Anglo-Saxon kingdom – above Mercia and below Northumbria
Dal Riata – Ancient kingdom of Scotland and Ireland
The Picts – Ancient kingdom of Scotland
Wessex – southern England
Kent – south east of England
East Anglia – east of England

Symbols

Chapter headings are surrounded by symbols, in an effort to make it easier to decipher the alliance each character subscribes to – some are intentionally left blank. ⌘✤

⌘ PROLOGUE ⌘

Penda of the Hwicce

I hear the news with sullen eyes and a spark of combined annoyance and excitement. I'm trying to look severe, aggrieved, dismayed, even emotional, but immediately all I can see are endless possibilities stretching out before me. With the news, all the kingdoms on this island have undergone another monumental shift. I just need to determine how I can best manipulate the sudden and unexpected, though perhaps not unlooked for, change.

The messenger, his appearance ragged and dishevelled, looks worried. I try to offer a reassuring glance to ensure it's clear the blame for bringing such dire news isn't levelled at his feet. Not that I believe the occurrence is as terrible as he thinks. But already, my mind is racing. It's all I can do to dismiss the man having summoned food and drink for his consumption. I'm trying to look stern, grieved, but it's not how I feel, a faint flutter of anticipation building in my chest.

My ally, Cadwallon of Gwynedd, is dead, killed in battle against the new king, Oswald, of Deira. That means two things to me. Firstly, my ally is over, and that's an unhappy end to what's been a profitable alliance.

Secondly, my ally is dead. And that might just be a good thing. I need to consider all the implications, but already I sense an imminent change in my fortunes. It should be for the better, provided I capitalise fully on Cadwallon's death.

In the past, I've been subservient to Cadwallon, never an equal. We've won a monumental battle together. We brought together almost all the kingdoms against the mighty upstart Edwin of Northumbria. We defeated Edwin and ended any chance of his dynasty regaining what he held. Only the events since then have strained the relationship and made my feelings towards Cadwallon's death ambivalent. I decide that's how I feel, ambivalent, neither sad nor happy. It's happened. Now I need to move on, realign the pieces on the board in my head once more.

I need time to think and to decide what to do.

I decide I require more details from the messenger. But when I look for him within my hall, the man has disappeared, no doubt to see to his needs or those of his horse before he eats. He'll be back. I know that.

For now, I fill my thoughts with what I do know. I still have my brother as an ally, even if I've started to question that alliance as well. I've begun to see that family is not necessarily the best way to keep an ally loyal. Eowa hadn't proved to be quite as effusive in his support and thanks following our victory as I thought he would. Even though he came so late to the alliance, and I had to work hard to have him included. It grates on him, having to be grateful to me, but I've been content to let my brother do what he felt necessary. Now I'm not so sure. I fear he no longer sees any gain in our union. I suspect his thoughts mirror mine.

This could be the perfect opportunity for my brother to wriggle out of our coalition. Eowa could announce that there's no longer any need to maintain the alliance without Cadwallon to unite all of the kingdoms against any possible aggression from a wholly subservient Deira and Bernicia. The intricate web of alliances formed to ensure that Edwin's pretensions to rule all of our island were stopped could be termed obsolete. Eowa will downplay the fact that he pulls away from me in doing so. I know he will, although it'll be his intent all along.

Eowa speaks of family and cohesiveness, but he's the older

brother, the weaker brother. He'll do whatever must be done to do to reverse that trend.

My other ally, Clydog, from the British kingdom of Ceredigion, is still just that. I don't know if Cadwallon's death will pull him from our close working arrangement. I don't see it. But it will depend on who becomes the dominant king amongst the British kingdoms in the wake of Cadwallon's death. It might be Cynddylan, or it might be Cadwallon's son. I'll have to wait and see, and patience is not one of my attributes.

So what should I do?

I did not gain as much as I thought from the victory with Cadwallon. He still saw me as his subordinate. My being here, whilst Cadwallon has met his death at Hatfield Chase in Northumbria, shows how far apart we've grown. I refused to fight his petty wars in the constituent parts of Northumbria, Deira and Bernicia because I disagreed with his tactics. I quickly realised that he hungered for Edwin's death so that he could become him.

I rub my hand across my face and down my neck, feeling the bristle of beard and short shaggy hair on the back of my neck. I'm still a young man. I've accomplished much, but I thirst for more. Need it even. I'm not about to sit around and wait for these men of the new but old Christianity to decide my fate.

The past year hasn't been at all what I imagined it would be when Edwin and his son, Osfrith, met their death at Hæðfeld. Those deaths opened the way for others to rule in Edwin's stead. Cadwallon, driven by his need for revenge, ransacked the kingdom that Edwin so recently presided over, Bernicia, and only met his match when he tried to do the same in Deira.

At first, I supported Cadwallon's intentions. But quickly, I grew tired of his contrary nature and inability to act with any sort of rationale, to see that he'd become what he despised.

The two kings raised in place of Edwin, his predecessor's son, Eanfrith of Bernicia, a man raised in exile amongst the Picts, and Osric, Edwin's cousin, the man who'd fought for us at Hæðfeld, fleeing from Edwin's side when he'd realised it would be impossible for Edwin to win, have both been killed on Cadwallon's axe.

Osric died in battle, a warrior's death at least, but poor Eanfrith, a man I respected and admired, met his death in peace, killed when he came to reaffirm his oaths to Cadwallon.

The slaughter sickened me. Even though I'm supposedly the more terrible man, the relic who believes in the Old Gods of our homelands. I'm not the enlightened man Cadwallon presented himself to be, the faithful follower of the new but old God, a man raised in Christianity and yet who acted outside of it.

For now, I think I should rejoice in Cadwallon's death. No longer will he be able to kill our allies and horde more land and wealth all for himself. No longer will he forget that between the two of us, we raised more than half of the kingdoms on our island to accomplish the task of killing Edwin of Northumbria.

Cadwallon called me to his service assured me he intended to stop Edwin from ruling the entirety of our island. But in the end, all he did was try and become Edwin. Cadwallon wanted Edwin's land, his wealth and his people. Cadwallon had no intention of sharing either.

I have a craving for land, but it's never been as great as Edwin's or Cadwallon's. Both men tried to claim too much land and lost everything due to their aggression.

I don't plan for the same to happen to me.

So what do I plan?

I need to know more.

The messenger is once more sitting within my hall. His face is cleaner now, and his hair tamed from the wild ride. I beckon him toward me. I need to know what he knows and how he knows it.

"Who sent you?" I ask, my tone cajoling. He might not want to tell me, and it never pays to upset the messenger.

"King Eowa," is his immediate response. Already this news starts to worry me. Why would Eowa take it upon himself to tell me? How would he even know before me?

"How did King Eowa come to learn the news?" I ask, sitting forward, my elbows on my knees as the messenger sits before me on the small wooden dais. He continues to eat as quickly as he can, his demeanour distracted. That's good. This way, I might catch him off guard and learn more than Eowa wanted to tell me. Or perhaps he's still worried? Did I dismiss him too quickly earlier? Did he have more bad news to say to me?

I get my answer quickly enough.

"He was at the battle," the man offers after a brief hesitation, eyes bright with the knowledge as our eyes meet. This is unwelcome news.

"Why was King Eowa at the battle?" I muse quietly, but the messenger answers, all the same, thinking I'm speaking to him.

"He's allied with King Oswald of Bernicia. They rode to battle together."

I bolt upright at those words, so casually thrown into our conversation. What game is my brother playing? It seems he'd already abandoned Cadwallon long before thinking to tell me the alliance between them was dead.

"You didn't know?" the messenger asks, thick eyebrows raised high in surprise at my reaction. I didn't bloody know because my brother didn't think to tell me. This messenger is telling me something important of which I should have already been aware. This means the messenger before me is more than just a helpful message from my brother.

My brother has abandoned our alliance, the one I've only been honouring because he's my brother, and I must do as my father commanded before he died. Our father left a proxy to ensure I allied with my brother, and we didn't become enemies. Our father told me of a prophecy when I was a child. To this day, I've honoured his injunction, anything to stop it from becoming the truth. Eowa doesn't share my compunction, but then, my father swore me to secrecy over the whole thing.

Eowa and the new King Oswald are allies, so my brother and I no longer are.

"What are your instructions now?" I ask the man, but he shrugs his shoulders. My brother didn't tell him what to do after delivering the message. The bastard. He sent this man to his death and thought nothing of it.

I make a small hand signal to Herebrod. He comes to lead the man away, kindly, taking him outside on some pretext or another. Herebrod carries grief for the death of Eanfrith of Bernicia at Cadwallon's hand. Ever since then, I've allowed Herebrod to kill anyone who needs to be killed. It's not a solution but more a balm to calm him until revenge can be enacted.

The messenger has just joined the ever-growing list of men who've disappointed me in their allegiances and their actions.

Fuck.

My brother has outmanoeuvred me, and any hope I saw for the future, now that Cadwallon is dead, has contracted before it had even become more than half a reality.

Now I'll need to fight for what little I already hold instead of trying to gain more. And the man I'll need to fight is my brother, the only person who could possibly have a claim on the land of the Hwicce and the land I claim as both my birthright and blood right. I won this land in battle. That's more than Eowa's ever done. Until now.

Fuck.

Lord Eadfrith, son of King Edwin, meets my eyes. He's my prisoner and my friend, but in the face of this news, he wears his fate in subdued eyes and the anxious twirling of a loose thread hanging from a fine tunic.

What use do I have for a man whose cousin has just stolen his kingdom? What possible reason would there be for me to keep him alive?

Fuck.

⌘ CHAPTER 1 ⌘

Penda of the Hwicce AD640

The kingdom of the Hwicce⌘

Gunghir is restless beneath my legs. I snap them back angrily to steady him, but he's ageing now, set in his ways, and he's not going to become malleable suddenly. I must still fight him every time I ride him, but I love the battle, the constant tension. I think without it, he'd have died many years ago.

Only his desire to piss me off keeps him going, and will do so for many years to come.

During the long dark days of winter, I feared I'd lose him when he contracted an illness that sapped his strength and made him almost timid. I tried to goad him to get well, but in the end, it was the tender ministrations of my tiny son that brought my horse back to his usual self. With my son, Paeda, he's a soppy wreck, but before me, he snarls and bites as much as he always did.

I'm grateful that my son rescued him and amused that even my foul-tempered horse has become a victim of his winning ways. My son isn't at all like me. As young as he is, I already know that what runs through his veins is different to the blood in mine. Different and possibly better, but time will tell.

I've time yet to give him the firm resolve and the desire he needs to win and hold a kingdom. But I fear for him. He's almost the age I was when my father gifted Gunghir to me, but I doubt he'd win a similar beast to him through the same techniques I used. No, I think he'd have to make the creature like him. I don't believe that Gunghir ever liked me. Not for a long, long time.

As I smirk at Gunghir's bloody-mindedness, I try to determine when our relationship changed. It was once one of the proud rider and even prouder horse. And now it's two old men, prepared to humour the other but without expecting either to be softer in their advancing years.

Gunghir side steps once more, almost losing his footing in a deep, frozen puddle. I snap his reins aside. I imagine his teeth are showing at such a harsh command, but I also know he'd expect nothing less. Neither would I.

"Father?" my son calls to me from his mount. I've not yet presented him with his own horse. For now, Paeda rides a pliable horse, not one of Gunghir's get, but a smoother horse, a calmer horse. One I'd never wish to ride, but my son is happy with him.

"Son?" I ask. It still thrills me to say that, even if my son isn't quite as I'd have hoped him to be. I'm not above seeing the possibilities in a son who might grow to be a man who employs different techniques to mine. As long as they bloody well work, I'm not going to scold him and force him to my viewpoints. Ruling through force rarely works. So I've learned.

"Uncle Eowa commands the land to this marker?" Paeda asks. He's keen to understand our family's history, to decipher why Eowa is known as the king of Mercia, whilst I'm simply the king of the Hwicce. I've brought him here to see for himself just how much land Eowa claims, and not all of it rightfully. Eowa's successes have come, not in battle, but in an alliance with King Oswald of the Northumbrians, a man who hates me because he blames me for his brother's death. How easily he forgets that Eowa was just as closely allied with Cadwallon as I was.

Still, a matter for another day.

"Yes, he commands to this field boundary. All the land to the north is his until he reaches the kingdom of the Northumbrians."

Paeda's eyes alight as he looks around him, and I don't blame him. Even on a chill, wintry day such as this, Eowa's land looks more promising than mine, and it certainly stretches far further.

"We sometimes come here to meet and discuss … family policy," I offer almost in despair. I don't know what to call the meetings I must endure with my brother. He thinks he's won the battle of the brothers, that I've nothing left to offer and that I've accepted my position.

He doesn't know me at all well. Not any more.

My son laughs at my choice of words. He's a scant nine years old, but he appreciates an evasion when he hears one.

"You don't like your brother?" he queries. As Gunghir reaches to snap at Paeda's horse, I almost think the old beast knows what we're talking about and is chastising him for his audacity.

I haul on the reins once more. The fact Gunghir obeys my wishes without even a token complaint makes me think he does indeed know the subject of our discussion.

"Do you like yours?" I ask tartly. Paeda laughs again. I like to hear him laugh. He might accomplish more with his laughter than he ever will with his sword. It's light and engaging, and almost all join him when he does laugh, even if they don't know what amuses him.

"He's a child," Paeda says in disgust. "He still pisses himself each night. Why would I like him?"

"Why would I like my brother?"

"Well," and Paeda is thinking of a suitable answer to give me. He's detected the edge in my voice. I wish I didn't show my anger toward my brother quite so openly, and certainly not to my son. "He doesn't piss himself," Paeda offers, hoping it'll make me laugh and dispel the tension. I let him have his way and chuckle. Herebrod joins in. He's a constant at my side. I know him much better than I ever have my older brother.

Paeda relaxes at my amusement, and if I could, I'd reach across and ruffle his full head of brown hair. But Gunghir is being difficult again. I don't want him to snap at the horse. He might like Paeda, but he only tolerates other males in his stables. If he can, he'll take a bite out of them whenever they get close.

I almost wish I could be as open in my hatreds as he is. But I have to play the game of politics for the time being until something else happens, and the kings and warlords within my island once more shift monumentally.

But it's been a long time. I think I might have waited for all I can. It might be down to me, just as it was once Cadwallon's duty, to foment trouble within the kingdoms.

"So why do you really not like your brother?" my son questions once more, and this time I give him my honest answer.

"He broke his oath to me. He decided family was less important than being king." I miss out all the gory details. I need to teach my son, but he doesn't need to know everything. I needn't mention how Eowa sent a man to tell me of his defection, not even telling me in person. How he turned King Oswald against me before I could even befriend him. How he presses ever further north with King Oswald as his companion. They're both land-hungry and care little for who they encounter along the way.

It seems that King Oswald has little regard for the men and women who sheltered him in his exile in the kingdom of Dal Riata. Now he tries to take their land and push his boundaries as far as possible. I only wish that Dal Riata was more able to defend itself. I yearn for all the old alliances formed by Cadwallon and myself to still be in force.

I must work to ensure they reappear if I truly plan to take back what my brother stole from me.

"He prays to the new god as well?" Paeda inquires. I'm not opposed to the new religion that's won the adherence of other kings. I even quite like some of their priests, but I'm content with my Gods. Gunghir has stayed true to me all these years. He serves as a living embodiment of my reverence of Woden, a stubborn relationship born of a desire to hold the upper hand, but a good one for all that. I like to be thwarted by something as simple but necessary as my horse. It reminds me that nothing in life will be handed to me. I need to fight for everything I want to hold and keep, even the love of my son and my other children.

"He does, but he only pays lip service to it." My son's face scrunches in concentration as he tries to decipher what I'm telling him.

"So, he doesn't believe it then?" Paeda finally mutters. I nod my head, once, sharply. As I say, I don't mind what men see in their hearts and feel the need to revere. I have my God. I'm content with the chaos he can bring. My brother used to be the same. Now I think he prefers the promise of order, but then, he's not a dynamic man. He likes rules and regulations.

My father would have pitied him. I don't, but I want to exploit his weakness all the same.

Herebrod grunts at my side. I look at him with interest. My eyes have been taking in the expanse of land before me, but Herebrod is indicating I should pay more attention to my son.

The lad is watching me carefully. It seems he has something to tell me. I'm reminded of something I overheard about the way he cured Gunghir. I see the conflict with me, but he's honest enough to want to discuss it.

"How did you cure Gunghir?" I ask him. Paeda's face lightens, seeing that I'm going to make it easier on him. His interest in the new God should be nurtured.

"I told him the stories of Christ and his Saint that Ohthere's told me, whilst he makes your swords and axes."

Ohthere is from Cadwallon's kingdom. I enticed him to my service after the victory at Hæðfeld. He's a good man, an excellent blacksmith and the sort of man who thinks before he speaks. I like him immensely. My son is drawn to him. He finds his work fascinating, as do I. So much heat, strength and labour to bring forth something so cold, deadly and beautiful.

"And what else did you do?" My voice is calm. I do not need to be angry with him, and yet his admission doesn't seem to be enough for him.

"Nothing, I talked to him, and he stood still then and let

Ohthere see to his bad hoof while Brunfrid asked me to feed him a thin soup."

"So you made him take his tonic and helped the men cure his hoof. What's wrong with that?"

"I did it using the words of the new God, but Gunghir is a horse of Woden. I've … I fear I've polluted him."

Paeda's voice is so worried, so earnest that I hold my laughter in check. I don't miss the quirk on Herebrod's face. He looks away into the distance, leaving me to answer my son's worried question.

"The new God didn't cure him. Ohthere, and Brunfrid healed him. You just kept him calm. He likes your voice. So do I." I hope this might stop Paeda's worrying, but I'm to be thwarted.

"So you don't think the new God has any power?"

"Did you pray to him? Offer him a sacrifice, or did you just tell stories?"

"Just stories," Paeda offers, voice perceptibly brightening as he considers that.

"And do the stories of Woden heal people and horses," I offer as an aside, "or is it only when we make sacrifices in his name and offer blood and gifts?"

"But Ohthere says that his God hears what we say."

"I'm sure he does, but if you think Gunghir," and here, my fractious beast finally sidesteps close enough to Paeda's horse that he manages to take a nip from his behind. The horse abruptly bolts as Paeda struggles for the reins.

Before my eyes, the horse and my son take off at a canter, and I curse loudly.

"Bloody hell, Gunghir, leave the poor beast alone." But I've kicked Gunghir to catch up with the other horse before he and my son plunge into some hidden ravine. At my side, Herebrod does the same. Sadly, we're experts at this. My son is an excellent horseman, but Gunghir is a spiteful old bastard. He often attacks the other horses in the herd, ensuring they know he's their lord, even if he's old.

"Penda," Herebrod shouts to me. I glance where he's pointing.

The idea is that I'll force Gunghir in front, and the other horse will veer away from him and into Herebrod.

I urge Gunghir onward, past my son, who shows no fear, but tries to calm his horse as they race across the wintry landscape. Gunghir, for all his age and foul-temper, manages to sprint in front of Paeda. Between us, we bring his racing horse to a halt. The beast is sweating and foaming at the mouth. He has an ugly bite mark on his back.

"I don't think Gunghir wants you to talk about your healing of him, but I don't mind," I offer Paeda breathlessly. Paeda eyes Gunghir with unhappiness before sliding from his saddle and walking up to him. At this moment, I see the bravery in my son. Not many would face a sweating monster like Gunghir, all unarmed.

I know a moment of fear, but then Paeda bangs Gunghir on the nose, with all the force of his fear and anger.

"Bastard," he shouts. Gunghir has stilled beneath me. I wish I could see the expression on Gunghir's face because Herebrod is cackling now.

For a long moment, Gunghir and Paeda face each other. Gunghir looks away, and Paeda, satisfied with what he's accomplished, walks back to his horse, exclaiming as he does so, for the wound on the poor horse's back is deep and long. He offers soothing words as he remounts the smaller horse and then throws Gunghir another angry glance before riding back the way we've just come.

"Frightened of nothing, that one," Herebrod offers. I nod with approval. It seems that my son has more in him than I thought.

"I need to find him a better horse," I acknowledge and then ride back, behind my son, to where the rest of my men are milling about. We're waiting for Eowa to make an appearance, but the git is late as usual. I've half a mind to turn around and go home, but I need to speak to him, my alleged overlord, and find out what he's up to now.

Damn.

I think I hate my older brother.

CHAPTER 2

Eowa, King of Mercia AD640

I ride slowly, purposefully, enjoying the very early summer's day, although the ground is still frozen. I don't wish to rush to yet another meeting with my brother that will only prove to be cantankerous and unproductive.

He'll never accept that I'm the better brother, the one who gambled upon the death of King Cadwallon. In doing so, I made myself the King of Mercia whilst he grovels before me, calling himself King of the Hwicce, a tiny kingdom. It's nothing compared to the lands I hold sway over. And worse, he's subservient to me for what he does hold.

And yet Penda continues to push. He wants to be a powerful man, as he thought he was at the end of Hæðfeld. Yet he's nothing more than the head of a roving war-band who take great delight in destroying King Oswald's carefully laid plans and setting kingdom against kingdom.

Penda's surrounded, more or less, by men loyal to Oswald. Only the men of Gwynedd, Powys and Ceredigion don't threaten Oswald's kingship, and they lie to the west of him. Cynegils is firmly Oswald's man to the south, for all that it was Penda who temporarily overthrew him before the battle of Hæðfeld. Now Cynegils holds his kingdom thanks to Oswald, and not only has he converted to the new God, but he's also father-in-law to King

Oswald.

To the north, Penda encounters my lands. Yet another king holds his kingdom thanks to Oswald's assistance to the east. And all this despite Penda's attempts to claim more land. Upon Cadwallon's death, he made a play for power, an audacious one as well, attacking and killing not one but two kings of the East Angles, one the Sigeberht who'd been Edwin's ally at Hæðfeld, and who'd lived to flee the battle.

Even that wasn't enough for Penda to hold the kingdom, and now Onna rules with the aid of King Oswald.

And to the far north? Well, Oswald and his brother push the boundaries of the kingdom ever further north, thinking nothing of taking land from men and women who sheltered them in their exile.

Penda is just about surrounded. He has no one to call his ally, yet he still refuses to accept Oswald as his overlord.

His determination to be independent in the face of such insurmountable odds infuriates me. As does Oswald's determination that Penda should be subject to him. So my task is never a simple one. I must work to reconcile Penda to Oswald, even though I know my brother so well that the impossibility of the situation isn't lost on me. He'll never accept another as his overlord, not after what happened with Cadwallon.

Penda plans on being subject to no one again. Only grudgingly does he offer me the oaths he needs to as his overlord.

Penda expects to call on other men's oaths to him and not to have to pledge himself to another, and certainly not his older brother.

I know all this. I've explained it to Oswald, but in his defiance of Oswald's wishes, Penda makes himself a powerful enemy, a man who likes being denied as little as Penda.

War will come between the two men. I only hope they'll reach an accord before that day.

Perhaps a marriage alliance? But I doubt it.

I imagine that just as Oswald labours to bring forth his string of alliances, so too does Penda. I know he has allies in Gwynedd and Powys. I suppose that he still has contacts with the kingdom of Dumnonia. I wouldn't be surprised to learn he continues to send messengers to the realm of Dal Riata and the land of the Picts.

After all, Cadwallon killed Lord Eanfrith of Bernicia, not him. Oswald seeks to undermine Dal Riata, no matter that they sheltered him when King Edwin claimed Northumbria for himself and Eanfrith and Oswald were forced to flee for their lives.

No, Penda is severely hampered in his efforts to claim more than he already holds. But, I'm not blind enough to see that his potential has been curtailed. He could cause a great deal of trouble for Oswald, and I imagine he plans to.

For too long, Penda's lain dormant. Five years have passed since his last battle, and whilst his wounds have healed, I know his ambition hasn't.

Penda sees a great future for himself, and only Oswald and his allies stand in the way of that future. Only Oswald, his supporters and, of course, myself, his brother.

This meeting today will be a waste of my time, and yet, I must meet with him, if only to satisfy demands from Oswald. Oswald wants me not only to try to bring Penda to his side but also to determine where an attack should take place on Penda. There was a time such a thought would have horrified me, but no more. I know that Oswald is correct to fear Penda. I'm Oswald's ally, so I have to fear my brother as well.

Quick thinking made me powerful, and slow thinking could just as quickly undo that power. Penda might have been peaceful for five years, but I doubt he's been doing nothing.

Of course, I have a spy within his household, but Penda knows who it is and only allows him to see and hear what he wants me to know. I assume that Penda has a spy within my household, but whoever it is, is too discrete, so he has me at a disadvantage. And what would I do if I did know? Would I act as Penda does? Yes, given half the opportunity, I know I would.

I often wonder where else he has spies? Does he know everything Oswald and his brother Oswiu plot, or is he dependent on the information I receive? I wish I knew.

Oswald hates Penda. He blames him for his brother's death at the hands of Cadwallon. He manages to overlook the fact that Penda wasn't with Cadwallon in Bernicia when Eanfrith was murdered when he assigns that blame. But then Oswald uses his piousness to ignore many facts he doesn't like. He's a man with a vision of the future as powerful as Penda's own. Only he's managed to bring his vision of the future to reality.

Oswald is the power within our island. Penda is no fool. He knows that. But Penda doesn't accept it. He still sees a future when he'll be the mightier king—the man to whom others bow. I can't see it. Oswald and Penda are of an age, and with each passing year, Oswald grows stronger and Penda weaker.

Six years ago, the loss of his strongest ally, Cadwallon, was a blow to Penda, although he didn't realise that. At the time, he thought he'd fill Cadwallon's position. Penda didn't expect Lord Eanfrith's younger brother to manage it in his stead, a man with nothing but his name to aid him upon his older brother's death. That seems to have been more than enough.

In the six years since he became king, Oswald's pushed his boundaries north. He's introduced into Northumbria the Christianity he learnt in exile amongst the Picts. And he's about to make his most audacious move yet.

This is why I travel south and meet with my brother along the way.

I doubt Penda knows why I'm going south. He's hemmed into the land of the Hwicce, and what news he receives is sent with the official blessing of either Oswald or myself. Although, well, he does have his spies. Perhaps he does know after all.

I need to be careful how I speak when I see him, giving him no idea of Oswald's impending move. Unless he already knows, that is.

I sigh with annoyance and run my hand through my long hair. I'm not riding with my helm on, although I probably should. Today feels like the first day of summer, for all that it's cold enough to have me sheltering within my great fur cloak. But the coming season is something to be celebrated. I want to feel the brisk wind in my hair and know that it drives the dark and chill of the winter from the land.

I always welcome its return come to the end of the summer, but I'm pleased to banish it for now. I have much to accomplish and little time to do so.

If I'm to take the land of the Hwicce from Penda, as Oswald demands I do, I need to undermine him in his court and find my own spies there. I also need a full assessment of his capabilities and whom he can call upon to be his ally.

I harbour the belief that the alliance Penda once held together with the support of Cadwallon isn't quite as dead as Oswald believes it to be.

Penda is, after all, not the only enemy that Oswald has. No man can rule such a massive piece of land and encroach on many other borders without making enemies.

Oswald is just as guilty as his uncle of underestimating the hatred of other men and the need to rule as he does.

He thinks he rules and shows men how it should be done, but really, all he does is rule and show others just how easy it can be to steal land, and people from whomever currently rules them.

The land falls and rises as I ride ever south, but then, cresting a final hill, I see my brother and his small party waiting for me. He hasn't invited me to his hall, nor have I asked for shelter within it. He thinks this is just a journey of a day or two for me. He doesn't know my ulterior motive.

I rein my horse in and simply watch the distant figures for long moments.

My brother continues to ride his old horse, a bloody-minded beast but one Penda values more than many of his men.

My own horse, gifted to me by my father, has long been dead, although his seed was used to swell my herd of horses. Yet, he was never as difficult as Gunghir. I've long pondered why my father chose the horse. It seems as though he cursed Penda with his actions. Or did he?

Perhaps he saw something in his younger son that I don't see in my brother.

My brother has his own son now. I consider if he'll gift him a horse as terrible as his own? I doubt it. News reaches me that Paeda is a far gentler boy than Penda ever was, perhaps more like me than his father.

I could use that to my advantage if I ever get close enough to the boy. It would be a coup to drive a wedge between the two of them before Paeda even knows his mind.

Herebrod rides with them. He's my brother's most faithful retainer, with a Pictish woman as his wife. Oswald fears Herebrod's influence over Penda. Oswald knows that it gives Herebrod legitimacy to claim loyalty from the Picts. Oswald wishes to solely hold that claim through his dead brother and his living nephew. He might mourn his brother, but he also sees infinite possibilities in his mourning. He uses them well.

Not for him, the Christianity preached from Kent, by Archbishop Paulinus and his connections to Edwin, the man who murdered his father and stole his kingdom; the man who was his uncle, no less. No, Oswald has turned to the religion of his youth, preached by the men who walk amongst the Picts, the men of the kingdom of Dal Riata. They kept the light of his religion burning whilst the rest of this island ran away from it, allowing the old Gods their resurgence in the wake of the arrival of my ancestors.

But as I say, it's Herebrod that Oswald fears almost as much as he does Penda. He would like him dead. I've been tasked with accomplishing it. In this, I think that Oswald has erred. He doesn't appreciate the warrior that Herebrod is or the counsel he gives Penda. Penda values him. He'll not allow him to be left unprotected. So Oswald has given me an impossible task, and I've no choice but to attempt it. For now.

Oswald is my ally, but he's also my overlord, and if I don't do as he asks, he'll replace me. I can only hope that I either manage to kill Herebrod during this meeting or through one of my spies or that Oswald doesn't grow impatient if I fail.

I smirk sourly. Perhaps Oswald isn't the best of allies. He is, however, undoubtedly the strongest one to have.

And then the time has come. Penda, impatient in waiting for me, has ridden to greet me. I mustn't allow my thoughts to show on my face. Penda knows me well, and he can read me too well.

I hope that this time his forethought fails. I fear that if he understands my intent, war will once more ravage our island. And I fret that he'll meet his death.

Or perhaps I don't worry about it all. Maybe I hunger for it and all he has.

I want my name to be remembered by the storytellers and holy men. My name. Not his.

✤CHAPTER 3✤

Oswald of Northumbria AD640

Bamburgh

My horse ambles along the sandy shore. It's a chill, cold day, with the wind blowing harshly from the islands out at sea. Most are flat, difficult to differentiate on such a bleak day. The sky flashes from grey to blue to grey once more, with the shifting clouds racing across the sky. Almost between breaths, they bring hail, snow and hard rain. One stands out amongst all the others, its white cliffs visible as the sun briefly flashes over its surface.

It won't be long until the cliffs are ablaze with sea birds, building their nests and raising their young, whilst seals beach themselves and bathe in the sun on the rugged rocks below.

This place brings me peace and reminds me of my youth before my uncle's ambitions overwhelmed my family and sent my brothers and me running for our lives. It fills me with the desire to succeed, to be better than my father ever was and to far exceed anything that Edwin attempted during his too-long life.

I only wish Cadwallon had managed to kill Edwin many years before, but then Penda brought my brother to their alliance. If Cadwallon had killed my uncle before Lord Eanfrith had joined the coalition, I don't think I'd be in my current position.

But then Cadwallon killed my brother too. For that, I'll always hate him and any who stood with him. Especially Penda. For him, I'll forever have mixed emotions. In some ways, I know I should be grateful to him, but I can't be. If he'd left Eanfrith amongst the Picts, he'd never have been killed by Cadwallon. But if none of that had happened, then I'd not be king now.

The twisted skeins of our lives tire me and brings me out here, in the cold and the frigid rain, to right my thoughts and think of the future, not the past.

And yet. My mind slips backwards, ever backwards. I remember vividly the day my father met his death, at the battle of the River Idle, against the combined alliance of King Rædwald of the East Angles. The latter had no business meddling in the affairs of the Northumbrians, and my uncle, Edwin. Edwin was a king of no land, not then, but desperate to claim his birthright. Edwin said my father had stolen that birthright from him by marrying my sister and begetting a herd of sons upon her, forgetting that he'd long ago lost his right to rule.

Too many of my father's men died that day, and yet somehow, the word was sent to my mother and her children of Edwin's ravaging intent. We raced to sanctuary, taking nothing but the clothes on our backs and the jewels and wealth we could carry. Without men to hold our fortress home, the very fortress that stretches across the land behind my back, there was no point in cowering inside it. It would only have led to our deaths. That would have pleased my uncle too much and made his usurpation that much more difficult to undo.

No, we escaped, and coming home, when I was a man, not a child any longer, was a sobering experience. This is my home, and I never plan on losing it again.

As such, I take my quest for more land, and more people to look to me as their lord, to the outer reaches of Northumbria, towards the lands of the Picts, and southwards, although I've had no success amongst the British. They're immune to my charm and my threats, even though I already claim the death of Cadwallon amongst my trophies.

That makes me nervous, especially as I think they still hold to some sort of pact with Penda. They share boundaries and borders.

The rain sleets into my eye. I turn my horse for home. As I do so, the holy island of Lindisfarne catches my eye, momentarily lit by the bright sunlight that flickers through the stormy clouds. It highlights another way that I'm enforcing my will. I wasn't raised in the ways of the Christian God. But I've embraced them in my time in the north, going so far as to visit their holy island of Iona and make myself acquainted with their ways.

As such, Bishop Aidan now resides on Lindisfarne, a man of my Christianity, not tainted by the false Christianity from Kent and its affiliations with Archbishop Paulinus, the man who made my despised uncle, Edwin, a Christian.

No, all traces of his religion must be wiped from my land, my people baptised in the correct faith, the true faith. It should fall to no other but Bishop Aidan to ensure it's done correctly.

He's an honest man, a good man. A man worthy of turning my kingdom to the correct religion. I'll use him, as I must, to accomplish that.

"Brother," the title is one I'm used to hearing, and yet I'll never hear it again from the man I wish to, Eanfrith. My older brother, the king here before me, a man who grew weak in the sight of so much wealth and power. He was too trusting, too scared. He'd been in exile too long, ignored by his saviours for too long. He'd forgotten how to be a king. I learned much from his mistakes, for all that they were too briefly made.

No, it's not Eanfrith who calls to me in the chill day but Oswiu, my younger brother, and the man with whom I've chosen to share my kingdom. We were kept together in our exile, and we think alike, scheme alike, and have long dreamed of making Northumbria as strong and powerful as we can.

Between us, Oswiu and I will make Northumbria impenetrable. We'll allow people to walk without fear from one side of our realm to the other, and we'll do it jointly.

"Oswiu?" I ask. He's windswept and riding his horse toward

me. I've not been expecting him, and my eyes narrow as I take in his stance.

He looks like me; we've always been told that, and it's strange to look at a man who carries my image and yet who isn't me. I hope I look as handsome as he does, even in the rain and the sleet.

"Oswald, why are you out here on such a bleak day?" his tone censors, as though he's the older brother to criticise me. I grin at him. He's probably been waiting for me in the great hall, before the huge fire burning there, but has become impatient, his biggest failing, and ventured outside to find me instead.

He could have sent a messenger but knows that I might send a messenger away. I never dismiss my brothers without listening to them first.

"I was thinking," I simply offer, shrugging to apologise for my whimsy. Oswiu shivers inside his great cloak. I grin at him. I'm sure it's not that cold.

"Are you sick?" I ask him instead. He shakes his head numbly, his long hair pooling under his chin and making it look as though he wears a long beard.

"No, but it's bloody cold, and it's snowing." The way he says snowing makes me aware of how strange my behaviour might appear. I glance behind me. The clouds are thickly grey, with the tinge of pink that means snow is on its way. Indeed, the golden beach is changing colour before me as it turns white. I hadn't even realised.

"Come, let's ride back," I offer, but he shakes his head again.

"No, we can talk out here, where the wind will take our words, and no one can overhear us."

My brother has been in the north. I wonder what he's learned that worries him so much that he agrees to stay in the snow and the wind. He's never appreciated the chill winds that chafe the coast.

"Your wife is well?" I ask, hoping that might be the cause of the problem, although I doubt it.

"Everything is well to the north," he says quickly, his tone aggravated. "It's events to the south that worry me."

"Penda is surrounded," I say sullenly. We've had this argument too often for it to be anything new.

"He's not, and he's stronger than you realise," he retorts immediately. "Is Herebrod dead yet?"

"No, but it's in hand," I offer, hoping to prevent any further debate. The snow is starting to settle on me, and my horse is growing restless, stamping his hooves in the cold.

"I doubt that," Oswiu says sourly. I hold my biting retort in place. We've long argued over Penda and Herebrod, but until I held almost all of the island in my power, there was no point in taking on Penda. He's the only king of the Saxon kingdoms who's not my ally, or if not my ally, then not my enemy.

"Why do you doubt it?" I grill. I fear he's come to argue with me just because he can and because he's a man of action, not words.

"He's travelled north during the winter to be with his wife's people. I doubt he's even with Penda. You should have permitted me to waylay him. I could have killed him, and no one would have known."

I know that Oswiu is lying to me. Herebrod is with Penda and has been all winter. My spies amongst Penda's court have assured me of it. I wonder at what game Oswiu is playing.

"Herebrod is with Penda," I state with finality, but his eyes blaze angrily. My brother craves war more than I ever did. He hates Penda with a greater passion as well.

"Do you wish to start a war with Penda?" I demand bluntly. It's often the best way to contend with his demands.

"No, with the Picts. They'll support Penda. We need to dissuade them before Penda can get to them."

"I don't think the Picts would side with Penda. They're not strong enough. We know that, they raised Eanfrith."

"They kept much from him and us," Oswiu mutters angrily, turning his horse toward the fortress. "I hear rumours that you wouldn't like," he continues to grumble. I feel my eyebrows rising in surprise. I thought Oswiu knew better than to pay any credence to gossip.

"I don't think they keep too much from us, Oswiu. They raised Eanfrith. His son, our nephew, is one of their royal princes. We know their military strength. Do you think they let us push our borders as far north as we did because they wanted to trick us? I don't think so. What's the matter with you? You never used to be so gullible."

His face turns thunderous at my words. He kicks his horse to canter away. I've upset him, but it'll make him consider his words and actions. He might even return to me with a decent answer to explain his unhappiness. He has a wife, land, and a future. Why would he be unhappy? Unless? Well, I don't know. Perhaps he hopes to be king after me after all, and the knowledge that my wife has recently birthed another son for me, and the child appears healthy, unlike our previous babies, has concerned him.

Perhaps it's that which upsets him. I'm sure I'll know soon enough.

Still, the snow falls. I think wistfully of my childhood, those scant few years when I saw all through the eyes of innocence and suspected deceit from no one.

Those times are long past, and my son, born before my marriage, has never even enjoyed them. All he's ever known is that he's the son of a prince, destined to be a king one day and that he'll have to fight to keep that kingdom for himself.

I've not expected him to have to fight his uncle, but then, I shouldn't be surprised. Lies and deceit seem to run through my family.

Dismayed, I finally turn my horse towards home. I'm numb from head to toe, and the only thing that keeps my heart warm, my very essence, my soul, is the knowledge that my brother hates Penda more than he despises me. That will, hopefully, keep him loyal to me.

For now.

✧CHAPTER 4✧

Oswiu of Northumbria AD640

Bamburgh

I guide my horse expertly along the small pathway into the fortress of Bamburgh. Ever since I was a child, I've ridden recklessly upon the path, and even being in exile for over fifteen years hasn't made my skill leave me.

Other men watch and gasp with fear and delight when they spot my erratic path. I grin to myself when I hear those gasps, but this afternoon, anger stalks me, not joy. In my rage, I nearly make a wrong step and plunge to my death into the crashing waves that bedevil the rocky ledge leading to my home. Only the horse's steadiness keeps me safely on the path. Instead of gasps of fear, I hear gasps of dismay when my horse regains its footing.

These men. They call themselves my allies, but they'd be happy to see me dead. All of them, even my younger brothers, those who would seek to leapfrog over me if I died and become confidants to my older brother.

How little they know him. He'll never share his kingdom with anyone. I see that clearly now. He intends for his son to rule after him and his son after that.

No matter how many times we've discussed our tactics, it seems that my brother has no intention of following my wishes or sharing his control. We've spoken about isolating the kingdom of the Goddodin so that we can take the land for ourselves. I've married to strengthen my ties with the British of the kingdom of Rheged and encircle the Goddodin. Goddodin is now almost ours to control, yet it would still be his conquest. If he doesn't even allow me to bring an end to the life of Herebrod, a nothing, a man with no great past, or future, to his name, I wonder why I ever thought he'd heed my words.

Herebrod is simply a man who's married to a Pictish woman who once knew my older brother. He shouldn't hold any sway about where the Picts direct their support, but he does. He should be killed because of that. His loyalty to my older brother was a fledgling thing that should be honoured far less than it is. He is, over and above all, Penda's man and always will be.

I wish I'd ensured Herebrod met his death years ago. Now he threatens the pretensions of my brother, and more importantly, of me. I was raised amongst the Dal Riatans, away from Eanfrith, but I still know the weaknesses of the Picts. I know I can exploit them in order to rule them better than they already are. But no, Oswald thinks that the presence of our nephew, Talorcan, amongst them will keep the Picts our allies. I disagree, but Oswald doesn't seem content to listen to me, as I've illustrated.

I growl between my teeth as I ride quickly into the enclosed area where the horses shelter. A man holds my horse's reins, and I stride angrily towards my brother's great hall, the hall our long-dead father built.

Edwin maintained it well, although it seems he used it far less often than my father did. Edwin favoured the royal residence of *Ad Gefrin*, Yeavering to some. He was there far more often, somehow thinking he was untouchable enough that he could afford to live without the protection of ramparts and ditches in the hills to the west. It's a great pity he didn't die within Ad Gefrin with nowhere to shelter, but an animal shed. Instead, Edwin met his death close to where he murdered my father.

Edwin was my uncle. I remember that I childishly once adored him, but he killed my father and almost made me an orphan.

I'm glad he's dead.

The great hall is situated in such a position that I need to walk through a tunnel of sleeting rain and heavy wind to enter it. I shudder into my cloak. I don't like being outside when the weather is so inclement. My time in exile showed me that men and women grow weak if exposed to the elements too often and for too long. The chill wind strips the flesh from their bones and the colour from their faces and hair.

Damn my brother for riding on the beach. I'm chilled to the bone now, and even my anger won't warm me.

I make straight for the vast hearth, thrusting my ice-chilled cloak from my back and handing it to a slave who happens to walk close to me at the required time. They'll ensure it's warmed before I venture from here again. Hopefully, I'll be able to restrain my anger until the weather clears or the weather will clear soon. Either way, I need to keep my unhappiness from showing too clearly.

I've no intention of losing what sway I have over my brother. Perhaps I should remind him of the role I played in our attack and over-running of the kingdom of the Goddodin? But no. My brother doesn't like to be reminded that he's accomplished all that he has with the help of other men. He thinks himself a holy warrior, a man come to correct the errors of Edwin's reign. And to restore Northumbria to its position under my father. But he reaches far and wide in his endeavours, preferring to think of what he could rule rather than what he already rules. Goddodin was ours for the taking, but he gifted it back to the ruling family. I'd not have done the same.

I love my brother, but I hate him too. He's no Eanfrith. Eanfrith would have made an excellent king if he'd only been less naïve, less trusting of Cadwallon. He should have made the connection that his alliance with Cadwallon was negotiated with Penda. He should never have allowed himself to think that Cadwallon regarded him with the same respect.

I harbour the hope that Penda hates my brother's killer as much as I do. But until I receive confirmation of that, it's Penda who feels my ire. It's Penda towards which I direct my vengeance.

And Herebrod is just the first step in accomplishing that. If only my brother would allow me a free hand.

I'm not alone in seeking my kingly brother during the bad weather. As I warm myself before the fire, two of my brothers greet me, Oswudu and Oslac. They're younger than I am, their faces flushed by the warmth of the fire, and no doubt, the amount of mead they've consumed.

They share my looks but not my personality, for they're both good-humoured and always smiling. I suppose being so much the younger brothers, with almost no chance of ever becoming a king, has made them so. They do not need to plot and scheme or try and find a way to become essential to their king.

They're simply his drunk younger brothers, and they're feted and indulged.

"Brother," they both offer me. I grunt an acknowledgement. I didn't want to speak to them, but I ignored them before seeking Oswald. There'll be eyes watching us, spies from the other great courts within our island, keen to exploit any possible division between us.

I try to lighten my face force the downward turn of my mouth upwards. Clearly, I fail because both of my brothers grin ever wider at me.

"What brings you here?" Oswudu asks, guiding me to a secluded corner around the hearth, where none of the women sits and sews as they sing.

"Does there need to be a reason?" I ask churlishly, but still, they grin at me.

"You never come unless you want something," Oslac offers evenly. He's the less drunk of the two, and his reasoning is sounder. I wish he were drunk. He has a way of looking at me that makes me think he knows things that even I don't.

"I came to ask how our alliances fare in the south," I try and evade. "I receive little news in the north."

I almost think that will satisfy the pair of them, but then

Oslac's face clears of his drunken stupor, deciphering the meaning of my words.

He's a young man, raised in exile, given little to call his own but his good looks and humour. But he's not an idiot. He knows when I'm lying. He always has. He could detect the condescension of those who cared for him during his exile. He didn't enjoy living off others' leavings. He never intends a return to that situation. As such, I think he uses his drunkenness as a mask to hide his intelligence and to gain information without even seeming to ask for it.

"Oswald sends messengers to you all the time," Oslac argues. "Why are you here?"

I sit down on the side of the hearth and stretch my legs before me. They're still bloody cold despite the blazing fire. I could do with something warm to eat.

I look around and meet the eyes of the slave who took my cloak. I gesture for food, and she turns to go about her business. I hope she brings me something good. It's the time of the year when even the wealthiest find their food resources running low. No doubt it'll be some sort of fish stew or baked bread with fish in it. At Bamburgh, there's always fish available to eat.

Oslac follows my example, but Oswudu has wandered off to refill his drinking horn. I watch him go with some anger. We could be a mighty force if we only chose to work together. But a youth spent in exile has made us keen to look for allies outside our family circle.

"How long have you been here?" I ask instead of answering Oslac. He might know Oswald's thinking more clearly than I do.

"Since the turning of the year. Oswald has done little but feast the men."

"Does he talk of war?" I demand.

"No, why, should he?"

"I think a king surrounded by his enemies should always speak of war," I retort heatedly.

"What enemies?" Oslac asks, raising and lowering his shoulders in surprise at my words.

This is the problem. Oswald has only held his kingdom for a handful of years, yet those he rings himself with already feel comfortable enough to think there are no enemies left.

This is why I feel I'm the only one who toils to keep the kingdom secure.

"Penda," I say with malice. Just saying that name makes my blood boil.

"He's been neutered," Oslac dismissed. He must know about my brother's plans with Cynegils and his son and heir, Cenwahl. "And there's yet more to come as well."

"He's not been neutered. He's too powerful."

"Not anymore, he's not." Oslac sounds so confident that for a long moment, I think that I must be wrong, that I must see phantoms where none exist. Only, I know Penda is still powerful. Anyone who thinks he isn't is deluded. He's not finished yet.

"He is, no matter what Oswald thinks."

"You speak very openly against our brother." It's not a question, but it should be.

"I do. No king should be advised by men and women who share only his opinions."

Oslac laughs derisively at my words.

"I can see why he banished you to the far north."

Oswald didn't banish me. I chose to go there, but Oslac's forgotten that, too keen to laugh at me.

"Does no one speak against Penda here?"

"Why would they? Eowa is Oswald's ally, and he's Penda's brother. He assures Oswald that he has him under his control."

I spit at that pronouncement. Penda is accountable to no one. Even when he was in his alliance with Cadwallon, he was far more equal than others thought. Eanfrith told me as much before his unfortunate death. No, Penda is a warlord, a king, and he plans to be a king of more than just the Hwicce.

"Eowa doesn't control his brother."

"No, but he hampers his actions whenever he can."

"When, tell me when he hampered him?" I ask angrily. This conversation is riling me, as I knew it would.

"He didn't send support to him when he attacked the East Angles and killed two of their kings. Remember, it's Onna who rules there now. Not Penda, and Onna rules with the support of Oswald."

"Eowa was only just Oswald's ally when Penda attacked East Anglia. The only reason for giving no assistance was because he didn't want Penda to rule any more land that bordered his. Or to encourage him to attack the Mercian lands."

"Eowa didn't support him when he took on Cynegils before Hæðfeld."

"Nobody supported him then because no one knew who the fuck he was back then." My tone's dripping with anger, but still, Oslac draws breath to dismiss my fears. I wave him away. I don't want to talk to someone who won't listen to my words. My brother has successfully encircled himself with men and women who believe everything he says. The whole court is infected with the belief that no one can challenge Northumbria.

I feel unwelcome. My views won't be heeded here. I quickly eat the bowl of food brought to me. It tastes good, and I can admit as much, despite myself, but I've decided I can't stay here. I need to go north, or perhaps south. Maybe I could travel to York and see what news I can garner from there. I need something concrete to present to my brother to assure him that Penda is more of a threat.

Oslac has gone, at my wishes, but it's not long before another seeks me out.

I don't know the man, although I think I should. I try to remember his name. He's not much older than me and dressed in the clothes of a monk. I want to send him on his way, but then I recognize him and realise he's one of Aidan's monks, brought here from Iona, a place I hold fond memories of from my youth.

"My Lord," he says with humility, bending his head. I indicate that he should sit with me, which he does gratefully. His face is blue with cold. He must have ridden here from Lindisfarne with some important message for the king.

"Hereric," I say. He glances at me in surprise. He hadn't expected me to remember him.

"I ride to the south on the work of God in a few days, but first, Oswald has asked me to speak with him."

This, at last, is something that interests me. Perhaps my brother is using his monks as spies in the southern lands.

"Where do you go?" I ask. He shakes his head and looks around to see if anyone listens to our conversation.

"To the south, to the court of King Cynegils," is all he says but his eyes gleam as he speaks. I think he must be trying to tell me that he's going elsewhere.

"You're going to work with the new bishop?" I ask, fumbling for the meaning in this conversation. He shakes his head, only slightly, and grins at me. His face is clean-shaven, and as the colour slowly leeches back into it, I see that he has a good nose, a pleasant mouth and teeth that he clearly cares for more than many others. If I needed to send a man to work on my behalf, I'd send a man upon who it was at least pleasing to look.

"I go via the kingdom of Gwynedd," he finally mutters. Now I understand his meaning. He's a missionary from Bishop Aidan, a man raised in the ancient Iona religion, so similar to that practised amongst the British. He's going to spy in Gwynedd, determine if Penda really does have allies there.

It seems I've misrepresented my brother.

Perhaps, after all, he does understand that he's not safe.

"My thanks," I say to the man. He nods and moves away from me, his eyes darting around the hall to make sure no one has overheard us. But I feel the eyes of another on me and raise my head to meet the gaze of a hooded individual who slips from the hall before I can determine his identity.

I rise to follow him, but Oswudu is back, his hand on my arm. He restrains me long enough that I lose sight of the man in the crowded hall.

I can only hope that he's a spy for Oswald and not one for Penda.

Only time will tell.

✥CHAPTER 5✥

Cynegils of the West Saxons AD640

I watch the bishop intently as he conducts his measurements and shouts commands to his workers. This project has been long in the making and expensive as well. I only hope that King Oswald, when he finally comes to make good on his pledge to support me, will be pleased with the endeavours of Bishop Birinus.

Oswald has made no secret of his distaste for those who preach the word of the Pope, but I could hardly demand one of the men from Iona, as Oswald did, when I considered allowing my people to convert. I don't have Oswald's sway with the men of the Ionan church, and so I've made do with what I have.

It will have to be enough.

I need Oswald to remain as my ally. He's strong enough to curtail any more attempts by bloody Penda to take my land. Penda's one time victory over us has never been converted to an all-out effort to claim my land for himself. But he grows stronger and stronger. I appreciate that if this alliance isn't reaffirmed soon, he'll launch an invasion against me once more. This time, he'll be more successful.

Whereas before, Penda was a young warrior, trying to make a name for himself, now he's a king of a vast land and has allies all over our island. No matter what Oswald thinks of Penda, he's a lethal force with which to contend.

I didn't much like Oswald's assumption that I'd follow his religion to win his support, but it's allowed our alliance to flourish. When I converted, and he took my daughter as his bride, I thought we'd always be allies. I was deceived.

My daughter was a beautiful young woman when she married Oswald, stubborn and determined. It was a relief to have her away from my home and married to a man who lived so far to the north. But I miss her. I didn't like to barter with her life for my safety, especially when I barely knew Oswald, other than by reputation. Yet I've had to rely on him to keep her safe from harm and provide her with a family of her own. In that he has, until now, failed, her tiny babies all losing their tenuous grip on life, although her most recent child is, so I hear, thriving.

By allying with Oswald, I also aligned with the kingdoms surrounding me, just as I did by becoming a Christian. The King of Kent looks kindlier on me for being a Christian, even if Oswald's relationship with that kingdom is more fractious than with others. He knows that Bishop Paulinus, the man who helped Edwin begin the conversion of the Northumbrians, came from Kent. He instinctively shies away from anyone who has anything to do with Edwin.

Still, to gain Oswald as my ally, I paid heavily, and now my son must also convert to his religion to ensure he succeeds to the kingdom on my death, which I know is coming soon. The portents have made it clear that I'll not live much past the end of the year.

My son is unhappy with my decision, but then Cenwahl has never feared Penda as much as I do. My older son fought with me when we were beaten by Penda when we were lucky to escape with our lives intact. Cenwahl is a warrior. He thinks we could outmanoeuvre Penda even if he did come and attack us. I wish I shared such conviction.

"My Lord King." Bishop Birinus calls for my attention. I look to where he's pointing. He's been discussing the placing of his altar and his shrine all morning. I've long grown tired of waiting for him to finish his minute alterations. Oswald will be with us soon, and all must be ready before he arrives. Birinus says that man will simply have to wait for his Lord's work to be completed, but after five years, even I'm tired of waiting.

"Bishop," I reply, watching him as he fastens his eyes on me. He's from a warmer climate than I am, and as such, he has unusual eyes amongst my people. They shine green in the lamplight, although they usually appear brown. I think this is part of his appeal. He offers my people and me something 'different' from the norm. It makes men and women more open to listening when he speaks of a God we don't understand and miracles we little comprehend.

"All is ready," he simply announces, sweeping his hands across his altar of wood. I can't see that anything has changed through the morning of my waiting for him to be finished. But he seems content. I'm happy to leave the church finally.

It's a small wooden building, with little to differentiate it from the rest of the buildings in Dorchester, but he's pleased with it. So I smile, mirroring his joy at what he's accomplished in 'only five years' as he says to me. I think it's a small amount for five years, but then, he tells me his God works in small ways to turn the minds of men towards him.

I can't say that I believe any of his words. They simply tumble over me in a torrent. Every so often, one phrase or another makes some impact on me, something for me to puzzle over and wonder why men think the miracles he speaks of mean so much more than they do.

But overall, I see this new religion as little better than the old one with which I feel more at ease. I'd far rather offer bloody sacrifices to my God than offer myself so fully. Yet I do what I must to ensure that King Oswald stays true to our alliance. Every day that I'm in Dorchester, I visit Birinus and listen to his words.

"When will King Oswald arrive?" Birinus queries as I leave the dubious shelter of the small wooden church.

"He said with the better weather, around Easter time."

This means something to Birinus as he nods, and I know it

probably should to me, but there are too many festivals I'm now supposed to adhere to, and I get confused.

"Good, we've finished just in time then." Birinus sounds a little smug with himself, although I can't imagine why. The church has been in the making for many years. Only the fact that Oswald deigned to come and visit has made Birinus speed his work in any way. I harbour the hope that he might not know what to do with himself now that his church is completed. Then I think again. These men of the new God always have new projects that they wish to put into action.

The man will probably never tire of his desire to build churches amongst my people. I almost wish I had the power to prevent it, but my concern is solely with stopping Penda, and that means Oswald, and in turn, that means Birinus and more churches.

I feel that I'm happy to pay the price for the future of my dynasty.

"Is he travelling by sea or by land?"

I'm sure that Birinus must know the answer to his questions. I wonder why he tests my patience as he does.

"By sea. He has some of the ships the men of Dal Riata use to travel between the islands they inhabit. He says he enjoys it."

I'm not a keen sailor. I have never been. The thought of spending any time onboard a ship makes me shiver with revulsion. But I stop my dismay from showing. After all, Birinus travelled by ship to reach my land. When he feels his missionary work is done, he'll travel home the same way. I don't want to give him another reason to belittle me.

"Will you be staying in the settlement until he arrives?" Again, Birinus must know the answer to this, but I grunt an acknowledgement all the same.

"Good. It'll give me time to finish instructing your son in the ways of my God. I'll ensure he's fully prepared for his welcome into the flock."

I just nod this time. I'm not prepared to enter into any debate with Birinus. Five long years of his company have taught me that it is not good to argue with him or ask him to explain his strange little phrases. I'm soundly of the opinion that his God is little more than a shepherd. When compared to the ravages of my old God, Woden, I think he pales into a meek eyed child. Birinus' stories fill me with no excitement and no joy either.

I must constantly remind myself of why I labour as I do.

When Penda attacked my son and me, he won an overwhelming victory. We were both lucky to escape with our lives. That knowledge haunts me. Penda was almost an unknown then, just the second son of a man who'd once ruled the Hwicce. His father had never worn a title other than war leader. His son was keen to be a king, but even before then, when he was only honoured as a member of a powerful family, he overwhelmed my men and me.

He could do it again, and he will. He just needs to remember that he has an argument with me, and his men will crash once more into my kingdom. Despite the precautions I've taken, the defences built around my homes and the centres of trade, I know that without the threat of Oswald inflicting retribution upon Penda, he'll not even consider the consequences, too sure of success.

Not that I'm a weak man. Far from it. No man could rule for as long as I have if he couldn't bring many men to the battlefield and reward his warriors handsomely. But Penda's renown grows with each passing year. As I said, he overwhelmed me when he had nothing. What could he accomplish now that he has so much?

My son joins me as I try to escape my conversation with Birinus. He's handsome and young. It makes me feel young to be around him, even when he's deeply resentful of the changes taking place within the kingdom and the personal price he must pay.

"Your older brother did the same," I say over and over again, but Cenwahl's responses have become routine. Cwichelm did convert when I did, but then he had the good graces to fall ill and die from a contagion, and in his death throes, he demanded a traditional burial, not one of the Christian ones.

"Oswald will be leaving warriors with us?" My son's concerns are all military. He hopes to break Penda's hold on the land of the Hwicce as soon as possible. The land is good there, the crops grow well, as do the animals. He hopes to rule it himself, either before my death or when I'm dead, and he can do as he pleases, with Oswald's support, of course.

"Yes, at least three hundred." It seems like a huge number to me, enough to add a full third more to my numbers. The only downside is that I must feed them as if they were mine, but their allegiance will remain wholly to Oswald. It's another warning, as if I needed one, that Oswald will support me, provided I precisely do what he commands of me.

Provided that Oswald and I continue to see the future in the same vein, I hope that his threats will never become anything more than that, just threats.

"Good. I want to attack Penda this year, just after the harvest. That way, we can steal their supplies and make the people of the Hwicce dependent on our goodwill."

My son thinks as a king should. He makes me proud.

"You'll lead the attack personally," I reiterate. "And you'll claim the victory as your own."

My son's eyes are hazy with the victory he already sees in the future. I hope he doesn't grow too used to the idea of the victory and give too little thought to how he'll bring it about.

My thoughts turn to my daughter once more. When Cyniburh left me, she was fearful, but for all that she's had little success in bringing forth healthy children, I understand that she's powerful in her own right. After all, what does she have to fear when she's married to the most powerful king within our island?

⌘ CHAPTER 6 ⌘

Domnall Brecc King of Dal Riata

My face is sour as I listen to the representatives from the three clans that form my kingdom. The men all have their ideas and prejudices. That's as it's always been, but they don't share my anger and fear toward Oswald, now calling himself king of Northumbria.

Oswald was raised within my kingdom, treated well, taught by the religious house on Iona. Yet for all that, he seeks to attack my land, to drive back or even obliterate the borders that separate us.

It always seems to be the way with the men who dwell north of the great river, Humber. One moment they're allied with the kingdom of Dal Riata. The next, they're enemies. With the virtual extinction of the kingdom of Goddodin two years before, Oswald's borders abut mine in places. I need to reverse his advances.

Only the three clans, with their eyes focused elsewhere, don't understand my fear or sense the urgency in bringing them together.

Last year, I broached the subject with them, told them of my wishes to attack Oswald and his brother, then living amongst the Britons of Rheged, the kingdom to the south of ours. I fully expected them to arrive with full ships and for their mounted riders to be close behind. Yet, no warriors are gathered here, none apart from the men and women who guard their clan chief.

This isn't what I asked for and not upon which I've decided. I'll have to wait another year now before I can attack Oswald. In that time, he'll have resumed his northward expansion.

Damn the bastard. He's too much like his father, King Æthelfrith, who practised the same deceits. I wish his brother, Lord Eanfrith, still lived, but he's dead at the hands of Cadwallon, his ally and supposed friend.

That angers me as well. I'm grateful to Oswald for ridding this island of Cadwallon and his anger and violence. Cadwallon gathered me to his great alliance against Edwin and then, once he was dead, became an even more bloodthirsty king.

Cadwallon deserved his death. He became what he swore he hated and in far less time than it took Edwin to become a tyrant. When Cadwallon died, I welcomed Oswald's kingship, but I no longer do.

I've sent missionaries to Oswald from Iona, as he requested. I've also sent men to speak with him and ask him to reconsider his intentions towards the land and people who supported him through his exile. The response I get is always less than I expect.

I want some sort of assurance that he doesn't mean to take my kingdom from me. But I know I'll never hear those words, not unless I attack him first.

With that in mind and listening to the excuses and arguments that my three clan chiefs toss at each other, I know that I need to take alternative action to achieve what needs to be done to secure my kingdom.

Lord Penda. He, too, is beleaguered by Oswald. His brother is a member of Oswald's alliance, but Penda is firmly aloof. Perhaps between us, and with the help of the British once more, we can curtail Oswald and his intentions to rule the length and breadth of our island.

I'll need to send messengers, urgently, to the men of Gwynedd, Powys, Ceredigion and to Penda as well. To arrange for a meeting of sorts, just as Cadwallon managed in the past. But first, I must appeal to them and ensure they understand the threat that Oswald presents. They may not be sympathetic to the dying kingdom of the Goddodin, the ancient British kingdom to the west. The British kingdoms to the west and east have long been separated and divided by the advance of the men of Deira, Bernicia and Mercia. The British may fear Oswald already but not as much as they ever feared Edwin when he held the land between them and Northumbria. Edwin meddled in events that were none of his concern and first earned the ire of Cadwallon, his foster brother.

No, Edwin was less devious in his wishes, more likely to simply start a war. Oswald is more circumspect. He doesn't so much take his time, as allow his holy men to spread their word before all. I admire his tactics, but they've been learnt in my kingdom, and they mustn't be used against my kingdom. I would have hoped he'd not turn his attentions towards my people, but if he's to be denied in the British realms to the west, then he's determined to succeed elsewhere.

No. I must ensure my future allies appreciate the danger we all face, not just myself. But how to do it? I can't appear weak or frightened of any possible attack. No, I need to be strong and stand firm before my clan chiefs and the allies I hope to gain.

I know that Penda has an alliance with the Picts. His man Herebrod, his go-between with Lord Eanfrith, is married to a wellborn Pictish woman. Although he spends his summer with Penda, he journeys to the north during the winter. Perhaps this year I could waylay him, ask him to broker an alliance with Penda, just as when Penda and Cadwallon made one. I'll think on it, but in the face of my clan chiefs, I know I'll not have their support, and yet I must do something to keep Dal Riata safe

As merely the son of the man who gave Oswald sanctuary within our kingdom, I'm to be disregarded and consigned to the list of kingdoms that he could rule if he succeeds in attacking and killing their ruler.

But, and he forgets this, I'm a warrior, trained and raised just as he was, and I'll not allow Oswald to override my position and wishes for the future.

No, I'll wage war as I must and keep Dal Riata safe. And I'll do it with the aid of Penda, for there's no other to take a stand against Oswald and his bloody brother, Oswiu.

⌘ CHAPTER 7 ⌘

Penda of the Hwicce AD640

Mercian/Hwiccan border

My brother finally rides into view, late as usual. I watch impatiently as his warriors arrange themselves into a position with which they're comfortable. They want to protect Eowa's rear, as well as his front. I think these men forget that Eowa and I are brothers and mean each other only good wishes.

Or perhaps they don't forget we're family.

I smirk at that. Families. It's no guarantee of loyalty, as I well know.

"Eowa," I call to him, foregoing any reference to his position as King of the Mercians. He knows he's king. I know he's king. There's no need for me to reference it any more than that, not when it's a constant source of strife between us. I wish I'd been the older brother.

I hold my kingdom with something like fealty to him. I resent it and acknowledge the fact as little as I can. Mercia, the land of the men on the borders. That's what Mercia means – the men on the borders. I often ask of where and then I look around. Mercia is surrounded by everyone. We have no coast to call our own.

Eowa's face, so like my own, although more fragile-looking,

with his long drooping moustache and shoulder-length dark hair, twists at my words. He would prefer it if I offered him a 'king' or a 'lord' before his name. But he's my brother, and he knows he's not going to get it. Ever, and certainly not whilst he toils with bloody Oswald. No matter if I understand why he does so.

"Penda," he retorts roughly, slightly tripping over my name, his eyes on my son. I think he almost called me 'lord'. That would have been amusing. It just goes to show how used he's become to being deferential to other men.

My father wouldn't have approved, and neither do I.

He's not seen my son since he was a tiny baby. With the slight opening of his eyes, I can see that he's surprised by Paeda's appearance. He must surely expect me to raise my sons to be the very image of myself, but I've learned many lessons since becoming a king and a father. One of them is that it goes against the constraints of parenthood to turn a child away from its pre-ordained course. My son will not be the same as I am. I know that already. He'll not revel in the blood of other men on his hands. But he'll command men to kill for him. Of that, I've made sure.

"You seem well," I offer, riding my foul-tempered horse to meet him. This won't be a long meeting, and as such, I've made no provision for a tent to be raised to house us. I've brought food and ale but nothing else to ease our conversation. This, I think, also surprises my brother.

He's used to more … sophistication when he treats with Oswald and his allies. It'll do him good to be reminded of our 'rough' manners and origins. We're kings of warriors, not bloody monks.

"As do you, if somewhat without warriors," he states, although it's a question. It amuses me more than it should. Why would I need warriors to meet my brother? He means me no harm, and I mean none to him.

We might not be alike, and I might not appreciate his new allies, but I don't wish to kill him. Not yet anyway.

"My warriors are close. You seem to have brought all yours

with you," I goad. It's always best to make Eowa realise that he'll never have the upper hand in our relationship.

"I ride on to ensure my boundaries are secure."

He thinks I don't know about his expedition to meet with Cynegils and Oswald. He believes I don't know they plan to strike against me soon. That astonishes me. I'm sure I've spoken of my suspicions in front of his spy at my court. I better make sure that I shout my suspicions before the old man. He might have finally become the drunk he always pretends to be. That way, he can account for his long absences when he travels to my brother's court by telling everyone he fell asleep under a tree and forgot his way home.

"Very good, brother, and what news do you bring me, and what should we discuss?"

Eowa's eyes flicker briefly to my face as Herebrod brings him a drinking horn to quench his thirst.

My few men and his are intermingled in a long straggling line. Many of them fought together at Hæðfeld. Many more are brothers or cousins, sharing some sort of family bond. After all, the land of the Hwicce is the heartland of our family's landholdings. I watch with amusement whilst Eowa looks uneasy.

Yet I keep Herebrod close to me. I've heard the unease that his friendship with me brings amongst Eowa's allies. Herebrod is too valuable to lose on the end of a sword or a seax. Herebrod knows of my concerns. He laughs them away, although he also heeds me when I command him to stay away from Eowa's men. I won't allow Eowa to kill my man unless he does it himself. Eowa doesn't have the stones to do that.

No man should command another to carry out his wishes unless he's prepared to do so himself. Oswald needs to learn the lesson. It's the very lesson I've taught my son. He might not want to kill men, he might take no enjoyment in it, but he'll do it when the time comes. Men will honour him for that and carry out his future commands and orders.

"King Oswald grows powerful in the north. His brother has claimed a great victory at Eten."

"Why did Oswiu claim the victory and not Oswald?" My mouth is busy devouring a piece of cooked pork, the juices dripping down my chin. My brother watches me with equal parts fascination and disgust.

"King Oswald has his attention focused elsewhere."

"Yes, but where?" I ask. He looks away, uncomfortable. It's a sure sign he's about to try and lie to me.

It's not a secret to me. I know Oswald's plans. I know how he uses his brother to further his ambitions to the north while he tries to both assist his ally, Domnall Brecc, and undermine his hold on the kingdom of Dal Riata.

Domnall and I have been in communication. I doubt my brother knows that.

We're allies, not bedfellows. I have many secrets from my brother.

"He seeks to spread the word of his God" is the lie my brother tries, the words uneasy and hesitant at first before then appearing in a rush of air as he decides he likes them.

I wish my brother had never allied with Oswald. It's made him weak when he should be strong. After all, he's the King of Mercia. It's not a tiny little kingdom wedged between Deira and the South Saxons and the lands of the Hwicce. No, the Mercian kingdom is a mighty creature, and my brother would rule it better if he paid less mind to Oswald's wishes and more to his own.

"I wish him luck with that," I offer flippantly. My brother glares at me. He sees his lies have failed.

"Who do you go to baptise this time?" I say instead, trying a different tact to see if he might inadvertently speak the truth for once.

"Cenwahl."

Oswald acts to secure his claim on that man's loyalty when his father dies. King Cynegils ails. I've heard it, and so have the traders who travel around our island. That means that there's truth in it. I'd be pleased to ally with Cenwahl. He's neither his father nor his dead older brother. Neither of those men should have ever called themselves warriors. I've tried over the past few years to taunt them into making a fresh war against me, but they're determined against it. Perhaps losing so much more of their land when I fought them at Cirencester, when I was no more than a child, has made them unwilling to risk more.

Parts of my expanding kingdom were once under their command, but no more. To their detriment, the hold on their land wanes whilst I carve out mine. When Cynegils dies, Cenwahl will attempt to take back what I took from them. He'll fail. He'll always fail, even with Oswald as his protector and overlord. He'd do better to be my friend—that way, he might avoid losing more.

"Won't you accept baptism?" my brother queries, trying a different approach and one that makes me chuckle. He looks at me in surprise. Has he forgotten so much about me?

I believe in the old Gods, my Gods, my ancestors. When Eowa talks about converting to Christianity, he talks about abandoning our proud heritage, forgetting that we're the offspring of Gods, the justification for ruling our kingdoms. This Christian God offers no such justification. A little dab of oil, or so I've heard, is all that's needed to make Christian men kings. A little dab of oil! What a ludicrous idea. We use it for cooking and burning the dead. Why would oil on our foreheads make us kings? It's swords and blood and death that make men kings—and having big enough stones to try it.

Men rib me about the size of mine. I let them.

I'm a man, just as they are, but with the ambition of a God and as such, I let them think that I rival a stallion in that regard. They believe me. Or at least, don't have the stones to doubt me.

What is it that the holy oil does? Does it make a man better than his fellow warriors? More inclined to rule well?

Not at all. It's just another way for this new God to try and displace the old Gods. But I do not argue with the old Gods. Not that I much care who other people choose to worship. I know why I'm a warrior king. I see the source of my power and my courage, rage and glory. I'm not trading it in for a dab of oil and some prayers for an after-life that seems dull when compared to the joys of Valhalla. Never.

"No, brother," I offer calmly, watching him intently. "Why, do you plan to convert?"

Eowa's expression blackens at my words. I think I might have touched on something here. Has he already been baptised and failed to tell me? I wouldn't be surprised if he's agreed to such a weak move.

Eowa is the King of the Mercians but only continues to hold it with the support of Oswald. Perhaps I should have realised that his conversion would be one of the terms on which their treaty rests.

I laugh again, pleased to see him so disgruntled. It worries me to think of the extremes Eowa is forcing himself to in order to remain king, to hold the kingdom against me, for all that we count ourselves as allies.

Eowa grunts angrily at me, his eyes once more on Paeda.

"I'll foster your son for you," he says, real malice on his face. He knows I'll never allow it. I'll raise my children, just as my father did before me. I might not plan on making Paeda into a likeness of me, but neither will I permit other men to try and mould him to their likenesses.

"I imagine you'd like that, but no, Paeda will remain with my men and me, with his mother." My wife, Cynewise, is a beautiful woman from the wilderness of Clydog's kingdom. She brought wealth and glory with her, but more than that, she brought joy to my bed and light to my life. She's everything I'm not. I've promised her that she'll have the care of her children—all of them.

"As you will, brother," Eowa concedes, but his eyes remain on Paeda. I consider allowing Gunghir to sidle his way into Eowa's horse as a means of distracting him. But I rein the beast sharply in before he can piss Eowa off even more than I can.

The two have never been allies, the man and the horse, even when we were allies. Perhaps Gunghir senses something in him that I don't. I almost wish the damn horse could talk to me.

In the interest of a more intimate conversation, I slide from my horse and hand the reins to Paeda, not Herebrod. I don't want to cause carnage amongst the sea of mounted men. Although. Well, it might be amusing. Herebrod thanks me with a curt nod.

My brother does the same with his horse, handing his reins to Herebrod. Eowa walks toward me, indicating that we should walk onto the bubbling stream to mask our conversation.

My brother and I have very different roles to play, but sometimes we have to let our guard down and talk freely.

"What the fuck's Oswald doing now?" I demand angrily. My brother chuckles, all pretensions of his unease around me gone.

"He has his visions from his God," he offers contemptuously. "And he must do what his God orders him to do."

"I don't know how you stand it," I offer with genuine sympathy. If our positions had been reversed, I'd have killed Oswald a long time ago. I've only met him briefly. He's nothing like Lord Eanfrith, who I loved almost like a brother. There's no humour to him, no modesty. He believes everything he does has been possible because of his God's gracious desires. The stories I hear about him bore me. I couldn't stand to be in the same room as him.

Eowa turns and looks at Herebrod.

"He demands Herebrod's death."

"I know he does. But he'll not get what he wants. Herebrod is my man, loyal to our family, not to Oswald."

"He thinks that Herebrod will force the Picts to battle against us all."

"I only wish he could," I sigh loudly. Herebrod has a small amount of sway in the Pictish kingdom but nothing to that which Oswald assumes he has. It's ludicrous how concerned Oswald is with someone who spends most of his life living in my kingdom and not with his wife in hers.

"He thinks that if he kills Herebrod, your power in the northern kingdom will be curtailed and that you'll have no choice but to become his ally as well."

"Doesn't he know about my alliances with Cynddylan and Clydog?"

"He does, yes, but he doesn't believe they have any strength to offer you."

"Has he forgotten about Cadwallon so quickly?"

Eowa's breath sharply catches as I ask the question.

"No," Eowa confirms, his voice almost thunderous. "Oswald forgets nothing about Cadwallon, but he thinks that power has been broken and that the other kingdoms will never ally without him as their head."

"He underestimates me then."

"Continually," my brother says with malice on his face. My brother never underestimates me.

"Why can't we just kill him?" I ask petulantly. Oswald is the only impediment to my brother and me commanding all the kingdoms on our island.

"He's too powerful," Eowa shrugs. "Warriors and priests always surround him. He's not easy to kill, and too many would seek revenge for his death at the moment. He has too many brothers to rule after him."

"Fuck," I say softly, cursing Cadwallon once more for killing Lord Eanfrith. He was a weaker man. We would have been able to rule through him easily. Cadwallon. He was always one step in front of his thought processes in his actions. Killing Osric was an unfortunate move on his part. Murdering Lord Eanfrith was catastrophic, as was allowing Oswald, a poor orphan from the lands of Dal Riata, raised in the ways of the Ionan Church, to not only re-soundly beat him in battle but to do it in his new God's name. That he killed Cadwallon in the process is even more damaging.

Oswald rules with the might of his warriors and the passion of his faith. It's infuriating.

I was pleased when Cadwallon died, I know I speak truthfully, but his death was the catalyst for my current predicament. In almost ten years, I've done little but hold my own against the growing power of Oswald. Even with Eowa acting for the good of our family, we've managed to make no progress in acquiring more and more influence.

"When can we force him to war?" I query. This is our intention. If we can't kill him secretly, we must do so in a great battle. We'll not have our names smeared as Cadwallon did by taking the lives of virtually unarmed men. His murder of Eanfrith, his loyal ally, has undermined my power. I'd kill bloody Cadwallon if only he weren't already dead.

"Soon. I can see it in the near future."

My brother has been saying this for the last four years, ever since we made our alliance against Oswald. It happened after Eowa failed to support me in the battle against the East Anglian kings and only afterwards realised the error of that decision. I hope he's not trying to delay the attack so that Oswald can grow even stronger. I hope he's not working as some sort of interloper in my kingdom to assist Oswald. I have my suspicions.

I love my brother. I don't trust him. Even now.

"Will we march north or entice him south?"

This has long been the debate, just as it was with Edwin. Do men fight more passionately for their land and lives or for others? We could attack Oswald in Northumbria or Mercia? Which would strike the most powerful message in the hearts of the men who want to rule in Eowa's place and mine? What would make me more powerful?

"Hæðfeld was in Northumbria," he simply offers. He always says that, and I've yet to decipher his intent behind the words. What does it mean? Was that a good thing or a bad thing?

"Clydog and Cynddylan say their men are more likely to fight closer to home."

"They bloody would," Eowa mutters. He's met with Clydog and Cynddylan, but he doesn't like them. He holds a dark opinion of them. He thinks they shouldn't be trusted and that when the battle finally comes, they'll run from the battlefield, taking their warriors with them.

I wish Eowa would try and trust someone. It doesn't help that Clydog and Cynddylan mirror Eowa's unease.

"It makes sense," I try and reason. I don't apologise for other people's perceived shortcomings, but in this, I think Clydog and Cynddylan might have a good point.

Cadwallon convinced many men to rise against Edwin because we wanted to attack the heart of his kingdom, but we only made it to Hæðfeld. The victory we gained didn't stain Northumbrian soil. As such, I think its impact was more far-reaching. It allowed Cadwallon to run virtually unmolested through Deira and Bernicia, take the dead king's men by surprise. I believe we should do the same.

"I'm going to attack your kingdom," I finally offer. I've thought about this for a long time. "Oswald is your overlord. He'll have to come to your defence."

Eowa turns to glare at me, his eyes oozing hatred.

"Why?" he demands, failing to keep his anger from seeping from him.

"As I say, Oswald will have to come to your defence, and then we can cut off any means of retreat he might have. We'll trap him in Mercia. If your people know that you're allied with me, they'll do everything possible to impede Oswald and his warriors."

There's so much logic in my words that, for all that Eowa hates to hear them, he says nothing further, other than, "When?"

"When the time is right. I think it best if you don't know the exact details. It'll make it look like a more genuine attack."

"I don't want you to murder my people?" he asserts. I'd not realised what a soft heart he has.

"It's not my intention to kill your people, but some will have to die, or Oswald won't believe the attack is anything but a ruse."

"Oh, he will," Eowa offers angrily, stalking back to snatch the reins from Herebrod, his intention to ride away clear. I'd not expected him to respond well to my words, but I'd anticipated a slightly more rational response than this. Although, well, it'll look as though we've genuinely argued, which is good for all those spies amongst our warriors to see.

I watch Eowa with interest as he jumps onto the back of his horse. He directs the beast away from me, back toward his men. Only then does he stop, pause for a long moment, before riding back my way.

I stand still, watching him, my eyes narrowed against the

glare of the sun. His warriors, alert to the fact that they're leaving, are starting to stream away from their small conversation groupings. At Eowa's reversal, everyone stops and watches him just as avidly as I do.

His men think we're almost enemies and that we'd kill each other before offering each other assistance.

He knees his horse back toward me. His expression is thunderous, and yet when he reaches down to me, his mouth pressed close to my ear, his words surprise me.

"Either Oswald dies in the battle, or you do. Either way. Mercia is mine, you cheeky fucking bastard."

He doesn't even look at me as he turns and snaps his horse to a gallop over the burgeoning growth of another year's bounty. My laughter follows him.

Gods, I love my brother.

This is going to be a monumental battle. Men will speak of it for years to come!

CHAPTER 8

Eowa of Mercia

Borderlands with the Hwicce

A sense of satisfaction fills me as I ride away from my brother. Just once, I'd like to upset him, leave him unsure as to my intentions.

His parting laughter, brought to me on the slight breeze, initially angers me and then makes me smile, all the time riding onwards, confident my men will fall into place beside me.

My brother. He's earned his name as a warrior and his position of respect amongst other men. Yet he's no ruler. Not as I am. He sees everything in terms of blood and violence, death and life; there can be no in-between for him, no haziness.

It's one of his downfalls.

The fact that I've just threatened his very life will have no impact on him. He knows he lives and dies by his battle prowess, nothing more. I almost wish he weren't my brother, but then I wouldn't want him as my full-blown enemy either. I could almost pity Oswald if I didn't appreciate the uncertainty that both he and Penda bring to events on our island.

My brother is a mighty warrior. He's shown it time and time again. Only circumstances beyond his control have prevented him from making far more of his victories than he has so far.

Most pertinent of those circumstances has been my lacklustre response to his triumphs and my failure to assist him when I perhaps should have done.

Yet, I do foresee a future where he's the king who holds the most significant sway over our island. In that future, men and women rush to do his bidding, both in fear and awe. He has an enticing personality. He listens and learns. He has a prodigious memory for names, and nothing, not one small piece of information, is ever forgotten.

But Oswald is the current king holding influence over our island, and he's come from nowhere to accomplish much in a short time. He's stolen, time and time again, the momentum that Penda carries with him into every battle and argument. That's why he's powerful whilst Penda tries to bait him into making a misstep.

I don't know if it'll ever happen. While Oswald shares my borders, I've no choice but to ally with him, bow before him and offer to convert to his Christianity, no matter how much I don't want to.

To remain ahead of Penda, I must be even more alert to events all over our island. I need to know what Oswald and Penda are doing before they even think about doing it, and it's there that Penda has a vast advantage over Oswald.

Penda is a man of action. He'd sooner march through a winter storm than sit in his hall, getting slowly drunk and lying with his wife.

Not so much Oswald. He needs time for contemplation. He's almost half a monk, and he's reliant on the portents he interprets as coming from his God. He talks and plots, and rarely, oh so rarely, does he strike, and every move he makes can be foreseen.

Yet as soon as Penda attacks my kingdom, Oswald will rise against him. He won't even consider not marching to battle against him. In that respect, Penda understands him better than he should. It won't be a quick decision, though. No, but it'll happen, eventually. Oswald won't allow Penda to try to undermine me. After all, I am one of Oswald's most powerful and staunchest allies. Or so he believes.

If Cadwallon had allowed Lord Eanfrith to live, Oswald would never have gained his position as king. No, Penda would have been king over all of us. I know that. It gives me some comfort to know that I supported Oswald in his victory over Cadwallon and that I stayed Penda's groping reach.

If Penda had moved to secure Deira for himself in the wake of Osric's death, instead of allowing Cadwallon to roam widely, Lord Eanfrith might never have died. In the end, I imagine that Penda would have been forced to attack and kill Cadwallon to stop his incursions. As soon as Cadwallon won at Hæðfeld, the joy of battle lust filled him and never left.

But the various scenarios I once envisaged would bring my brother to the position of king of the Saxon kingdoms have bled away, just as Osric and Lord Eanfrith did, on Cadwallon's sword.

Penda can blame his current predicament entirely on the shoulders of Cadwallon. If he publicly does so, he'll lose the support of Cynddylan and Clydog. The British don't take kindly to others, Saxons no less, criticising one of their numbers. It's only amongst themselves that harsh words can be spoken and revenge taken.

I can see how my ancestors managed to take so much of Britain, driving the ancient tribes to the edges of our shared island. I can also see that they'll happily accept my brother and me as their allies in the right circumstances. But never as king of Northumbria or its constituent parts. Never.

There are too many dominant kingdoms to the north of Northumbria or Bernicia to give it the correct title for the northernmost part of the kingdom. They haven't yet finished standing in opposition to the Saxon men and women who try to farm and rule their land.

Oswald might think his alliance with Domnall will protect him while also allowing him to override his kingdom as well. But he's wrong to think so. Even I know that. I've fought against the men of Eten as a member of Oswald's host. I know determination and strength when I see it. The land of the Goddodin might have suffered a reverse, but even now, they work to carve out their kingdom once more. Oswald is deluded if he believes he's won that engagement already.

I could be a great king. I know it. But too many men contend with me. Unless they all drop dead, I'll never have the momentum they do.

No, Oswald not only stole the wind from Penda's sails, but he also did the same to me. Every day since, I've laboured to undo his influence, realising that I'll only regain what I've lost if I become his ally and remain as such.

I play a dangerous game. Penda and I are allies of a sort, but more through our blood than a shared vision of the future. He sees this island as his, with me as just an annoyance or an encumbrance to be born patiently. I see the future as belonging to my family, not Penda's.

I'm also an ally of Oswald, ostensibly because Penda and I decided it would be the best course of action to keep Mercia safe. But also because I wanted to be Oswald's ally. Until all the men who thwart my plans are dead, I must be a friend to them.

Should Penda fall, and he just might, if his arrogance gets to be too much for others to stand, then Oswald will rule without impediment. Oswald will need me to rule Mercia for him. All of it.

Still, I don't like my predicament, mainly because I don't know how I want the future to evolve. Do I want to be ruled by my brother? Or a man with no blood ties to me, who could turn on me at any moment and accuse me of aiding his brother's killer to gain control over the British Isles?

I don't know. It's that which keeps me awake at night. Not the fear that I dishonour my family with my alliance, and not the worry that I might support the wrong person. No, it's the knowledge that I don't know who I want ultimately to be victorious because, in my mind, I want it to be me.

Should a great plague kill Penda and Oswald, it could be me, but I'm not lucky enough to have both men drop dead before me, paving the way for my success.

Penda has the luck of the Gods. That's why I toy with Oswald's new Christianity. He doesn't seem to have great warrior as a prerequisite for being a king over other men and women. No, this new God might offer me more chances of gaining what I want. But I'm not convinced. He seems a vengeful sort of God, more likely to demand that the victor pays penance for his success rather than be a justification for that hard-won success.

I might have offered to convert to keep Oswald as my ally, but it's only a half-hearted conversion. I'm no Christian. It must just be that I'm no longer a worshipper of Woden either. Time will tell.

For now, my men ride with me, Penda far behind us now. I savour the time alone with my thoughts. When I ride, my worries fade to nothing. My hopes become the possibilities of dreams. Only when I reach my destination does reality crash down around me.

I'm the king of Mercia, but only because Oswald supports me and, for the time being, my brother as well.

It won't always be that way.

No, I didn't lie when I warned Penda as I did. Whoever is the victor, or likely to be the victor, will support my warriors and me. Until then, this delicate balancing act must continue. That's why I now ride to meet with Oswald and his newest convert, Cenwahl. Cenwahl was a pagan but now wishes to be a Christian. I'm intrigued to watch his baptism, to see if he suddenly becomes infused with a new Christian spirit that drives out his pagan one. I believe he simply acts now as a means of securing Oswald as his overlord, the only man who could beat Penda in battle.

Cenwahl's father ails, and Cenwahl knows that on his father's death, Penda will attack his kingdom again. Oswald foresees the same. He'll act as soon as possible, despite anything that Oswald tries to do. The net tries to close around Penda, but he'll have thought this through.

War is coming, and any who can't see it are blind to my brother's ambition and Oswald's vision for the future.

I consider what it would be like if the two decided to cast their hatred aside and work together. They'd rule every kingdom between them. There'd certainly be no room for men such as I in their plans.

However, neither Oswald nor Penda will ever take the first steps to uniting for a single purpose. I know I'm safe. For now. Until one or other of them makes too great a demand on me and punishes me for failing to carry out their instructions.

My destination is Dorchester. It's a long way for Oswald to travel and shows his confidence in the alliance with the men who control the kingdoms along the route. He helped Onna of the Eastern Angles after Penda's attack five years ago. My kingdom won't attack Oswald while I'm absent. Oswald even draws close to Kent and relies on those men not to attack him.

I'm sure that Penda would confront Oswald for all that this expedition was supposed to be a secret. But Penda doesn't wish to show his power yet, his prowess in battle. Penda hides his strength well, but his very arrogance in travelling with so few men to meet me highlights how strong he is as well as the intense loyalty of his men and his innate belief in his Gods and himself.

If Oswald only knew the enemy he'd created, I doubt he'd be as comfortable and assured in his current power base.

Time will tell.

I've been to Dorchester-on-the-Thames before when Cynegils underwent baptism, and his sister married Oswald. It's a fair settlement, a place of trade and where Bishop Birinus has built his first church. From it, the bishop labours to convert Cynegils' people. It makes excellent use of the River Thames as a means of enticing traders to and from it, and yet I hold no thoughts of owning the site or taking it from Cynegils. There are settlements with more wealth and more effective defences throughout Cynegils' kingdoms. It's also far too close to Penda's powerbase.

I wouldn't want that. Not unless he were my brother.

It only takes the rest of the day to reach the place following my meeting with Penda. Along the way, my thoughts turn away from Penda and focus on Oswald. What will he demand from me now?

Oswald troubles himself with events to the north of his kingdom. The Dal Riatans raised him during his exile. As such, he simply wants my kingdom that of Cynegils, that of the East Angles and Kent, to remain peaceful whilst he wrestles control of the northern lands out of the hands of the Goddodin and into his. Oswald has more than a passing fascination with becoming king of Dal Riata himself. I don't think he fully comprehends his ambition. But I see it, and so does Domnall.

Only two years ago, Domnall attempted to exert his command over the kingdom of Alt Clut. When that failed, Oswald took advantage by attacking Eten, at the heart of Goddodin, while the kings and warriors of those lands were busy fulfilling their obligations to their lords.

Oswald means to be more than just king of the Saxon kingdoms. He intends to take as many of the British domains as he can. Perhaps then, he'll turn his eye towards the land of the Picts. Not that I think he has the means to accomplish all he wants. He faces opposition wherever he goes. Only his brother's firm hold on Rheged and Gododdin keep Oswald's position safe.

Oswald demanded I support the attack on Gododdin. I did, but only because it allowed my warriors to practice their skills, not because I thought he had the right to claim the kingdom. And as I thought, his rule was only fragmentary. Gododdin still lives as a separate entity.

Within Dorchester itself, I find myself drawn to the church built by Bishop Birinus. The last time I saw it, it was barely begun, just a few wooden struts sticking up through the mud of the recent rainstorm. Now, its wooden structure rises high on those wooden struts, and I can't help thinking that it would make a fine mead hall. Perhaps not for what Birinus was hoping?

Most of my men take themselves away to find room for the horses and themselves, but a handful of my chosen warriors walk with me through the neat streets to seek out Cynegils in person.

A smirk crosses my face as I near his hall. It's almost identical to Birinus' church. Servants and slaves alike carry great jugs of mead in and out of its open doors. Night will fall soon, and when it does, the doors will be closed, and the heat and the smoke locked up tight inside. Until then, men and women, children, stray animals and dogs have free and easy access to their king. It's a sure sign that Oswald hasn't yet arrived.

Oswald employs more ceremony within his hall, making it akin to a religious service where everything must be done in the correct order than a warrior's mead hall.

As we were challenged at Dorchester's set of defensive earthworks entrance, Cynegils has already been informed of my presence. Yet he doesn't rush to meet me, not even sending his son to make such a greeting. I could be annoyed, but instead, I think it speaks more of Cynegils apathy at his position. He's an old man. He'll die soon, and when he does, he's left his son nothing more than a kingdom that must do fealty to Oswald to survive against Penda's reaching grasp.

Cynegils has nothing about which to be proud. I think he knows it.

Stepping into the gloom of the hall, lit by a substantial central hearth and smoky lamps at its periphery, I'm not surprised to see Cynegils almost sleeping in his ceremonial chair, his son at his side, looking anything but pleased.

Cenwahl wears his hair in the way of a Saxon warrior, his long moustache dripping long past his chin. He was always a pleasant man in the past, but his brother's death and impending conversion have soured him. He glances my way, gestures half-heartedly for me to join him, and turns to nudge his father awake.

It's not exactly a scene of martial glory.

Cynegils grunts to wakefulness. I attempt to show him the respect he's due. Old men deserve to be remembered for what they've achieved, not what they've become.

His eyes blink in the dull glow, and he looks about as though surprised to find he's in his hall at Dorchester by the Thames. I hope I never grow old.

Cynegils wipes drool from his mouth while pushing his body back into his chair. His clothes are fine but have probably been repaired numerous times, and they've certainly been taken in now. Some men grow fat in old age, but Cynegils is skinnier than a youth.

"My Lord King," I say hopefully, looking at Cenwahl as I speak. He rolls his eyes at my words and tuts loudly. I don't know if Cynegils hears him or not, but he ignores him if he does.

"Who are you?" Cynegils demands, his voice rough with age and lack of use.

"Eowa, my lord king, King of Mercia." That causes him to harrumph and fiddle with his clothing, reaching for the emblem of his new God around his neck. The cross flashes more brightly than Cynegils does. He must have invested a fortune in that simple piece of jewellery.

"Yes, yes, I'm expecting you," Cynegils replies, his face a puzzled frown as he tries to remember if he's speaking the truth or not.

"Yes, you are, and it's good to be here."

Servants and slaves are meandering around the hall, trying to find mead jugs and cups for my men. It seems that it's not only Cynegils who ails here. I'd not realised just how weak he'd become. Does Penda not realise how easy it would be for him to take the kingdom now? What sort of game is he playing if he does know?

I reconsider. My brother doesn't like an easy challenge. He'll think it beneath him to attack an old, dying man. No, he'll wait for the son and attack a youth who should be his equal in battle. He has much to prove to himself and his followers.

"Is Oswald here?" he asks cantankerously. "My daughter?"

Cenwahl grunts angrily at the words and doesn't seem inclined to answer.

"I don't think so, My Lord King. I've only just arrived myself."

I'm trying to dilute whatever tense atmosphere exists between the disgruntled son and the confused father, but it seems

I'm failing.

"Are you a Christian?" The question comes from Cenwahl, although he doesn't look at me or meet my eyes.

"I'm undergoing instruction," I lie smoothly. It'll do me no favours with Oswald if he's reminded that I've yet to convert fully. I might have to speak with Cenwahl and tell him to shut the fuck up. This isn't about my conversion. It's about his.

"You should come and listen to the good Bishop Birinus this evening," he answers glibly, smirking at me now. Cenwahl has decided he's no ally of mine. I'm tempted to leave before Oswald arrives. It might be better to upset Oswald by my absence rather than by my perceived continued apostasy.

Only, as with all things, Oswald chooses that moment to make his presence known, with one of Cynegils' men rushing into the hall to inform his lord that the King of Northumbria has arrived, Oswald Whiteblade.

"I'd be delighted to listen to Bishop Birinus' words," I say into the immediately soured face of Cenwahl. He'd hoped to have some fun at my expense, but Oswald's arrival has reminded him of the events of the following day when he'll become a Christian and I won't. He growls, making as though to stand, but then slumping in his chair once more.

I'm still standing, and so I move back toward the door. I think I'd rather meet Oswald away from Cynegils and Cenwahl. Perhaps I could even warn him of the unhappiness his arrival brings. But no. I've no reason to try and win his appreciation. I'm his ally. He can deal with his other allies on his own.

Outside, the atmosphere is clearer but also colder. It'll be frigid tonight. It's too early in the summer, and ice often mars the early mornings. I hope I warrant a sleeping place close to the central hearth.

There's far more activity at Oswald's arrival than at mine. I even see Bishop Birinus himself hustling across the hard ground to reach the hall. I can only hope he presents as a more convivial host than Cynegils. I bow my head so that he doesn't see me, but it doesn't work. My fine clothing sticks in his hurried glance, and before I know he's standing before me.

"King Eowa," he offers, inclining his head just a touch. These holy men from the Pope believe they're superior to the 'pagan' kings of the Saxons, as they refer to us. I'm surprised they manage to convert anyone to their religion with their unapproachable manner.

"Bishop Birinus, I hear you're to preach this evening," I offer before he can invite me. He looks too pleased with my words. I appreciate that his preaching is intended to astound Oswald and will probably last well into the cooling night.

"You'll come and listen?" he gushes in response. I nod just once, my gaze distracted by the horses being ridden into the area before the hall. Why hasn't Oswald left his horses near the open field with his men? There's no room here. Someone is bound to be trampled.

Oswald rides his white horse before the assembled crowd. He wears a helm embedded with jewels and layered with different colours of gold and silver. His cloak is heavy fur, no doubt from his time in Dal Riata, and beneath it pokes the handle of his sword, the sword with which he earned his name.

It flashes white in the dying daylight. I believe he's timed his arrival to look as magnificent and munificent as possible. He understands the ways of the kings of Dal Riata. He comprehends the importance of showing his wealth and power.

If Lord Oswiu were with him, his dourness would only make Oswald appear to glow even brighter with the light from his God.

I'm jealous. I know it. I wish I could arrive with such fanfare making my presence and wishes known with seemingly little effort. But I'm a warrior king, if not a warrior king like my brother. I'm not a Christian king, and this is how Oswald presents himself in his shining metal helm and carefully crafted sword.

I'm reminded all over again of the reasons that men and women follow his words and strive to bring his wishes to fruition. Oswald has a persona that makes men and women want to be seen in his reflected glow.

I don't. That's all I know.

Although, I would quite like his sword and his reputation.

Perhaps I should have been raised in exile by men who fight every season regardless of whether they have an enemy or not? Oswald's honed his skills against the legendary warriors of the ancient tribes of Ireland.

Oswald notes me, but his eyes widen with joy on seeing Bishop Birinus. I remember my ire at his treatment of me in the past. My belief in the Old Gods still causes rancour. Oswald accords me only as much respect as he feels he should.

I wished I'd stayed with Penda and ridden to war now. I'm sure that if I'd given the matter more thought, Penda and I could have taken the Northumbrian kingdom while Oswald sits on his bloody white horse, extolling his Christian virtues.

I smirk dourly at the thought. Perhaps I'm more like my brother than I care to admit. I need Penda to win the coming battle. If he doesn't, I'll be stuck with Oswald until he does me the courtesy of dying.

Bishop Birinus walks sedately toward Oswald, his hands clasped together in prayer. Oswald removes his helm to receive whatever blessing Birinus offers him. I hope it won't be a long one. It's cold outside, away from the heat of the fire.

Before Oswald can slide from his horse, Cynegils shuffles his way into view. I can see why he ails so quickly. He must have an old wound to his left leg. Blood seeps through a padded wad of bandages as he walks. Every step must be agony for him. I can also see, in the outside light, that his skin is greying and hangs in folds around his slack face. I can only assume that his injury is slowly poisoning him.

I pity him for such a poor death. Better to die on a battlefield than to be the victim of such an injury. I try to think more considerately toward him, but then he opens his mouth to welcome Oswald, and I immediately forget any kindly thoughts I might have had about him.

"The great King Oswald," he somehow manages to shout, his

voice causing everyone in the space before the hall to lapse into silence. "You're most welcome in my kingdom. It's an honour to have such a mighty warrior and Christian king visit with me."

Cenwahl's face briefly mirrors mine of disgust. Oswald gets this sort of response, whereas I had to tiptoe before him and wake him. Perhaps I should work on my aura.

"King Cynegils," Oswald responds in the same vein, and so it goes on, both of them trying to out-do the other with their praises. Oswald's horse's legs start to shift at being forced to such inactivity after so long on the road. I, too, begin to tire of the display. Surely they could call each other such grand names inside the hall and not outside?

Only when a drenching rain begins to fall do either of the men move to enter the hall. Oswald hasn't so much as spoken to me, brushing past me as he goes to stand before the fire. By now, I'm cold and hungry and angry.

If only he hadn't seen me, I'd be on my way to Penda. I don't wish to play any more significant part in Oswald's plans to surround Penda and force him to war. He doesn't seem to appreciate that Penda has no other intention than war. He welcomes it. He wants it.

Oswald takes Cynegils arm in a warm welcome, and the pair of them saunter toward the great hearth. I trail in their wake, as does Cenwahl and a woman I don't recognise but think might be Oswald's wife and Cenwahl's sister. She seems serene. Her conversion hasn't embittered her as its promise does her brother.

It makes me appreciate that Oswald has a spy here. He must have warned his wife of her father's illness. Perhaps she hopes to rule here one day, or rather, allow her son to rule here. Oswald's ambitions in that regard wouldn't surprise me.

I look around to see if others bow before Oswald or if it's just myself and Cynegils. My eye fixes on Bishop Birinus. The man is beside himself with satisfaction. I'm sure the Christian priests aren't supposed to be so self-righteous. I look away quickly. I don't want to meet his eyes and have him seek me out again, personally. He'd only drone on about his God, and I'm in no mood to listen.

In the time we've been outside, the hall's interior has transformed into something that resembles a warrior's mead hall instead of a shabby hovel. Fresh herbs are hanging from the rafters to add the scent of very early summer freshness to the occasion. The fire has been rebuilt, made huge by adding several split logs to its bed. The temperature has increased ten-fold. Huge pots of food steam merrily, and a boar is roasting over the licking flames.

I must ensure that my appearance is met with as much pomp and ceremony as this in future. I hold just as much land as Oswald.

Without being invited to the conference, I push my way through the throng of people so that I stand before the crowd, not part of it. But there I wait. I don't want to force my way into the conversation. I just don't wish to be ignored entirely.

Cenwahl follows me, standing awkwardly to my right, whereas Bishop Birinus takes it upon himself to walk directly to Oswald. The relationships in this hall are out of line with the prevailing atmosphere. I should stand by Cynegils and Oswald, not the bloody bishop.

I could make a small scene, push myself to the fore of the group, but one look from Cenwahl, and I know he's not only thinking the same as I do but also pitying us both as well for doing so. I hold in place.

I'm prepared to play this game for just a little bit longer, just to assure myself that I'm not better off with Oswald for an ally. I want Penda to be my best choice, the ally I should turn to naturally, but I know that blood ties, even the ties of the same parent, mean nothing.

Edwin stands as a testament to that. Both of his sons turned against him, even his cousin. Edwin's a cautionary tale in trusting family too much. I don't want to make the same mistake.

A few moments stretch into an almost interminable amount of time. I begin to uncomfortably shift as I wait for Oswald and Cynegils to finish whatever their business is. Surely everything has already been agreed far in advance? They must both know what's planned? I've been riding all day. I want nothing more than to sleep, but it seems I'm to be denied any respite from the events that Oswald has arranged. Before I can so much as lay eyes on him again, he's leaving the hall in a swirl of cloak and a passing aroma of the outside world.

I look around in confusion, and Cynegils takes my arm and guides me after the small train of primarily men, with just Oswald's wife amongst them.

"The Church," he simply says. I groan. I'm too tired even to pretend to be interested in their prayers and exhortations to their particular God.

Cenwahl chuckles darkly at my side.

"What price we must pay for security on our island." I find myself cursing my brother. If he were dead, then there'd be no need to ally with Oswald.

Or would there be?

I shake the thought aside. I'm about to step into one of their holy places. I need to force my thoughts to blankness and allow their words to wash over me without making any impact.

I long for Oswald to have stayed in the kingdom of Dal Riata and for Penda to have taken control of the Northumbrian lands. Perhaps Penda still can. With my help, of course.

✣CHAPTER 9✣

Oswald of Northumbria AD640

Dorchester

I observe Eowa as Cenwahl is submerged into the water on the narrow ledge that juts out into the menacing River Thames.

He's watching carefully, his expression bland. I know he plays at being a Christian. That he listens to the words of the priests and bishops I send to him but without them having any impact on him.

I've spoken to Bishop Aidan about the unwillingness of the man to convert fully, but all Aidan says is that men's hearts move slowly and that I must wait.

But I don't wish to wait. Not anymore.

I've waited for over five years, and he still has no intention of converting. I'd have demanded the conversion as part of our alliance with any other ally. With Eowa, it was different. He came to me when King Cadwallon was ravaging my family's lands. He offered me his support, an untried prince, with nothing to offer other than the potential to kill Cadwallon.

Not that we became firm allies then, but his support assisted me greatly. I've ensured that the written record preserved by the holy men under Bishop Aidan's direction makes no mention of him. For how could I have won a holy war against Cadwallon when Eowa, my ally, was little more than a pagan? And that's with making no mention of the fact that Eowa had been a supporter of Cadwallon until the Welsh king had run rampant across Northumbria, killing men who'd been his allies.

I think that Eowa must have feared for his life. Why else would he have come to me, offered me his men and his sword, if not for that reason? Certainly, Eowa didn't follow my religion and still, apparently, doesn't.

It was only when his brother flexed his reach attempting to take East Anglia that our alliance became solidified. Only then could it be spoken about. Still, in deference to his initial support, I let him remain as he was. Now I look like a fool, although Bishop Aidan assures me that I do God's work even with Eowa as he is.

I don't see it, and I don't feel it.

No, he must fully commit to being my ally, and I'll have to tell him as much. He's failed twice now. Herebrod still lives, and Eowa still practices his pagan worship of the old Gods, offering blood sacrifices to see him through the winter season.

Eowa's damaging my reputation. How can I be the holiest Christian king on this island with a heathen for an ally?

Eowa meets my gaze. He always knows when I'm watching him. It's an uncanny ability. He raises his hand somberly, aware of the importance of the moment, yet even in that, I sense deceit. Eowa understands the customs; that's plain to see. But he doesn't embrace them.

No, if he wishes to remain my ally, to know that his borders are secure, he must convert sooner rather than later. He must do it before men like Cenwahl question why I make them listen to the one true faith while allowing Eowa such freedoms.

Whatever Eowa sees in my eyes, he nods, just the once, and turns back to focus on Cenwahl and Bishop Birinus. Birinus allows his Latin words to flow above the noise of everyone assembled, his speech somehow elongated and elaborate. I much prefer listening to Bishop Aidan when he baptises the Northumbrians. I wish Birinus would hurry up with his farce. He neither explains Cenwahl nor describes the significance of his actions, not as Aidan would do.

I sigh loudly. My wife looks at me pointedly. I note Cyniburh's expensive dress and the jewels that flash on the brooches securing that dress. She wears a shimmering piece of silk around her blond hair. She looks every part a king's wife. It's a blessing that she's so comely.

She knows what I'm thinking as her lips turn slightly upwards. She and Bishop Aidan are good friends now. She trusts his teachings and listens attentively. I feared when I took her as my second wife that I was making a terrible mistake, but I was quickly proved wrong in every respect other than our ability to have children.

Only now do we have a son who lies in his cradle, breathing freely and growing by the day. It's a poor result for over five years of marriage and no end of praying, but she's happy, and so I am. I hope this is just the first of many sons who'll be born to us and who'll serve their older brother when he becomes king in my place. Not that I anticipate that happening anytime soon. Other than Penda, my position is secure. Oswiu is my trusted commander to the north, while I maintain peace to the south.

The Saxon kingdoms are almost too pleased to have someone to command them, as I do, and to help them rule and grow stronger as they counter Penda.

Yet I don't understand their worry about Penda. He's a bloodthirsty warrior, nothing more. He was once lucky enough to be associated with Cadwallon, and now he isn't. He has no skill to rule. I imagine his men are restless at his ineptitude. I'll support Cenwahl when he tries to overrun his kingdom after this baptism. Then Cenwahl will be just like the rest of my supporters. All of them, apart from Eowa, are welcome to my warriors and my blessing.

But not Eowa. He needs to prove himself to me, finally, and this will be his last time chance.

✟ CHAPTER 10 ✟

Oswiu of Northumbria AD640

The Kingdom of the Gododdin

Despite the gloom that infects the day, I feel free. My visit with Oswald was a total failure. He'll never listen to my concerns regarding Penda. I shouldn't have wasted my time and effort trying to convince him otherwise.

Yet something productive did come from my journey, his permission to attack the kingdom of the Gododdin once more. Two years ago, with an alliance of Oswald's oath sworn followers and with the support of the kingdom of Dal Riata, we took the attack to the very heart of their kingdom. But we left too soon before our hold was secure, and ever since then, I've wanted to return, to finish the takeover of the kingdom.

I still don't know why Oswald withdrew, but as it gives me the chance to deal with my anger and frustration with events further south, I'm not about to complain. I think it might be because he argued with Domnall Brecc about dividing the spoils of war. Domnall resents that neither Oswald nor I are bending to his will.

It was Domnall's father who provided support to us during our exile. Domnall has always resented it. I don't understand, and neither does Oswald, why Domnall believes we owe him anything for his father's generosity.

This kingdom of the Goddodin, perched on the top of my brother's land, is in its dying days. Its royal family is weak. Its warriors were almost destroyed by an attack my father led nearly forty years ago. They've tried to rebuild, but after Oswald and Domnall's attack and my failure to adhere to the terms of the peace accord, they're even weaker than they were. Although I have only two hundred men to my name, it'll be more than enough.

The British kingdom of Gododdin has outlived its usefulness, isolated so far from the other remaining British realms. It's archaic and has outlasted its ability to survive in the face of the advances of the Saxons, in which I include myself.

Oswald assures me that once I've expelled the remaining royal family, he'll allow me to rule here, alongside my British wife from Rheged, to ease the transition. Then, when the time is fortuitous, we'll simply amalgamate the Gododdin into Bernicia, and Oswald will have grown his kingdom with my help. I need to ensure he never forgets that.

My warrior, Willyn, has been scouting the settlement at Eten for me, and he returns with a smirk to his youthful face, a spring in his step as he bows before me. We're out of sight of the settlement but near enough that we'll overrun it quickly once I give the order.

"They've barely rebuilt their defences. We could just walk in and take what we want." I imagined those were the words with which he'd greet me. The kingdom of the Goddodin has lost most of its warrior class. Few can fight for its survival now. They have only babes and old men to stand and face my fury. I could almost pity them.

"I don't want just to take it," I say moodily. I want a battle. I want to be *tested*.

Willyn grins at me. He shares my frustration. He knows me too well as he pulls his seax from his weapons belt and examines the sheen to the sharp blade.

"If they offer it to us instead of a battle, we'll have to take it.

We can't exactly turn down a kingdom. My Lord," he offers as an aside.

I growl. He speaks the truth, but it's not what I want to hear.

Rheged, my wife's kingdom, will never be mine, and I only married her to ease Oswald's transition in becoming the king of Northumbria. She might be the granddaughter of the mighty Urien, the much-lauded warrior king, but she has brothers who'll rule in her father's stead. I need somewhere to call mine. Although I understood that Oswald would share Northumbria with me, he hordes it to himself, under the belief that his reputation will prevent any from attacking him.

Oswald deems he has everything he needs; a wife from the southern kingdoms; a bishop from the holy island of Iona to tend to him; a son from a previous marriage and a new one, still in his cradle; his reputation gained fighting in the kingdom of Dal Riata, but he's weak. He believes the stories men tell him about how powerful he is, and he'll not divide his kingdom or allow others to share his duties.

Northumbria is his to rule as he sees fit. He'll hear nothing said against him.

Yet, he's my brother. I love him and respect him.

But for now, I need men to wage war against, to erase my anger against him, to make me into a warrior of greater renown than he is, Oswald Whiteblade, exiled orphan and now king of a mighty kingdom.

No matter how short, this battle will be my opportunity, and I don't intend to squander it.

✤CHAPTER 11✤

*King Cynegils of the West
Saxons AD640*

Dorchester

I'm dying. I know that, and so does everyone within my mead hall. Yet no one speaks of it. Not out loud and never to my face. Well, no one apart from bloody Bishop Birinus and his droning discussions about the afterlife and how I'm going to a better place than this horrible world in which we live.

I wish I could tell him to shut the fuck up, but the last few weeks of my illness have sucked everything from me. Since Cenwahl's baptism, I've faded, little by little, day by day. I wanted to die the death of a warrior, with my sword in hand, but I'm to be denied even that by this bloody God about whom Birinus speaks so often. It seems he'd rather I suffered and malingered, cared for by slaves who'd rather not touch my decaying body, my skin shrivelled and stinking from the disease that ails me.

Cenwahl is gone as well. He wasted no time demanding that Oswald's warriors follow him into battle against Penda. I don't know why he's so keen to try his luck against Penda. Cenwahl believes he's a warrior. But when he meets Penda for the first time, adorned in his battle rage, Cenwahl will wish he'd not been quite so outspoken with his claims that he'll kill the Hwiccan warrior, despite, and because I failed to do so.

Oswald took him to one side as soon as he was baptised, spoke to him of the battle to come, and made him promises. I can only imagine what those promises were because in the eyes of the younger men, I'm already dead, and they disdained to consult with me on matters that affect my kingdom.

I could be angry. I think I'm angry. But it also pleased me to see that Cenwahl is confident enough to make the decisions that need to be made.

My kingdom has stagnated under my rule, my oldest son's death doing more harm than having Penda living on my border. Men followed Cwichelm because they believed in his skills and decisions. Men only follow Cenwahl because no one better fulfils the position.

My dynasty is weak. It'll only survive under a strong king, but I fear Cenwahl is not that man. I wish I'd had more sons or that my daughter had been born a boy. Then I could die knowing that the kingdom of the West Saxons wasn't under imminent risk of attack from Penda and his allies to the west, the men of Dumnonia.

But no, I must die knowing that only through my alliance with Oswald have I managed to hang onto the kingship for as long as I have. Provided Cenwahl learns some military prowess and the art of bending low before another warrior, one who can offer protection and support, the West Saxons might survive intact. But I hold out no hope of that happening. My son knows how much I doubt his skills.

Ever since he was small, I've criticised and found fault. I couldn't help myself. He was a big boy. He should have put his skills to greater use than bullying any smaller than him. He believes physical presence is all he needs, but he's wrong. He also requires some skill in speaking with his followers.

I fear that when this attack on Penda is an utter failure, men will call for Cenwahl to be replaced and elect another in his place. I think they'd be right to do so, and that knowledge is no secret from my son, and it burns him.

I breathe deeply, labouring under the light furs that cover my chest. The room is dark apart from one candle, guttering in the slight breeze. There's no sound from outside. I've lost track of time. Is it day? Night? I assume it must be nighttime, and everyone sleeps, but I could be wrong. It could just as easily be the middle of the day and everyone busy about their duties, in the market or attending upon Bishop Birinus in his church.

I laugh at the thoughts, and a great wracking cough echoes through my body.

It'll be one of these attacks that steals my life once and for all, but this isn't the one, and so I live another day.

I'm woken later by Bishop Birinus. He looks sombre in the dull candlelight, even in his robes of office. Still, what brightness there is hurts my eyes.

I wrinkle my nose. I stink. I wish the slaves looked after me better, but then, I should have looked after them better in the first place. I've no one to blame for my plight but myself.

I should have been a better king, a better father, and a better master. But there's nothing I can do about it now.

"King Cynegils," Birinus speaks formally to me, and I wonder what's happened, my hazy thoughts trying to connect so that I can remember what he might need to tell me.

"Bishop," I croak. He helps me to a small sip of water without even grimacing that he has to touch me. At that moment, I respect him more than I ever have before. Perhaps this is all his Christianity is, a little kindness to ease the passing from this world to the next.

"I bring ill tidings."

Immediately my thought centres on Cenwahl, off on his expedition to tackle Penda, but Bishop Birinus surprises me.

"Your grandson, My Lord King, the blessed little lad, I'm afraid he's died." The news is like a knife to my heart. My poor daughter, Cyniburh. So many babes gone before their time. It seems my family line is poisoned. Even my sons have struggled to bring forth live kin.

"How do you know?" I ask.

"King Oswald is often in contact with me."

I shouldn't be surprised by the news. After all, Bishop Birinus and Oswald have a shared spirit; they both wish to convert men and women to their way of thinking.

It's also another way for Oswald to keep a pair of eyes on what I'm doing within my kingdom. Oswald protects his interests within those kingdoms subject to his whims.

I feel tears leak from my dry eyes. I wonder where the moisture comes from, for I'm drier than a husk.

Birinus watches me expectantly, and I realise for what he's come. I might be dying, but he wants masses said for the soul of the babe, not even a year old, and who's done little but be born to Oswald. I feel bile in my throat. All this time and I'll be less well-remembered than the child. Yet I feel his loss strongly and don't wish to stint in my remembrances for him.

"Have a service arranged," I manage to cough. Bishop Birinus, so slow in his actions, caring in his treatment of me, leaps to his feet, no trace of remorse on his face.

He has a service to organise that he hopes will please King Oswald.

I sigh heavily.

Will this damn life never be over?

⌘ CHAPTER 12 ⌘

Domnall Brecc of Dal Riata AD640

A hand on my shoulder has me fully awake immediately. I've only just closed my eyes in sleep, but I'm to be denied any rest.

I assume it's one of my clan leaders, causing problems once more, but the man who wakes me shakes his head at my question and gestures that I follow him outside.

Whatever he knows is more secret than I at first thought.

Outside, night holds sway. I can barely see in front of my face, let alone along the pathway he takes me down. Luckily, I know the route well and follow more through feeling my way than by seeing anything.

I'm angry at being disturbed when I'm trying to sleep but also feel a little flutter of excitement. Such a covert approach must mean something important. When I finally step beneath a huge tree close to the riverbank, I realise I'm not to be disappointed.

I vaguely recognize the man waiting for me, but it's the ship that gives me all the clues I need. It's a Pictish ship, similar to mine. There's only one man I know who'd have access to such a vessel and who'd wish to speak to me.

"Herebrod," I utter, and he grunts an agreement.

"My Lord, King Domnall," he offers. He speaks my tongue, but it's mangled by the Pictish he also knows. Not that I'm about to mention that. He's a tall man, well wrapped in his cloak, beneath which he'll wear byrnie and be fully armed.

It's dark and stormy. I shelter inside my great cloak pleased I managed to scramble into my boots and fling its comforting warmth around my shoulders.

"Has Penda sent you?" I demand, and he grunts.

"He wishes to know your intentions towards Oswald and Oswiu. Do you propose to reenact the old alliance that stood before Hæðfeld, or do you plan on supporting them?"

I'm pleased to see Herebrod, but he must know how dangerous it is for him to visit my kingdom. Should Oswald learn of this visit, he'll react angrily. I'm in no frame of mind to offer Herebrod any assurances.

"Yes, is my simple answer. I allowed Oswald to decide once before. I told him all he needed to know, and still, he chased after Edwin. He's unreliable and thinks nothing of the support my father and I gave him."

I feel Herebrod's approval in the relaxing of his tense posture. Penda must have sent him hoping that an alliance could be agreed. But Herebrod will have known that my connections with Oswald may have meant I'd be more inclined to kill him on sight than speak with him.

"That's excellent news, My Lord King," even Herebrod's tone has warmed toward me now." Oswald isn't to be trusted."

"Don't I bloody well know that," I counter. Oswald and Oswiu have disappointed me. I continued the support that my father gave them when they were exiled. I gave them Bishop Aidan. All I ever did in return was call on them to assist me in my wars against the men of the kingdom of the Gododdin. Not only did they only make half an effort and lose the advantages I'd gained, but news also reaches me that Oswiu is now attempting to take the kingdom for himself once more.

If I didn't want the kingdom of the Gododdin as my neighbours, I certainly don't want their place to be taken by the sons of Æthelfrith.

"The rumours are true then?" Herebrod queries, his furrowed

brow just visible in the deep gloom.

"Yes, Oswiu moves against the kingdom of the Gododdin."

Herebrod sighs unhappily at that news.

"Penda's allies will be furious to hear this."

Ah, it seems I'm not the only one who sees Penda as the only real counter to Oswald's advancements. Not that I ask the identity of Penda's other allies. I have a fair idea that it'll be the men who stood against Edwin at Hæðfeld. Where those men have died, it'll be their successors.

"How does Penda plan to make war on Oswald?"

"He has some firm allies and ideas, but much of it's still to be decided. But be assured, your military might will be called upon, either in your homelands, on the northern borders of Bernicia, or even in the Saxon lands."

I made many journeys to ensure the success of Hæðfeld. While I believe they were worth the effort, with Oswald and his kin so keen to forget any sense of obligation placed upon them, I'd rather attack them from here. I wouldn't want them to sneak up on my borders when I was elsewhere.

Herebrod senses my hesitation and is quick to reassure me.

"Lord Penda is no fool. He understands it might be difficult to stand shield to shield with him. He would just as much appreciate your men causing a distraction for Oswald and Oswiu as actually making the long journey south once more. This time, Penda believes that Oswald can only be beaten if he's forced to fight away from Northumbria."

I leave aside my questions about how that can be accomplished and instead ask another question that's been worrying me.

"What of Lord Penda's brother, Eowa. Isn't he the king of Mercia?"

Herebrod stiffens at my words. I'm sure I've heard reports that the two men are enemies, not allies. I hope I've not poured oil over their differences.

"King Eowa has an alliance with King Oswald, as do many of the men in the Saxon kingdoms. None of them is strong enough to stand against Oswald and his Christianising ways."

I've managed to find the flaw in the alliance, but I'm remembering Hæðfeld and looking around to ensure, even in the dull gloom, that no one overhears our conversation, I whisper to Herebrod.

"Is that the truth?"

He starts at my words. I'm not sure what Penda has told him to tell me, but he needs to speak no further.

It seems that King Oswald finds himself with an ally who's not an ally after all.

That makes me smirk. It's past time that Oswald knew the feeling of betrayal, knows how it can twist a man and make him bitter.

Without waiting for a verbal response, I speak in a low voice.

"Tell Lord Penda he has the pledge of my support. Inform him I'll do all I can and tell him that I need to be kept informed of all developments. I'd rather our alliance was kept just as secret as … other elements of his actions against Oswald."

Herebrod nods, the sound of his helm moving beneath his cloak attesting to his actions.

"It's always good to speak with you, Domnall," he mutters, and then he's gone. The only reminder of his presence is the ripple of the water over which he's made his escape.

I've got to hand it to Penda. He knows how to keep secrets secret, and he's blessed to have a man as loyal as Herebrod amongst his followers.

When the faint noise of oars on the water fades away, I return indoors, discarding my cloak and my boots before I slide back into my warm bed.

What started as a night I knew I'd lie awake throughout, worrying about the future and my clan chiefs, has suddenly become far more convivial. I feel my eyes close, and sleep claim me.

Oswald will pay for his arrogance and his lack of respect.

I anticipate it eagerly.

⌘ CHAPTER 13 ⌘

Penda of the Hwicce AD641

Southern Mercian/Hwiccan border

The day's mild, the hint of warmth making itself known in the soft fragrances that manage to make their way past the smell of my body and that of my warriors.

We only left my stronghold a week ago, but a week on the road can make even the dirtiest man dream of being clean once more. It's the height of summer, or soon will be. The crops grow thickly in the fields, the new lambs almost the size of their mothers. I feel emboldened with the joy of so much new life burgeoning all around me.

I move against my brother, as long-discussed, but first, I must meet with my allies, Clydog and Cynddylan, and any others they've managed to coax along the way. I harbour the hope that Domnall will have arrived at our muster point as well. But Oswiu presses him in the north. We've already decided that it's as well to keep Oswald and Oswiu divided. They're both warriors of some renown. Although I'm not scared of attacking them together, I'd prefer to kill one and save the other for later. There's more pleasure in such a course of action.

Domnall's rage at Oswald's less than graceful repaying of the debt of keeping him safe throughout Edwin's tenure as the king has made him a valuable ally. Domnall may have failed in his attempt to subdue the kingdom of Alt Clut a few years ago, but that makes him no less of a warrior in the eyes of his people. Oswald should be more careful who he upsets.

We've arranged to muster close to the borderlands between the Saxons and the British lands. It is the fairest way of sorting out the difficulties of our partial trust in one other.

Clydog and I have long been allies who want to better each other. We're very similar, which makes us dangerous unless we choose to put aside any slights we might inadvertently give to each other. It's an interesting alliance, not without difficulties, but Clydog was as good as his word at Hæðfeld. All one hundred of his men fought well and achieved victory. I'll not be forgetting that, and neither will Clydog. He likes to remind me of his loyalty with every messenger he sends.

Yet, I can rely on him. He's unswervingly loyal, provided I don't offend him. It's good to have an ally, almost a friend, on who I can wholly rely. The security of our alliance has allowed us both to grow into our positions without fear of threat or retaliation. It's rare to have such a surety in the troubled times in which we live.

Cynddylan is an easier ally. He didn't fight with Cadwallon and me at Hæðfeld, but he shares our passion for removing Oswald from his position of power. He resents the wars that Oswiu enacts against the British of the kingdom of the Gododdin. He tolerates me as the lesser of two evils because I've made it clear that I've no intention of attacking the Britons. I don't want their kingdoms. After all, I'm a Saxon, not a Briton.

These are the two men who've chosen to wage war with me and muster their men. There are others, most notably Domnall and Petroc of Dumnonia, who've decided not to take advantage of my distraction and invade my kingdom. Petroc has informed me he plans to attack Wessex whilst I'm trying to entice Oswald to war in Mercia. That means that Cenwahl will be kept busy trying to defend his lands of the South Saxons and won't respond to any summons from his overlord.

I like those odds.

As to the rest of Oswald's alleged supporters, I doubt any but Onna of the kingdom of the East Angles will heed his request for help. Why would they? The men of Kent are secure under their new king. I don't want their kingdom. I certainly don't want their religion.

No, my intention is clear. To attack Oswald, kill him if possible and drive back his pretensions, if not. Above all, I hope to show my brother that between us, we can rule this island with far more stability than Edwin or the power-hungry Oswald has ever offered. I'm convinced of our victory. How can I not be? Eowa and I have carefully arranged every one of our attacks. Settlements will be burnt, but only after the inhabitants have been told to leave. Our battles will be bloody but short. We need to make our attack as realistic as possible. We want to make Oswald heed the call of his ally, but we don't desire our people to suffer in the process.

We'll have a battle or perhaps two, but it'll all come down to a final fight. It'll be the one where Oswald is far from home and cut off from any possible hope of retreat that will mark our campaign as a success or not. Cynddylan knows it, and so does Clydog. Much of our summer will be spent perpetuating a ruse, no more.

I grin with delight. The intrigue of what we're about to attempt excites me. At Hæðfeld, it was an all-out war against Edwin, and it didn't work. We killed too many future allies, too many enemies, and Cadwallon allowed the victory to sour him. I won't act in the same way. I've assured my men of it and my allies as well.

We want to get rid of Oswald and his pretensions to other kingdoms and push the presumptuous kingdom he rules back to the northern side of the great Humber River.

All I need to rely on now is my brother's ability to engage Oswald in a battle that's really of little interest to him. As I said to Cadwallon many years ago, to destroy the Northumbrian king, we need him outside of Northumbria, away from any easy means of retreat and escape. When Oswald is in Mercia, he'll be cut off from his brother, wife, and young son. He'll want nothing more than to kill me and get back to Northumbria. I plan on ensuring that doesn't happen.

I ride with over eight hundred men. It's a huge number and reflects how much I've grown in stature since Hæðfeld. Oswald might assume that I've achieved little in the intervening years, but he needs to look further than the end of his nose. My power base has grown. The trust men place in me has ballooned. When I fought with Cadwallon, he was the uniting force in the alliances we grew now, I'm that unifying force, and Oswald has overlooked that.

Neither has he ever actually faced me in battle. I know he was Edwin's ally before Hæðfeld, but he never brought his men to the battle site. I'm curious why he was scared off, but I don't think I'll ever know. Perhaps Lord Eanfrith reached out to him and asked him not to offer resistance when he finally made his move and joined our alliance.

Herebrod rides with me. His weapons have been honed to razor-sharp edges, his shield and byrnie repaired so that nothing can get through them. His horse is as keen to face our enemy as he is. All of my men are keen to engage the enemy, and by that, I mean the men of Northumbria. I've assured them all that they'll be richly rewarded for obeying my orders in the run-up to the final battle.

And those I've left at home to guard my family and my children? They'll be even more richly rewarded for not only enduring the demanding ways of my wife but for ensuring my son and daughter come to no harm from my actions. Should the worst happen, they're to escape to the kingdom of Petroc if they can. From there, my wife will decide on where they can live in exile until Paeda is old enough to use his winning personality to gain back the land I've foolishly lost.

I hope my son never has to endure an exile and know the impotent rage that has made both Oswald and his brother Oswiu so keen to overpower all who stand in their way.

I kick Gunghir to greater speed. He obliges by thundering in front of my warriors, those who tasked with keeping me safe throughout the summer.

Herebrod yells in annoyance, but I simply laugh and allow Gunghir to do what he must. He doesn't like to be led.

He's as cantankerous as he's ever been, and I relish his strength and his stamina, leaving my men in the dust of his hooves, my laughter on the breeze the only indication that I still ride before them all.

The coming battles fill me with anticipation and excitement.

All the years of hard work, building my network of alliances, convincing my brother to our partnership. Soon it'll all have been worthwhile.

CHAPTER 14

King Eowa of Mercia AD641

Shifnal - Mercia

I curse softly beneath my breath as I watch Penda and his warriors form into their shield wall, appreciating the difference between hearing that Penda has a force of over a thousand men and actually seeing it in the flesh.

I have five hundred men, no more. They're unhappy and uneasy. Penda might have trusted his warriors with the details of what we hope to accomplish today, but I've not been able to do the same with my warriors. Too many of them would run to Oswald with the news of our carefully orchestrated plan. My trusted commanders are aware, but not the men who look unhappy at such overwhelming odds. I can't blame them. The rumours of Penda's attacks have run like wildfire through my kingdom.

They don't know just how soon I'll be giving the order to retreat, allowing the men to run for their lives. Neither do they know that Penda and his allies have no intention of chasing them down.

Today is a sham, nothing more. Provided no one acts too irrationally today, few should lose their lives, if any. Or so I hope.

Yet, I wouldn't put it past Penda to take advantage of his superior numbers to put an end to my warriors and me. I berate myself. I have to learn to trust my brother, assure myself that he means no harm to me. He might have stolen the reputation that belonged to me, but he's never intimated a wish to steal my life as well.

At least never to me.

The past year has been challenging. I've had to convince Oswald of my total allegiance to his alliance by listening to the word of his God and, in the process, losing the support of some of my warriors who now face me on the battlefield. They've chosen to stand with Penda, who holds to the old Gods.

I've also had to listen to the news of Penda's warriors amassing on my borders and take no action until now. I've had to pretend to fear his strength and work my guile on Oswald so that when my message reaches him, that I need his support against my over-mighty and war-hungry brother, he believes me.

And all the time, I've not even been able to speak openly with my wife, or indeed Penda. None of our plans would have worked if we'd met and news had reached Oswald that I still spoke with my brother.

No, it's been a challenging year, and this coming battle might be the most difficult part of it yet.

"My Lord King?"

I turn slightly sour eyes to look at one of my warriors, a man I know who reports directly to Oswald about my every move. He's called Artair. His name is imprinted on my memory, along with his long sly face and constantly shifting eyes.

"What is it?" I ask, shielding my eyes from the glare so that I can calculate exactly where Penda is making his stand. We have an agreement that we'll not fight each other directly. One I hope he keeps.

"The scouts are saying that Penda has more men in reserve, some of the British. We should find another site for the battle. There's nothing to commend this stretch of land to a battle."

Shit, Artair has a point and one I'd hoped no one would appreciate.

I'm stood on a slight grassy rise in the heart of my kingdom. It has little to advocate it for the coming battle other than that it's far from any settlement and will allow my brother to push my men back the way we've just come when he wins. The land tapers slightly to the east, serving as a natural funnel for my allies to escape through. It'll ensure that Penda's warriors and mine are kept apart. The lay of the land will force my warriors to step foot on Watling Street, and provided they follow it back to Tamworth, no one will know how staged the clash has been.

It would endanger our plan if my men encountered my brother's and could speak freely. Who knows what they might inadvertently say?

"Penda's men are readying themselves for battle. We must meet them here," I say hurriedly, hoping that my voice carries the correct amount of urgency and fear. I don't think the fear is forced. My brother and his warriors are formidable. I'd not fully appreciated how hard it was to pretend to do something when you know the opposite to be true. As I toy with the idea of whether I trust my brother or not, fear is my honest reaction

Penda definitely has the more straightforward role in this regard.

The man looks unhappy. For a moment, I envision the joy of thrusting my seax through his chest. I quickly abandon the idea. I can't kill him. I need Artair to run back to Oswald and offer his opinion of this battle. It must be an opinion that entices Oswald into Mercia. I need to look weak. I'll have time to rebuild my reputation once Oswald is dead and the truth of this farce is known.

Not that Oswald has an aversion to leaving his kingdom. Far from it. But I think he suspects my loyalty. For that reason, I've converted fully to the Christian faith. I ride to war with a large wooden cross around my neck and not Woden's wheel. I'd feel far more protected if I had Woden's wheel as my emblem, so similar in design to the Christian cross and yet so very different as well. Its weight, made of precious silver, would be a comfort in and of itself. But I don't even wear Woden's wheel under my cross. I wouldn't want it to be mistakably glimpsed by Oswald's spy.

"As you will," the man says, clearly unhappy with my decision. I gaze at the horde of men before me and swallow thickly.

I trust my brother.

I'm sure I do.

It's Penda who gives the command to form his shield wall first, as though he knows I might procrastinate about it all day. My men are quick to reciprocate. I march with them, just as Penda does with his men. The flash of sunlight on metal is as blinding as the bright summer sun. We're dressed for war.

The ground is soft beneath my feet, and the air chill with the morning dampness. The sun rose a long time ago, and yet the birds still sing their dawn chorus. I offer a quick prayer to Woden that it won't be the last one I hear.

I trust my brother.

I'm sure I do.

All too soon, the two sides meet in a clamour of wood on metal, the men grunting their efforts, some whispering prayers to the old Gods, some to the new, but the majority simply concentrate on what they must do to stay alive. I include myself in that number.

My closest warriors surround me, where I fight in the second line from the front, holding my shield above the man in front of me. Another has his above mine. Few spears are being thrown by Penda's men, something about which he was keen to reassure me. Although few in number, Spears can be decisive in any battle, terrifying those at the rear of the shield wall, sometimes scaring them so much they force their way through the carefully ordered battle lines and upset other warriors along the way. No, a lack of spears is a good thing.

Immediately, I feel the strength of Penda's force. Almost twice as many men as mine, and they're happy to expend their energy on shoving my shield wall back because they know they'll not have to do any heavy fighting. When I call to retreat, my men will flee quickly back to their horses. Penda's men will only threaten to follow on behind.

I call encouragingly to my men. I don't want this loss to damage my reputation more than necessary. Penda has to win convincingly. He doesn't need to annihilate my warriors. My words are repeated up and down the long line of men. I hear the scrape of metal on wood as those at the front of the shield wall prepare to begin battle as soon as the shoving and pushing are finished.

I steady myself on the damp ground and ensure my feet are well planted. In my right hand, I hold my shield and in my left, an axe. It's my favourite fighting weapon, and although, as I say, I trust my brother, it has a winter sharp edge to it. I could sever a man's neck with my axe or his hand from his body. I could kill and maim at will if my trust ends up being misplaced.

I can even hear Penda's voice over the roar of men shouting, praying, breathing, and even crying. He commands his men to do well against my warriors, to spare no one when they break our shield wall and retreat. His warriors snarl their approval, and doubt assaults me. What if he means his words? I wouldn't be the first brother to have trusted too willingly.

But no, I trust my brother as I must.

"Attack," I hear the words pour from Penda's mouth, filled with hate and revulsion for my men and me. Yet, although there's a massive outcry of battle rage, the expected assault doesn't follow. Not immediately. My brother's biding his time, ensuring the battle lasts just long enough that Oswald can be convinced of its authenticity.

It's not his standard fighting technique, but as Oswald never showed up at Hæðfeld, he'll not know that Penda is acting contrary. Sooner or later, the real work will begin, and I lick my dry and cracked lips.

I trust my brother.

I'm sure I do.

Penda's voice rises again, urging his men to more extraordinary efforts, urgency in his voice. I wish I could see him. I want to know if he speaks with his customary smirk of derision or whether he can barely hold his mirth in place at the lie we're enacting for Oswald's benefit.

Then I remember that he's simply waiting for my words. This has been agreed, only I've forgotten because of my fear. I imagine that he's cursing me for an arsehole.

"For Mercia," I shout, at last, and that's the signal for which he's been waiting. His men surge against mine. Despite all our hopes, I know that some men will lose their lives here today. The hatred the Mercians feel for my brother's Hwiccan warriors will quickly get out of hand if this isn't accomplished quickly.

An axe is battering the man in front of me. I stand as close behind him as I can, ready to step into any breach that might happen in the shield wall. This needs to be a defeat, but not a blood bath.

My weapons are slick in my hand, despite my gloves, and all around me, the grunt and groaning of warriors fill my head.

Any moment now, I know that Penda will make his move, force this battle to a quick ending. But as I say, the struggle needs to last more than the few heartbeats of which it currently consists.

I wait. I'm ready if my trust is misplaced.

I wait, and I wait, my mouth dry.

Any moment now.

And then I hear it—the roar of angry men. I smirk. Penda is as good as his word, after all.

Above my head, I detect the sound of running feet on the shields. I hear a groan of anger from my warriors closer to the back of the shield wall. They'll be the only ones who've seen what's coming.

For just as Artair said, Penda hasn't come alone. Although I can't see, I know the warriors of Powys and Ceredigion are not only reinforcing his shield wall, they're also moving to encircle us, having used the forest to our right to mask their movements.

My warriors still fight, but Penda's men are starting to advance, their footsteps forcing me to retreat faster and faster. Worried voices rise, my men calling to each other and hoping that I have some sort of trick to help them win the battle. But I have nothing. All I want is for Penda to win and my men to withdraw, with or without my command, although I hope it'll only come when I give the order.

The man in front of me stumbles to the ground, and my eyes close in grief as I see the wound that marks his neck. I'd stoop and help him if I had the time, but I don't have the time. He'll be dead soon anyway, trampled by the feet of Penda's warriors.

A man tries to squeeze his way through the gap formed by my warrior's impending death, his face almost hidden by his helm, only his grinning and bloody mouth visible, and anger consumes me.

Penda demanded an oath from his men that they'd not kill my own, other than by chance. Now, seeing the man's face, I think my warrior's wound was intentional, which infuriates me. This man has allowed the joy of battle to infect his actions.

I step into the breach, taking hold of the fallen man's shield where it's been held in place by the tight formation of warriors for all that no man lent his weight to it. The handle is slick, and my brother's warrior grins at me with delight.

I try to meet his eyes, but his helm has been knocked askew. I see nothing but his gaping mouth, blood dripping down his bearded chin. I wish I knew who the man was, but I don't.

My foot impacts my dead warrior's head with a sickening crunch. I appreciate that he's well and truly dead. My axe, sharpened to use against my brother should he prove me false, is suddenly attacking the warrior before me, without thought for who he is or whether my brother values him or not.

I know I shouldn't fight him so brutally, but he's killed my warrior, and he needs to die.

Concerned voices fill the air above the tide of the battle. I think I should probably be giving the order to retreat. I will, once this man is dead.

He still leers at me. I don't think he knows whom he faces. His focus is exclusively on my axe, watching to see where it'll fall next so that he can deflect the blow. I watch him, watching me, and suddenly I know the man and distrust once more guides my hand, for the man is none other than one of Penda's most trusted warriors, a close friend of Herebrod's. Has he been sent here to kill me? To rid my brother of his older brother?

Suddenly, my axe moves without thought, just as Aldfrith once taught me when I was a boy. I know this warrior will be dead at my hand, and my brother can bleat about it all he wants.

I think he wanted to kill me, despite his words.

At my strokes, the man holds his shield tightly against his chest but continues to lash out with his axe. We're evenly matched. For all Penda's boasting about how strong and lethal his warriors are, he taught most of them, and he was taught, just as I was, by Aldfrith.

I strike left, then right, my axe trying to find a way through his shield. I try high, then low, and then I hear his laughter. He's playing with me.

I growl, the voice vibrating deep within my chest. He killed my warrior intentionally, and so I'll repay his kindness.

As he laughs, his shield falls slightly, fractionally. I don't even think he notices. I drop my shield to the ground, where it tangles with my legs, but it doesn't matter. I can use his shield to protect me from his attacks just as easily as I can use mine. With both hands free, I reach for my seax, as well as hefting my axe.

The man doesn't even notice until I'm standing with my body pressed against his shield, my axe behind his shield, and my seax against his neck.

Only now do his actions still.

But before I kill him, I have a question I need answering.

"Did Penda tell you to kill me?" I ask. Only as his head tips back and he looks into my eyes do I see shocked recognition in his eyes.

"No, My Lord King, never. He forbade it" he stumbles as my blade bites into his neck, perhaps hoping that I'll spare him. For all I think he tells the truth, otherwise, he'd have known me for who I am; I allow my blade to bite deep, feeling his blood gush over my hand before dripping to the ground.

He dies surprised, but I whisper of the dead warrior to him, and at that moment, he understands my rage.

He glides from my blade, a small hole now forming in Penda's shield wall, but my mood for this battle has soured.

"Retreat," I shout, and my words are echoing up and down the shield wall.

I feel the ricochet effect of men peeling away from the front line, but I stand still, surrounded by my warriors, keen to at least cast my eyes over Penda to see if he's bloodied himself against my combatants as I have against his.

Penda's warriors jeer as they watch my men run away, but only a handful of them chase after, the rest looking as though they want to, but held in place by the commands of my brother.

I was wrong to doubt my brother after all.

My warriors try to hasten my steps, but I wait, breathing hard, my heart heavily pounding as I look for Penda, aware I stand between his dead man and mine. Neither are these the only two casualties. I want him to see what a mess we've made in our attempts to trick Oswald.

The day is young, and death has cast a dark shroud over my enjoyment in it.

I hear my warriors race away and then their horses puffing with their exertions.

"Do they go towards Watling Street?" I ask of no one, but I hear a reply, all the same, my brother, standing almost opposite me, his axe dripping with gore, his moustache riddled with bloodletting.

"Yes, they do," he says, but his voice is filled with sadness and grief. I gaze at him across the area where our two forces met moments ago.

He seems shrunken, his grief and sorrows a cloak that's shrouded his enjoyment in battle.

"Apologies, My Lord King," he offers me and turns away. He's never acknowledged my status above him before. It's a sobering moment and one that spurs me to walk away from the scene of my rage.

I can trust my brother.

I see that now.

This pseudo battle has been as hard on him as it has been on me.

Perhaps, after all, he's not made of stone as he so often pretends.

"Until the next time, My Lord," I call back. He turns to gaze at me once more, removing his helm as he does so, his long hair flopping into his eyes for all that it's supposed to be bound and tied back from his face.

He offers me a tired smile and then leaps into the saddle of Gunghir. The horse growls fiercely at me. I grin at Penda.

That damn fucking horse. He has a long damn memory.

Penda yanks Gunghir's head around, and then he gallops away, back the way he'd come. I see he doesn't need to do so. He's not going even to pretend to follow my warriors, who're streaming towards my home.

A mere handful of his warriors are mounted, and from the safety of the wood, they're hurling abuse and pretending to rush my men, but they're under the firm command of Herebrod and will do nothing that goes against Penda's wishes. These are the men he trusts more than any other. I should have had faith in my brother.

I shake my head.

Damn bloody Cadwallon for cocking up all our plans. We need never have come to this.

⌘ CHAPTER 15 ⌘

Penda of the Hwicce AD641

Shifnal – Mercia

I ride away from Shifnal disgruntled.

It's one thing to talk about pretending to battle, but it's quite another to caution men so used to maiming at will that the battle is just a game, nothing more. It seems I fared poorly with my commands. I don't think I even want to know how many men lost their lives to force bloody Oswald to stand against me.

This idea of mine is starting to curdle.

I should have marched through Mercia and taken the fight directly to Oswald. It would be better than knowing that good men lost their lives today for no reason.

Herebrod is commanding those men who pretend to harry Eowa's warriors. He warned me against these actions, and I laughed aside his concerns. Now I don't. In him, I know I have a man I can trust implicitly.

Tomorrow, when my rage has subsided, I'll return to the battlefront and personally build a monument to these men. Their sacrifice won't have been in vain. Their deaths will make Mercia stronger. But first, first, I must ensure that Oswald meets his death on the end of my sword, or more agreeably, on the side of my axe.

My allies respect my unhappiness, riding close to me but not trying to speak with me. Our camp is within our eye line, my men's voices reaching me through the air. It seems that they share my unease as well. Some cast dubious glances my way as Gunghir frets and tugs at his reins. The damn horse. I slap him hard, and he turns his long head to both glower at me and bite my knee.

I slap him again, but he just shows me his teeth and turns back to watch where he walks. The campsite is ordered, but tether lines are running all over the place, and Gunghir is very aware of his role as a leader here. He doesn't wish to fall or injure himself.

If I weren't quite so dissatisfied, I'd find the pretensions of my horse amusing.

I know I need to speak to my warriors, thank them for their efforts, force myself from my discontent. Only my tongue seems stuck to the roof of my mouth. In the distance, I can just make out the retreating back of Eowa and his men. I wish we battled together, not apart.

I look forward to warring with him once more, together, when we finally attack Oswald.

"My Lord," Clydog is watching me intently.

"My Lord?" I ask, trying to force the words past my dry lips and tongue.

"May I thank the men?" he asks, and at that moment, I realise that even he's unhappy with the extent of our deceit. I should have just sent an assassin to kill Oswald. It would have been far preferable to this. But I'm not a snake. Other men battle dishonesty. I want to allow him to better me, but I need to tempt him to that battle, and in that lies my deceit.

"My thanks," I simply say and wait for him to speak.

We've long been allies, grudging at first, too alike in many ways, and yet he's my brother by marriage, and I respect him for managing to live with his sister for as long as he did. She's a beautiful woman, and she lets no one forget how powerful she is, and also how powerful before becoming my wife. The Britons respect their women, treat them well, would have them as their queen or war leader. I've often wondered what my life would have been like if she'd been the brother of the two.

"Warriors of the Hwicce, Powys and Ceredigion," Clydog raises his booming voice high. All activity in the camp stills, apart from Gunghir, who still worries at his reins and tries to escape my command.

"Today, we've fought, as we must. Those of our warriors who met their death did so for our cause. They understood what was being asked of them when they stepped into the shield wall. Their deaths will be mourned and won't be forgotten."

His words seem to raise the spirits of the men, and downcast eyes turn a little more hopeful. Cynddylan listens carefully. This place is so close to his borders that he could almost claim it himself, but we've made an agreement. I don't want what's his, and he doesn't desire what's mine. Yet this alliance has been a test to see if our men can adhere to our terms as well. He needs to see if they will.

"Tomorrow, we'll build a monument to their deaths. The following day, we'll march towards Eowa's stronghold, prepare for Oswald's arrival, for he'll not let our attack go unanswered."

As we've moved from the borderlands with the British kingdoms, we've ensured that we've set massive fires to mark the landscape as far as the eye can see. We might pretend to this war, but we need to in order to ensure that Oswald comes to fight us.

The men mutter at the thought of burying the dead, but Clydog is right to command that we do so. We could use it for a double-edged purpose to mark the battle and delineate the borderlands with Cynddylan. I don't for a moment think that he'll not demand extra land for joining my alliance. He might be welcome to this strip. I might never wish to see it again, but that'll be for Eowa to decide when he finally joins us.

"Tonight, we'll toast our success, mourn our losses and dream of a future when King Oswald, that most holy king of Northumbria, is dead and gone."

Clydog speaks well, with just the right amount of respect and disdain. Those words are greeted with a huge cheer of consensus, and even I feel a smile tug at my face. I couldn't have done better myself.

"To our alliance," he finishes, indicating Cynddylan and myself. We both raise our bloodied arms to accept the acclaim of our warriors.

Today hasn't been the best day, but it's only the start. We have much to do.

"My thanks," I say to Clydog after the men have turned away to their tasks, and he grins at me from horseback.

"Ah, come on, Penda. You can't possibly have expected to walk away unscathed. When the battle rage takes men, they don't know their mother, let alone their ally dressed as an enemy."

Clydog dismisses the inevitable outcome of the battle. I wish I could do the same, but I shrug instead.

"I always forget how bloody stupid men are," I offer, taking the sting from my words by grinning. "Think with their swords and their cocks, never their bloody heads." Clydog laughs at that, slapping his horse's shoulder before meandering away to speak with his men. Cynddylan stays with me. I believe he wishes to say something, but although he opens and closes his mouth, he shakes his head and goes to mingle with his warriors. I'm left to wait for Herebrod alone.

I turn Gunghir to gaze at the tree line before me. It almost masks the battle site, but I know where it was. I can see it in my mind and fear I always will.

It was an excellent place to join battle, the ground relatively gentle underfoot, but its proximity to Watling Street, the great road that splits much of this kingdom, was what made it so appealing. That, and of course, its distance from my brother's stronghold. From here, we can delay for as long as we must. We already know where the next battle will occur, and it's a far more promising site. Its land is already soaked with the blood of dead kings. There we'll chop Oswald down and take his warrior crown from his head.

It's there that my brother and I will reunite and show the

people of Mercia that no quarrel exists between us. In fact, the exact opposite.

Eowa has suffered enough. I'll not let it continue after our next attack.

✤CHAPTER 16✤

Oswald of Northumbria
AD641 Summer

I'm approached by two men, both looking as worried as the other. I can't imagine that they carry the sort of news I wish to hear.

The one I know intimately, the other is one of Eowa's men, no doubt come to barter for something.

I'm at Bamburgh, enjoying the early summer breeze on the beach when they're ushered before me. I've been biding my time, waiting for Eowa's messenger to reach me, and also one of mine, sent to infiltrate his warrior band and tell me exactly what's happening. Both of them show signs of having seen a recent battle. None of this is news to me. I've heard of Penda's ravages within Mercia and his tenuous alliance with the British kings.

Since Cenwahl's baptism last year, I've only been in communication with Eowa occasionally. My disappointment in him is immense. Despite my unhappiness, he looks to me as his overlord. I won't be able to ignore his request for assistance against his brother. Neither is that what I wish to do. This is the excuse for which I've been waiting. I'll be able to bring Eowa to my Christian faith while being presented with the opportunity to meet his brother in battle. And kill him.

Once Penda is dead, I'll decide how I want to proceed. It might be that Eowa doesn't keep his kingdom for long after my victory. After all, he's been not only my longest supporter. He's also been my most contrary. I've had no choice but to tolerate him for as long as I have.

I need Eowa to get to Penda. Now, I'm going to be given that opening.

I signal that Eowa's messenger should be allowed to speak with me first. He looks delighted to be allowed to present his petition first. I hazard a guess at how the two men have striven to outdo each other to get to me first. Ironically, they've arrived at the same time.

"My Lord King, Oswald," the man begins; his words are slow and meaningful. He means for me to listen to everything he has to say.

"King Eowa of Mercia sends warm greetings and wishes for your health and well-being."

I allow a small sigh to escape. I insist on such formality within my court, but I'm desperate to hear what it is that Eowa wants from me. Yet I can't rush the man. If word seeped out that I hurried him to a conclusion, others would understand that I'm desperate to gain influence in Mercia and the British kingdoms to the far west.

"My thanks for his wishes," I acknowledge with a faint smile on my face. I hope the man will take courage from my reception and speak more quickly.

"I bring tidings of … difficulties … within the Mercian kingdom, between Eowa and his brother, Penda." He stumbles over the words. I feel my anticipation build.

I've heard of trouble in the borderlands between Mercia and the kingdom of the Hwicce, but perhaps events have spiralled out of control.

"Lord Penda won a great victory at a place called Shifnal, near Watling Street." The man explains as though I know my way around Mercia far better than I do. I know where it is. I know the kingdoms that border it, but the details of its make-up confuse me. I know my way around Mercia but never through it. Not until now.

I nod as though I know of where he speaks.

"It was a brutal encounter, and Lord Penda's men had already caused untold damage amongst the farmers of Mercia, burning crops and settlements as they sought out Eowa. Lord Eowa fears that Lord Penda and his allies are too great a force for him to defeat without reinforcements."

The man is worried but also trying to act as an official messenger from one king to another. No doubt, Eowa filled him with the correct words to use, but in his joy at finally being able to speak them, the man has given away more than he should have. Eowa is facing a combined attack and without adequate resources.

Eowa and his brother have long been enemies, or nearly so, ever since Eowa supported me against Cadwallon.

I wait for the man to give me more details, but he's expectantly waiting for me to say something.

"Did many men perish in the battle?" I think to ask.

"Too many, My Lord King. Too many and more only survived because Lord Eowa gave the command to retreat."

"Were you at the battle?" I ask, eyeing the other man with interest. I know he'll have been there. Artair was tasked with being in the thick of any altercation between the two brothers. I'm surprised that Eowa wasn't better prepared. Surely he was aware that his brother would attack? Cenwahl's failed attack on Penda's southern borders last year has made Penda keen to assert himself over others. I've been forced to send a permanent force to Cenwahl to keep his kingdom safe and to stop his sister, my wife, from fretting too much.

Since the death of our only surviving son, she's become weak in spirit and difficult to please. I should cast her aside and take another wife, but I have a son already, almost a man grown. He'll be able to rule after me, regardless of any other sons I might father. It wouldn't be Christian to cast my wife aside when she's so ill with grief. Bishop Aidan and I have discussed her struggles at length. She blames herself for her non-Christian upbringing while Bishop Aidan labours almost daily to assure her that his God isn't so cruel as to punish her by taking her children.

Yet, in this, I find myself questing the power of my God. I don't understand why he'd claim innocent babes, extinguishing their life before they've had time to live it. Bishop Aidan assures me that I can't know everything our God has planned for me and that it's simply a further test.

His words eased my conscience, but sometimes I think I'm being punished for failing to make all the Saxon kingdoms Christian.

"Yes, My Lord King, I fought in the battle. It was terrifying. Lord Penda has amassed a huge force, and few of their warriors died on the battlefield. Some were even arrogant enough that they used our shields to get behind the shield wall and attack our men from behind as well as from in front."

"What is it that Lord Eowa wants from me?" I suddenly find I don't want the details of the battle. This is the crux of sending a personal messenger. Eowa wants more than just my men.

"Your presence, My Lord King. He believes that only with you leading the counter-attack will he be able to hold firm against Lord Penda's aggressive stance."

Ah, at last. Eowa's words are exactly what I want to hear, even if another speaks them.

"I'll think about it and let you know soon. First, I must speak with Artair."

Eowa's messenger briefly looks worried and can't stop himself from turning back to me.

"He's a traitor, My Lord King. He wasn't ordered to come here. He ran from the battlefield."

The man's voice is filled with accusations. I simply nod.

"I know Artair and his ways. Don't concern yourself any further with him. I'll speak with him now."

The messenger is amazed to hear my words, but already I'm walking away from him, to stand with Artair. He'll have a truthful accounting of events in Mercia. If his words mirror Eowa's messenger, then I'll know that my chance has finally come.

Mercia will be open before me. The irony isn't lost on me. While Penda works to control Mercia for himself, all he's doing is making it easier for me to assert my claim to it.

I allow a smirk and then turn to Artair. His posture is as submissive as Eowa's messenger. I already know what he's going to say. I allow a myriad number of scenarios to run through my head.

What should I do first? What second?

Mercia beckons me, and I only just stop myself from leaving immediately.

I hunger for that bastard Penda's death. It can't come soon enough.

✣CHAPTER 17✣

Oswiu of Northumbria
AD641 Summer

I don't hear of my brother's intentions directly from him but rather from Oslac, who's sobered up long enough to ride to me in my home at Rheged.

In his haste, Oswald has ridden south, leaving his kingdom in the hands of his wife and Oswudu. Oswald's arrogance astounds me, as does his decision to summon me as though I'm no more than one of his oath sworn men who must do whatever is asked of me.

Oslac, patently expecting my rage, smirks as he imparts his news. It takes all my self-control not to slap his face and command him from my sight.

Oslac resembles Oswald, yet his belly has swollen over his belt and hangs low. He could no more fight in a shield wall than he could birth a child. I'm ashamed to call him my brother, and what's worse, he knows that as well.

"Tell me again," I demand. He swills his mead and launches back into his account of events in Mercia. His words fill the gaps in my knowledge and, more, make sense of Domnall's cooling attitude toward me. After I reclaimed Eten once more, only to walk away from it because my brother commanded it, I thought that Domnall would be keen to aid me again. But in fact, he was the opposite, more intent on ensuring that the royal family there survived.

I've half a belief that he sheltered some of their exiles during my too-brief attack. I wish I'd had the numbers to hold the kingdom and keep it, but instead, I needed to appeal to Oswald for more warriors. As is his way, he was so slow in providing them that Eten was saved from my ravages. I was expelled with no ceremony.

Why then does Oswald rush so quickly to Mercia? He can't possibly expect to hold Mercia as well? Surely? Rumour has it that Penda has such a massive force, reinforced with men from the British kingdoms, that it would take fully over two thousand men to obliterate them.

I shake my head angrily, the grip on my cup so tight that I hear it crack and fracture, spilling its contents onto my lap.

Oswald is prepared to offer support only where he sees a chance of success for himself.

He's too confident and too sure of himself. But, I'll do as he commands and return to Northumbria, specifically to Bamburgh, and rule in his stead.

Oswald says it'll be a quick attack, but even getting to Mercia will take time. So even though I know Oslac will have dawdled on his way here and that the battle might be half won, I call my warriors before me and tell them that we must ride to Bamburgh.

Many of them are pleased to hear my words. They've been away from our homeland more than they've been in it. After our shared years of exile, I know they hoped for a warmer reception from Oswald and their relatives. But that's not what we received.

Perhaps this time we'll be allowed to stay for longer.

I eye my wife. She's never been either a pleasure to bed or a pleasure upon which to look. This might just be the opportunity I've needed to get away from her. Maybe this time we'll stay for good.

She meets my gaze squarely, no doubt thinking the same of me.

This could work out the best for all of us, but I think that Oswald has jumped into the fray too soon and that he'll come to regret it.

I'll travel to Bamburgh, but from there, and once I've assured myself that all is well, I might travel south, ready for the inevitable demand for reinforcements that he's going to send to me.

I grin at that. I don't so much hate Penda as I admire him. This altercation between the two of them might be as profitable for me as it could be for Penda.

Only time will tell.

✠ CHAPTER 18 ✠

Domnall Brecc of Dal Riata
AD641 Summer

My men stand ready to ride to war. I inspect them, glad to do so. The warriors of my kingdom have different techniques to the Saxons, but it doesn't make them lesser warriors. In fact, in the wars against the British kingdoms and the Saxon kingdoms, our differing techniques, our round shields, just like the Picts, and our reliance on the spear, mean we often succeed just because we're so different.

It'll be different when we ride out this time. We go to harry the border with Northumbria or Bernicia, to be more accurate. The men and women there are used to our fighting styles. They share many of them.

Not that I'm unduly worried. My intention isn't to force Oswiu to all-out war. Instead, it's to annoy him enough that when he receives the call for reinforcements, if events in Mercia go poorly for Penda, Oswiu will be unable to take all of his warriors with him.

I know that Petroc of Dumnonia is readying his men to the south. We've both decided that we can't leave our kingdoms to swell the battle lines, not as before. Oswald is simply too powerful, his spider web of alliances stretching across our island and yet at this moment, we stand our best chance so far of ridding ourselves of him.

I pray for Penda's success and that Clydog, Cynddylan and he will tempt Oswald to battle and then overpower him. I long to reclaim my hold on Dal Riata, to wipe away the stain that my father's support of his exile has brought to our family name. I'm not deluded enough to think that if Oswald dies, his brother won't claim his place, or at least try to. I know that given the opportunity, Penda and his brother will reverse all of Oswald's gains and cage Oswiu back into Bernicia alone.

That's as far as Oswiu's family can claim. As much as I appreciate his vigour in spreading Christianity, he's gone about it the wrong way. I'm sure that Bishop Aidan can't have advocated his approach.

No, I ride with my warriors to the south, to disrupt the border regions, to perhaps have another attempt at unseating the ruling family in Alt Clut whilst reinforcing the floundering Gododdin. Amongst my warriors, I have fifteen men from Gododdin, warriors all but unable to stand against Oswiu. With Oswiu's view elsewhere, I can enable Gododdin to grow strong once more. I need the kingdom to survive and remain as a buffer state between my realm and Bernicia.

It's proven difficult enough to manage the kingdom I rule without worrying about an external attack. My clan men don't share my views of the wider world we live in, content only to worry about their harvests and feuds. Without their support, it'll be almost impossible to fend off an attack from Oswald or Oswiu. But in infringing on Oswald's kingdom, in meddling in affairs Oswiu believes should be none of my concern, I'll pay them back for the disservice they've done me since they left.

I still reel from the utter lack of appreciation from any of Æthelfrith's sons and how they've repaid what my kingdom did give them by trying to attack it, in attempting to undermine my kingship and have it collapse.

No, despite our past relationship, Oswald and his brother are no allies of mine. Just like Cadwallon and his foster brother, Edwin, it seems that men raised together, as brothers but of different blood, can never have their divergent views reconciled.

Like Cadwallon, I must fight to thwart my foster brothers, Oswald and Oswiu. And damn it, I'm going to enjoy it.

⌘ CHAPTER 19 ⌘

Penda of the Hwicce AD641

Wall and Lichfield

The old road has brought my men and me, my allies as well, almost directly to the place that Eowa and I have chosen to be the final part in our staged battles against King Oswald. It's here that Eowa will cast his lot in with the alliance I've created with Cynddylan, Clydog, Domnall and Petroc.

I know that Oswald is riding south with his men to support Eowa. I also know that in the northern lands, Domnall is keeping Oswiu too busy to leave by offering support to the men of the kingdom of the Gododdin. Our plans have fallen nicely into place, yet much could still go wrong.

My men are setting their encampment in the remains of an old hill fort, used by the Britons to defend themselves from attack from other tribes, and when the Romans came from their hot homeland, against them as well.

The banked walls are crumbling away, but they still offer more protection than camping on flat land. That's a good thing. They also protect a water source, and that too is a benefit. We don't want to be caught by surprise by Oswald. But if we are, I want to know that we can defend our stronghold, not retreat before him.

Tomorrow, I'll take Cynddylan and Clydog to view the final battle site. But today, I must ride out and meet with Eowa. We need just one last meeting to assure each other of our intentions. Herebrod will rule the men while I'm gone, telling the men that I need some time alone to pray to Woden and offer a sacrifice for our success. They need not know that Eowa and I are meeting. They believe our agreement has long been settled. They don't know just how much Eowa distrusts me. How Eowa showed that during the battle at Shifnal when his hooded eyes met mine, and he failed to give the command to attack when we'd decided it should come.

I'd blame him for the slaughter of our men, for heightening the tension, but I don't have the heart or the desire to do so.

The place we've chosen to meet is a small forested area, not far from his stronghold at Tamworth. It means that I'm taking all the risk today, not him. He need only send a small group of his warriors to waylay me, and he could kill me and claim my kingdom for himself.

Yet, I know he won't. I know my brother well. He might have threatened me that he'll side with Oswald if I look like losing, but as that's not going to happen, I won't concern myself with his threat.

My warriors have had the summer to practice, to get used to fighting with the Britons, and friendships and rivalries have sprung up amongst them all. But they all share one desire. To get rid of Oswald.

Gunghir is unusually quiet beneath me as we ride in the sleeping countryside. We might have fired some of the settlements we've passed along Watling Street, but here, to the east, Mercia is relatively calm and secure. Eowa has ensured that his warriors will leave their land safe in the knowledge that they won't be attacked in their absence. I've ensured the same in my kingdom. My wife, my queen, rules there with the full weight of my authority. Already I've had word that she's sent her warriors to dispel trouble brewing on the border with King Cenwahl. I knew he'd not be able to resist the chance to meddle when I moved inland. A pity that he's disregarded Petroc's border skirmishes.

Once this battle is won, I'll take my vengeance against Cenwahl. He hardly knows his own thoughts and can only be acting because Oswald has ordered him to do so. He doesn't deserve to rule the kingdom of the South Saxons. It should have been left in the care of one of his nephews, sons of Cwichelm.

I might have triumphed over Cwichelm in battle, but at least he was a warrior who thought before he fought. It's a pity that Cwichelm died before his father and could never hold full authority in his kingdom.

I'd have allied with Cwichelm, but not with Cenwahl. No, Cenwahl has started on a path that can only end with his death or with him handing his kingdom over to me. I don't mind either way. But his death would make my advance into the southern lands far easier. If only his sister weren't married to bloody Oswald. But not for much longer. Oswald will meet his death soon enough.

Eventually, and with due diligence, just in case Eowa has had second thoughts about our long-standing arrangements, I enter a small wooded area I remember from my childhood. I'm sure we used to play here – play at warriors and savages – using the trees for our defences and the slight rise in the ground as a hill fort. I smirk at the memories. I'm not so old that they feel like they don't belong to me, as though I dreamt them instead of living them. I am old enough to appreciate the innocence of my youth, to honour my father for securing his power base so that we could live without fear.

I reconsider, never wholly without fear, for how would we win any battles when we were men if we'd never known fear? No, my father might not have been in such a high position as Eowa and me, but he was still a member of the ruling family. He watched, and he waited, ready to take advantage of any possibilities that came his way. I miss him.

The weather is warm, Gunghir unhappy. I almost think that I should read something into my old horse's behaviour, but he's become difficult lately. I think he smells the tang of the coming battle on me, and I worry that he fears himself too old to carry me to another altercation. I hope not. Gunghir and I are the staunchest of allies. I'd be uncomfortable with another horse beneath me.

I manage to force him through the tangled growth from the small wood that allows me to overlook my brother's stronghold of Tamworth. The trees are filled with new leaves, the smell of damp and dry mingling enticingly in my nostrils, the odd scurry of small woodland animals not alarming Gunghir, simply adding to the tranquillity of the moment.

This is what life should be. Quiet and peace, not death and blood. But if that were to be my life, then bastards like Oswald and Edwin would never have been born. I blame their God for that, and then I thank Woden as well. My life would be boring if not for good enemies who need to die on my blade.

I lead Gunghir to the stream I remember from my childhood and allow him to drink deeply. It's hot work riding the countryside, but it's cool and filled with shadows inside the wood. Not a day to talk of war, but that's what I've come here to do.

I slide from his back and pat his head while he drinks. His head swivels quickly to take a nip from my ear. I bat him away. His eyes are clear and bright. He might think he's old, but he has fight in him yet. I laugh at his attempt to annoy me. It's too hot, and his action is just a token movement, born of too many years together.

I chuckle and then hear the tread of another and turn sharply, my hand on my seax at my waist, but it's only Eowa, laughing sourly at the antics of my horse and me.

"I see he doesn't improve with age," he adds almost jovially. The two would have made a fine couple if Eowa had chosen him. But Eowa left him for me because I wanted him. I often wonder what sort of horse Sleipnir would have been under my tutelage.

"He simply gets better, brother," I smirk. Eowa reaches forward to greet me, his hand wrapping around my forearm and then into an embrace. Here, in the woods, it's easy to forget that we're enemies, and perhaps always have been.

He looks around me as though expecting to see Herebrod, surprised when he realises I'm truly alone.

"You fear me so little," he asks it lightly, but he means it. Have I angered him by sticking to our agreement?

"I know these lands as well as you do," I respond, hoping for some tact. "There's nowhere I could hide from you where I'd be truly hidden. You know this place as well as I do."

His eyebrows rise at that, and he acknowledges my logic with a nod of his head.

"You're right. You wouldn't leave if that weren't my intention." I don't know if he's trying to menace me with his words, spoken with a hard edge, but I do know that Eowa wouldn't kill me. Just as I wouldn't kill him. We're enemies, and allies all rolled into one. But to kill my brother would lose me more than just a firm ally.

"Neither would you," I laugh darkly. His eyes meet mine with fire raging inside them. Perhaps my brother is more conflicted by our actions than I thought?

Yet he says nothing about it.

"Oswald is coming, any day now. He sent word of his intentions."

"Good, then everything is proceeding as planned?" I half-ask. I know the answer. I have my spies watching events at Eowa's and Oswald's court. I'm also that Oswald comes alone. Oswiu remains in the north.

"Yes," my brother says slowly, pondering his words as he finds somewhere to sit along the riverbank. The trickle of the water over the rocks adds a soundtrack to cover our meeting. Any who saw us together might not hear what we say, although being seen together would be catastrophic enough.

"Shifnal. It didn't go as I thought," he admits slowly, as though the words weigh too much for him to say with a mortal tongue.

"Well, some men died. Unfortunately. There was no need for them to do so." I felt their loss just as keenly as my brother. I'd hoped to talk of other matters now, not about something that neither of us can change.

"I killed one of your men," Eowa announces as though the admission costs him dearly.

"I know you did. Men die in battle, no matter how much we wish they didn't." I'm trying to sound pragmatic. I'm not used to speaking to my brother about such things.

"Is that what you'd say if I died in battle?" Eowa asks the question blandly, as though he speaks of the coming rain or the winter snows, something that just happens each year, not an extraordinary occurrence.

As I've said, I'd miss my brother if he died. We're more than brothers, more than enemies and beyond allies. I almost don't know what to say to him.

"You're my brother," I try. I know I have strong feelings for him, but I've never put them into words. "I'd miss you if you were gone. I don't want to kill you in battle." I know my words sound shallow and inadequate, but I came to talk of war, not of death.

His eyes, still blazing with an intensity I'm not sure I understand, rake me with their gaze and then turn away.

"As I thought," I think I hear him whisper, but then he stands and begins to speak of the coming battle as though nothing's happened, as though we've not just shared our most intimate conversation ever. I don't even know if I pleased with my answer or angered him. I feel uneasy. Should I have asked him the same question? Is he trying to tell me that he wouldn't miss me if I died?

I don't even know what he hoped to achieve by speaking as he did.

"We plan on meeting at Barrow Hill?" Eowa confirms. I attempt to return my thoughts to the purpose of the meeting.

"Yes, yes, at Barrow Hill. You'll hold the position, and we'll attack up the hill, but also from the side."

"How big will your force be?"

"As at Shifnal. My allies are keen to engage against Oswald."

"Where will you be?"

I eye him critically. His voice quivers a little. Does he worry about the coming battle? I know it's a risk, but we need to attack Oswald away from Northumbria, away from the support of his brother and where there is no place to which he can retreat.

"In the centre of the attack. Cynddylan and Clydog with each take a wing. I'll face Oswald, and you'll face Cynddylan. You and he are allies. He knows not to attack your men too harshly."

"What if Oswald doesn't agree to the placing of the men?"

I laugh at that.

"Oswald has his reputation to protect. Oswald Whiteblade. He'll want to be where he thinks there'll be the greater ferocity."

"And what if he kills you?" Eowa asks, his eyes now back on mine. The thought of my death doesn't worry me, but it would be bloody inconvenient. My wife might never forgive me.

"Then he kills me, and you become king of Mercia and claim my kingdom as well. We merely need to ensure that Oswald doesn't take our land and that it stays in the hands of our family."

"Can you truly speak of your death so lightly?" I'd not expected my brother to show fear. Not now.

"Have you been listening to the words of one of Oswald's priests?" I query, hoping to have discovered the root of Eowa's unease.

"I hear their words. I have no choice, not anymore."

"What? And you dream of going to their heaven instead of to Valhalla?" I'm taunting him because I'm amazed to hear my brother speaking as he does.

"I simply don't wish to go to their Hell," he says defiantly. Suddenly, I consider if I ever knew my brother at all. We've been raised in the presence of the old Gods by men who've made their pacts with Woden and who accept the risks they take whenever they face another in battle. When we go to Valhalla, we'll be feasted and feted and speak of these days as though they were a dream. Why does my brother suddenly worry so much?

"Then don't go," I offer wryly. Eowa's conversation isn't what I expected to be greeted with today.

"I might have no choice," he mutters.

"You've been baptised?" I utter in amazement—my brother. I'd never have thought it.

"It was a condition of his support," Eowa offers the words darkly. This can't have been an easy decision for him to make. I walk before him, roughly grabbing his arm.

"Brother," I turn him to meet my eyes. At that moment, I see him as a young lad, barely older than me, and yet forever marked as the older brother, the one to whom the family's future was always attached. How was he to know that his younger brother would challenge him every step of the way? Eowa looks young, unsure and uneasy.

"You didn't need to go so far. We can undo any harm this new God might have caused you. We can rededicate you to Woden, to the father of our family line."

I little believe that lie my father perpetrated, but others think it's good and only right to have a ruler who claims descent from a God.

"Did the baptism mark you in some way? Will Woden even know of what you did?" I believe that Woden has power, but to date, I've not been shown anything to make me think the Christian God has any power at all. I don't mind who my men worship, as long as they fight. I thought my brother shared my viewpoint.

"I feel it, in here," Eowa almost screeches, pointing at his chest, where his heart beats. His voice, so loud, echoes above the gurgling stream into the clear sky, sending birds from their nests in panic.

My brother killed a man in battle at Shifnal. Not his first, and certainly not his last, but this new Christian God has rules about killing and maiming.

"Woden is in there," I say savagely, jabbing his chest to reinforce my words. This talk of Gods and nonsense is infuriating me. We came to talk of battle glory and formation, not of a man's conscience.

Eowa can hear the anger in my voice, but still, he looks apprehensive, scared almost.

"I hear about the power of this new God. Oswald is always

speaking of him. He raised a banner, a holy cross before he defeated Cadwallon. There's power in it. I saw it, remember."

The admission hurts him. I grab him by the shoulders and shake him hard, his head lolling from side to side as though he's too weak to counter my sudden attack.

"This new God is weak, and anyway, Cadwallon was a believer in Oswald's God as well. He didn't protect him in battle."

"But against 'pagans', as Oswald calls you, against you? What might happen then?"

I'm growing frustrated with my brother's inability to listen to reason. I wish I'd known of his conversion, that he'd even hinted at the fears it's aroused in him before this moment. I'm starting to worry that he'll change his allegiance to Oswald in more than just name now.

"You're descended from Woden," I growl at him. "He gives you strength, legitimacy to rule. This new God does nothing and touches nothing. Oswald can say his victory is because of him, but he lies. You win victories, or you don't. It has little to do with who you worship. We pray to Woden, and the Christians pray to their God. But really, all that matters is who's the better warrior, the man better able to read a battlefield. And in this case, it's me and you, brother. We know how to fight. We bloody should, the amount of time our father spent teaching us. We have the experience and the skills here. Oswald has fought Christians in Ireland and Dal Riata and even against Cadwallon. We fight differently. We don't fear death as they do. Death is just the next step for us when Woden and his ravens will claim us." I fill my voice with confidence. I must make him understand.

I'm hoping that my words reach whatever dark fear under which my brother currently labours. If not, this enterprise is doomed before it's even begun. If he sides with Oswald in the battle because of his bloody Christianity, then I'll have no choice but to kill him. I'll not allow the spiritual needs of men to get in the way of my victory. Not now.

I lapse into silence, releasing Eowa from my firm grip. He's silent, thinking as he gazes into the distance. I wonder if he sees the fires of Hell he speaks about or whether he's reminding himself of the joys of Valhalla, where allies and enemies are reunited to feast until the end of eternity. I grunt at the thought. Surely, I'm living through something similar at the moment anyway, with my brother.

Valhalla is my eventual destination. But not yet. I've much more to accomplish, and Woden seems to prefer his warriors alive rather than dead. Dead warriors can cause little harm to their enemies.

"My thanks," Eowa says softly. I don't know for what I'm being thanked. I hope it means he's re-orientated his viewpoint, changed it from that of a scared man to that of one who's ready for this battle. Eager for it to start so that we can build on our positions on this island.

"We never said this would be easy," and that's the only concession I'm prepared to make. We need to discuss the next few weeks, not the afterlife.

"No, we didn't," Eowa confirms, turning to greet me with his eyes dimmed by his religious fervour, his whole demeanour now more as I'd expect it.

"No, we didn't," Eowa reiterates, "but it must be done."

"It must, yes. We need to undo Oswald's advances. At the least, it'll be him who dies in battle."

I want to be the one to kill him. That is my hope. I'm not sure if my allies realise how much I hunger for Oswald's death, and even more so, now that he's made my brother question his beliefs, wants and wishes, desires and needs.

"You'll attack Oswald," Eowa acknowledges. "When his attack falters, as it will," he speaks with firm resolve, convinced that Oswald is no match for me. "I'll turn my force, and Oswald will be trapped between us all. You in the centre, Clydog and Cynddylan to either side and then my men will wrap around yours as well."

"How will your men be told?" I ask, but he smirks at that.

"It'll be fairly obvious by then that we're supporting you. Don't fret, brother. This will be easy. Barrow Hill is the perfect location. It'll make Oswald feel strong when he isn't. As you say, we know this land too well. If Oswald does manage to escape, they'll be nowhere for him to hide that we can't unearth."

My unease at my brother's initial attitude, and his startling fears about his religion, are starting to lift. Yet I still perceive on my brother. I think his relationship with Oswald has caused enough damage. If we weren't so close to the battle, then I'd send an assassin now to kill the bastard. How dare Oswald undermine my brother's confidence? I'll kill him. I'll feel his blood on my face, and then I'll burn him, or leave him for the crows, or perhaps I'll crucify him as his bloody God was once murdered.

Anything to ensure that his power over Eowa diminishes.

"We'll win," Eowa says confidently, but all of a sudden, his fears are resting on my shoulders.

Oswald, rumour has it, is a great warrior, but I'm better, I always have been. I foresee every eventuality, every possibility, and for that very reason, I'll be speaking with Clydog and Cynddylan later of my qualms.

I think my brother might have become a Christian. I fear he might well be about to try and play me false, just as happened to this Christian God, the one betrayed by his ally.

I'll need to be wary of Eowa. Watch him.

I curse. Oswald employs a more serious threat than just brute strength. He meddles with the minds of men, with my brother's belief in himself, and worse. It's now started to infect me as well. I see an enemy where before I knew I had an enemy and an ally combined. Now I'm not so sure.

"Until the battle," I say, reaching for Eowa once more. I need to leave here before he sees my doubts.

When he meets my eyes, his face is once more ablaze with an inner fire.

"Yes, Penda. Until the battle. We'll arrive as enemies and leave as allies. I hunger for it."

"As do I," I reciprocate, reaching for Gunghir, who nips me once more as I walk past him. Bloody horse, but his nip makes me pause, turn to face Eowa, and what I see fills me with foreboding.

I need to shore up my alliances with Cynddylan and Clydog.

No matter what my brother does in the coming altercation, we will defeat Oswald.

We will.

CHAPTER 20

Eowa, King of Mercia AD641

Near Tamworth

I watch Penda ride away. I know he's disappointed in me. I'm disappointed in myself. Where have these doubts come from, these fears that Oswald might be right in pursuing his new God?

I've always been less secure in my beliefs. I've never enjoyed the blood and sacrifice that must accompany our family's links with Woden. But, and it's a huge but, I don't feel entirely convinced by Oswald either.

I almost wish these Gods who allegedly war for our souls would leave me alone. I've long been content with my version of our religion. I can accept Woden as my ancestor. I don't have to follow all of his ways, but Oswald's God seems to offer more and for less. His God doesn't demand blood and death, but rather life, and perhaps blood as well. Or so it seems to me at the moment.

For too long, I've been toying with the ideas, but it was Bishop Birinus who finally managed to slip the seed of doubt into my mind, him and Oswald's insistence that I convert.

I thought nothing of it, but then when I heard the words wash over me and the chill water that followed, I can't deny that I did feel something *different*. I've tried to dismiss it as nothing. I wouldn't be the first man to convert and then recant, return to my old religion. Yet it seems to have been a small thing for all the others, done in a moment and then forgotten. It's not that way for me. I see and hear things all the time that make me question myself.

If I weren't about to go into battle with Oswald against my brother, I'd have the time I needed to consider my options. But I don't. I could die in this battle, or worse, Penda could. Then I'll be left with little but Oswald as my ally and a lifetime of listening to men like Bishop Birinus who twist their words and ensure that they somehow penetrate my resolve, for all that I don't want to hear them.

Bishop Birinus uses words more cleverly than weapons. I feel Birinus' scars every time I move. I fear they do more damage than a blade. Their impact is just as long-lasting, the scars never seeming to fade away. The flood of holy water over my head seeming to mark me and give me new skin that fears what will happen if I die.

Never once in my life have I known dread quite so deep. Never have I doubted my brother's prowess in battle. But now I dread, and I doubt, and it's no way to go to war.

I need to kill Oswald almost as desperately as Penda does. Then I need to kill his priests and bishops and forever drive the stain of their holy water from my skin.

But I can only do all those things if I allow myself to believe, as Penda does, that the holy water had no impact on me, that it's not changed me beyond return to Woden and his ways.

Long after Penda has left me in the woodlands, I linger, my horse eager to graze on the river rushes. Content that he has water enough to last him all day long, I sink to my knees, allowing the water in the secluded place to wash away the sting of the baptism.

I allow it to soak through my trews and my cloak. Welcome it dragging me down into the shallows of the brook, tears streaming down my face. My hands become bloodied from where I thrash against the chill of the water and the feeling that I'll never be free from the Christian God, from Bishop Birinus' words, from King Oswald's exhortations.

I want only to be king, to be a warrior, to be lauded on my death and to feast with Woden, my brother and my father in Valhalla. Yet my baptism has prevented it from being anywhere near as easy as Penda implies.

I wish to be free from my doubts and worries. I demand to be set free to war and toil as I must. To create the sort of chaos upon which Woden thrives. Yet, the calm I need, the strong beliefs in Woden, elude me, even as the day turns to dusk and the creatures return to the brook, ignoring my presence and that of my horse, as though we've become part of the landscape.

I need some inner hope, some inner calm.

It seems I'm not about to get it.

✣CHAPTER 21✣

Oswald of Northumbria AD641

Mercia

Eowa greets me beside the river. The water is a welcome sound in the still day. It's the height of summer, and it's too warm, far too warm this far inland. I'm used to a constant sea breeze. The windless days are more notable in Northumbria than when the wind does blow because they so far outnumber them.

I've ridden my men hard to get here and come to Eowa's aid as his brother rampages through his kingdom. I've chastised the men for their complaints about the heat and the sweat, but here, beside this river, I share their frustration and anger. It's too damn hot. How are men supposed to fight when sweat trickles from the top of their head, down their backs and into their boots? I should have delayed, have the men travel when the season was beginning to turn. But there was no guarantee that Penda wouldn't have taken control of the whole of Mercia by then. Eowa might well have been dead.

Eowa isn't the fully-fledged convert I might have hoped he'd become, but he's still attempted to reconcile his views to mine. There's no other who could stand firm against his brother and hold the loyalty of the men of Mercia away from Penda. No, I had no choice but to come as quickly as I could, with my warriors in tow. I might have to start praying for rain and a storm, however. The air is sticky, clammy, here in the heartlands of our island. I wish that Penda had chosen to attack Northumbria directly. At least my men would have been more comfortable then, with the sea breeze and the nearly constant wind.

Eowa waits for me, patiently anticipating our conversation while his horse drinks deeply from the river. Eowa's wearing his battle equipment and doesn't appear as uncomfortable as I am. He's used to this heat and stillness. No trace of sweat mars his face.

Eowa's surrounded by his warriors. They're ready to fight Penda once more, but Penda has managed some substantial gains throughout the summer raiding season. From his heartland of the Hwicce to the west, he's attacked and now holds much of Mercia. Eowa is encamped at this place he calls Tamworth, hovering on ground he once held confidently and which he now fears Penda will snatch from him.

I think of my brother as I watch Eowa. I'm glad Oswiu knows that I'm the king, not him. But how would our relationship have developed if he'd made himself a king of somewhere else and then tried to challenge my kingship?

I'm a fine warrior, trained and bloodied in the many battles between Dal Riata and the old Irish kingdoms. But Oswiu's reputation is more to be feared because he gained it fighting on our island, against the men of the kingdom of the Gododdin and the wilder tribes that live in the mountainous region occupying the centre of the land opposite Northumbria. My reputation is more distant. It means less to people who've never seen the deep blue sea that lies between Dal Riata and the Irish kingdoms nor experienced its beautiful but deadly landscape.

"My Lord King," Eowa breaks my reverie. I stride toward him, trying to ignore the fresh trickle of sweat that beads my face.

"Lord Eowa," I offer. He's my ally, and he's asked for my help. When Penda is dead, he'll still be king of Mercia, so I offer the honorific.

In the distance, I can smell the tang of burning and wrinkle my nose against the smell of roasting flesh.

"An attack, only yesterday. It was less than a day's march from here." Eowa's eyes briefly close as though to fight off the pain of that admission. I look where he points. Penda has continued to make headway in Mercia, even after I sent word that I'd assist Eowa. I'd hoped it would drive Penda away, or at least scare him enough that he decided to find an old stone ruin and shelter within it. It would have been far easier to attack him then.

"He grows bolder and bolder with his movements," I offer sourly. Eowa doesn't even provide an answer.

"How many men do you have?" Eowa asks eagerly. I see before me a man who's keen to regain his kingdom from the clutches of his brother. He's not given up or been beaten yet, and the considerable number of warriors he still controls shows that the people of Mercia want him as their king, despite what Penda might think.

I've followed the correct course of action in coming to his rescue.

"Nearly a thousand men," I respond quickly. "We'll attack as soon as they're rested, no more than a day. We need to stop Penda before he advances further. Have you found a favourable position for our battle?"

"I have, My Lord King, yes, and my thanks for coming to my aid. I'm grateful for our alliance."

"As am I," I retort quickly. I want to discuss tactics not to hear simpering thanks from a man who's been put in an unwinnable situation by his brother.

"You have a place in mind?" I demand. Eowa, no doubt sensing my impatience, turns away from me to look to the west.

"Not far from here, a great hill which is easily defensible and which Penda must strive to attack up if we can hold the top. We'll encircle him if we can just entice him there in the first place. It'll leave us plenty of opportunities to retreat if we must. Not that we will," Eowa adds hastily. "It's a good site. And it has a bonus. The people who live here speak of a great battle in the mist of time when three kings were slain. It has a reputation as a place where kings die and a small barrow at its peak where their bodies are said to lie."

Eowa sounds smug as he speaks, for all that he's fighting for his kingship.

"Does it have its own defences?"

"A small earthwork, the positioning of the land will disorientate the men. We can set traps all around the base of the hill and to its rear as well."

"I'd like to see the place before I agree." Eowa has considered the needs of the coming battle well, but his words mean nothing to me. It's as though he tries to describe colours to a sightless person, a task Bishop Aidan once undertook and told me about, at great length. How can you *see* a colour when there's no comparison? I need to see this place for myself.

"Tomorrow," I say with finality, turning to lead my horse away from the stream. My men are busy setting up a temporary camp, well those who haven't fallen to the ground in exhaustion or run into the river to cool their steaming backs are. It's not the most promising of arrivals at a battle, but I've had worse. Time will show that my warriors are the better fighters. When I stand against Penda, with Eowa at my side, not his, I'll win the day. I dream of Penda meeting his death on the end of my sword. It would be an excellent story to hear retold around the fires in the depth of winter.

I can taste my victory.

"My Lord King?" Eowa recalls me to the here and now.

"Do you have other men coming? Have you called on any of your other allies?"

The question mildly torments me as I watch him, eyes narrowed, trying to determine my strength. Why should it matter if I have? Perhaps he just hopes to put the warriors of other men at the front of the battle and leave the meat and bones of the fighting to men he'll not miss.

I tut with annoyance, but against the rush of water in the stream, Eowa doesn't hear me or chooses not to do so. Either way, I don't much mind.

"No, I've sent word to Cenwahl of the South Saxons and Onna of the East Angles, but I've not demanded their attendance at the battle. It doesn't mean they won't come. It just means that if they do, it's their choice. I've not called on their support as their overlord, only as their ally. It would do them well to fight Penda, to prove to themselves that they can beat him. But then, both men have faced him before, something I've never done."

Eowa considers my words pensively. I don't know if he's unhappy with the lack of support or whether he's just thinking of the coming battle against his brother.

"Penda's skills aren't to be underestimated," Eowa finally offers. His words mask a wealth of information that I should perhaps know, such as his true feelings on the matter, but I let the topic slide without comment. I'm just as fractious as my men, and I'm in no mood to discuss family relationships.

"I've heard," I mutter as I walk away from him. I can feel his eyes on my back. I consider if he genuinely trusts me or perhaps knows my plans for his kingdom. It would be nothing to me if he died in this battle, alongside his brother, and left all of Mercia open to be ruled in my name as well. My brother would happily come to Mercia from his place of power and position in the north, and I have more brothers yet as well, and sons as well. Perhaps my wife could rule here for me? I'd like to reward her for the loyalty she shows to me.

I sink to my campstool, grateful to whoever has placed it beside my tent, the front door thrown wide open to allow any stray breeze inside. I know it'll be a hot and sticky night.

I certainly don't wish to do more than rule this kingdom in name alone. Hopefully, I'll never have to revisit the place once Penda is dead.

My eyes close as I lean back against the side of the tent. The heat has drained my strength, and I allow my mind to drift.

I foresee a great future for myself. I must thank my Lord God for his favour.

Tomorrow.

CHAPTER 22

Penda of the Hwicce AD641

Barrow Hill, Mercia

The journey from our encampment has been short, with no need to bring our horses. Should the worst happen, not that it will, we'll run away quicker if we're not worrying about retrieving them.

Some of my older warriors instead guard the animals, disgruntled to be left out of the main fighting but reasonable enough to appreciate that their skills have diminished with time. Even Aldfrith, a man so old he has no teeth left, stands and personally takes control of Gunghir. They respect each other. If I weren't about to attack King Oswald, I'd amuse myself with tales of what the old man, and the old horse, will today tell each other? What aches and pains will they complain about, and what will they say, eyebrows raised, about the headstrongness of young men who want to be kings?

Not that Gunghir let me go easily. He fought and bit and stamped on my foot, ensuring I heard his unhappiness and understood it as well. He was bred for war. He wants to be with me, but no horse can stand in the thick of the fighting. No, I need my shield, sword, axe, and spear for that. Nothing else will kill Oswald.

Cynddylan and Clydog march with me. We've decided to go to the hill together, to show the men that we're united in our purpose. To present Oswald with a united position from his enemies. We might hope to know the outcome of this battle already, but we still need to fight it and maintain the illusion that we don't.

Oswald can't know what we've planned.

Oswald can't know that Eowa isn't his ally.

Behind and also in front, men stream through the bright morning sunshine. It's the summer. The sun has been high in the sky since long before the birds woke. But the day is still young. Our advance scouts have hunkered down and watched Oswald and Eowa form into their battle lines last night. Oswald might believe this battle will surprise us, but it won't. We're prepared.

Yet, we've not made ditches or raised vicious wooden stakes against any attacking force, for we're the attacking force. We'll be rapid, like lightning, streaking up the hill, steep but not steep enough that spears thrown from the top of the old barrow will give the enemy any sort of advantage.

No, our assault will be quick. We'll overpower Oswald as soon as we can. Then Eowa will make his intentions clear. Before the day ends, another king will have lost his life on this fabled hill, the subject of many a tale when I was a small boy.

Clydog's encumbered with weapons, his shield, sword, war axe, spear and knives, with his helm shining brightly. He looks like an avenging God come to restore order to the world. I think that's what we plan. He's a Christian, and I'm a believer in Woden. Still, neither of us agrees with Oswald and his desire to turn the whole world to his one true God. Clydog and I, so similar in so many ways, come to seek vengeance against Oswald and to stop his converting practices. We must kill the man who replaced King Edwin, another man who fell beneath our blades long ago.

Cynddylan is just as resplendent in his battle wear, but he strides with a different purpose. He, like myself, labours to drive back Oswald and his intentions to rule every kingdom on our island. Cynddylan's domain stretches almost into Mercia. It's land that I'd welcome into my kingdom, but which I'll never take for Cynddylan is my ally. I'll not take what he holds.

All three of us have different hopes for the coming battle. But we share one, to kill Oswald. I hope that blood flows freely on Barrow Hill today.

My scouts have told me all of Oswald's and Eowa's movements. I know that Oswald holds the centre of the hill. He has men in reserve to the north. I'm also aware that Eowa has warriors in reserve, hiding in the very woodland where we met only a handful of days ago. I believe he'll send them to join me, but equally, he might have commanded them to protect his family should the battle go badly.

I see it as a sign that Eowa's not yet fully recommitted himself to our cause. That upsets me. My words weren't heeded. Only my victory will convince him that I'm correct in what I say, that his baptism means nothing and that he's still a descendant of Woden. Nothing can wipe that stain from him.

The top of Barrow Hill is shrouded by streaming clouds as we near it, but my scouts and those that Cynddylan and Clydog dispatched return to us. They inform of what they've seen during the night and what they think is happening now, and all too soon, the cloud cover clears, the bright summer sun striking through to illuminate the might of Oswald's warriors.

There must be at least a thousand men staring at us as we march toward them. The hill seems wreathed by precious and deadly sharp metals. The men's shields are smeared with Oswald's God's emblem, a cross daubed in white against a dark background.

Our approach is no surprise, for Oswald and his chosen few stand at the top of the hill, for all to see, their banners trying to fly in the still air. I notice his special royal banner, the one that shows his affiliation with his God, his wooden cross. I also observe that Eowa stands beside him, Mercia's eagle-headed banner still. It's not the most promising of views, but it reveals one crucial thing; Eowa has done as we arranged. He flanks Oswald. His intention is still to fight for our alliance.

I imagine that Oswald would like to make a pretty speech for my warriors to hear. That he'd like to appeal to the Christian men who march with Clydog and Cynddylan from his place at the top of Barrow's Hill. But we've decided we'll not give him the time he needs to do so. The sooner the battle is started, the sooner we'll be victorious.

Quickly, our men file into position, Clydog to my left and Cynddylan to my right, their oath-sworn warriors joining them. We're all warriors here. We'll fight with our men at the front of the battle lines.

We've already given our speeches and roused the men to battle rage. All that remains to be done is to attack. With barely a moment to catch our breath from the brief march, I raise my shield high, ensuring it covers my body from any stray spear. Then, the men and I are racing up the hill, taking the strain of the slope within our long strides. It's nothing, really. But to Oswald, it will have looked like a massive advantage from the top. He shouldn't have listened to Eowa. Oswald should have realised that brothers don't suddenly become enemies.

I watch Oswald hurriedly disperse his small collection of men and banners, dispatching Eowa back to his side of the battlefield. I smirk at the ease of it all. I'd hoped to meet the attack near the top of the hill, but I think that by the time the enemy is ready to attack, we'll be at its peak. Oswald will have lost all of his advantages.

Yet, Oswald doesn't dawdle as much as I thought he would. Soon my racing run is stopped by the first thrown spear. I shout for my men to form up, to make the shield wall that will protect us all. They do as I command almost immediately, as spear after spear hits our shields, sails overhead, or stops well short of the battle line. I look around quickly, lowering my shield as I do so. Cynddylan and his men are ready, so too are Clydog and his. I roar once to my men, not knowing what I say, just that the sound of my voice will inspire them and bring on their desire for revenge against Oswald.

Amongst Cynddylan's warriors, the roar is even louder. They hate Oswald more than I do. They have a score to settle, for Oswald killed Cadwallon, a man they once looked to as their king. I grin. Oswald has allowed himself to be lured by the hope of a quick victory.

Herebrod stands to my left, Wiglaf to my right. Both are men I'm proud to stand beside as Oswald's warriors finally form their shield wall and rush to meet our attack. They don't want to lose all the advantages that holding the top of the hill gave them.

Grunts and groans reach my ear as the two shield walls meet in a thunder of metal and men. This is where we're at our weakest, for it's easier to force a man down a hill than up it. My warriors shout encouragement to each other. I appreciate that the shield wall will hold for the time being.

Now comes the time for those men with long spears and daggers to do their work from behind us. Three rows of men hold the shield wall in place. I'm at the front, my eagle-headed shield in front. Behind me stands another man, his shield above my head, and behind him another man, his shield above the head of the man in front of him. After that, the remaining rows of men are ready to reinforce any who fall and to add their weight to the line should it falter. Those small, wiry and agile enough crawl between the legs of the men before them and try and attack the exposed parts of Oswald's warriors; their feet, their ankles, and sometimes, their faces, where they might peer beneath their shield to determine how well the attack is going.

This part of the battle is where warriors can lose their strength without realising it. When others can slash their ankles and allow their blood to pool on the ground beneath them where it might make them slip or stumble, or even bleed to death without even being aware of the danger.

Yet Oswald's men are thinking the same as me. I feel the telltale sign of a foe-man attempting to attack my legs.

"Lower," I holler. Along the shield line, the probing spears are snatched back. The shields are all forced to the ground, catching unsuspecting hands and weapons in the act.

I feel a crunch beneath my shield and stamp down hard, feeling a wisp of air that assures me the shield above my head has followed my downward movement. A sharp cry of pain reaches my ears. I hope it comes from whichever little bastard was trying to slice my leg open.

"Higher," I call again. Quickly the shields are all back in their original position. Leaving shields low for too long allows the enemy to attack exposed chests.

The enemy's shields move with ours; the effort needed to shift the pieces of wood far above the normal strength because of the weight of the enemy pressing down on them.

Still, in that movement, we accomplish much. A stray cry of pain isn't the only one I hear.

My muscles strain as I hold my weight against my shield. I know I can keep up the same pressure for a long time yet. I don't want this to be a long, drawn-out battle but rather a quick one. I command those in the second row to begin attacking our enemy.

I feel the blade of the warrior behind me as it pokes through the gap between my shield and the open sky. I hold firm to my shield as my warrior tries to work the dagger behind our enemy's shield, to attack his exposed side or his neck, anywhere that flesh might be showing.

I hear a muffled command from the other side of the shield wall and brace myself for Oswald's attempt to repel the attack. His accent is thicker than mine. I blame it on his time in Dal Riata. I struggle to understand his shouted words. Not that I give too much time to them. There's little more to be done until one side gives a little.

I consider my options. I want it to be a quick battle, a short and resounding victory.

Above my head, I hear the whistle of arrows, unable to determine if they come from Cynddylan's archers or Oswald's. Only the noise masks a more worrying sound as I hear the thump of feet over the shield above my head.

Damn, are they my men, those who've decided to prove their

strength by using the shields as a handy stepping platform to reach Oswald, or are they his men, using the same tactic against us?

The man behind me grunts at the weight on his shield, and then the man behind him, and I have my answer. It's Oswald and his men. They've decided they want a rapid battle as well.

I lick my lips, thinking quickly. All the time, I can hear my warriors at the back of the shield wall assaulting however many of Oswald's men risked attacking in such a way. I've used the tactic before, but as a means to distract my enemy or as a way to make a battle appear more vicious than it truly was, just as at Shifnal.

Ah, distraction. That must be what Oswald intends.

I dare to lower my shield, to look about me, but all I can see are men straining, one against the other. I turn to Herebrod, but his expression is fixed, his concentration intense. I should have stayed at the back of the shield wall, kept my eye on what Oswald was doing. Now I feel as though I'm fighting in the dark, for all that the sun blazes overhead, and sweat is forming on my face and running down my back.

"Take my place," I command the warrior at my back, Cudberct. He grunts, taking hold of the strap on the shield. I force my way back through the press of men. Two of my most trusted warriors quickly surround me to ensure I'm not attacked. But as I fight my way to the rear of the shield wall, going against the natural flow of events, I see that Oswald's men number too many. My men here fight a more deadly battle than those at the front.

I rush through, taking the shield of one of my men as I do, for I've left mine in the shield wall. I heft the comforting weight and step into a clear space, breathing deeply for the first time since the attack started. I can see that at least fifty men fight our rear down the slope. I break into a short run. I need to see what's happening on the battlefield. If I had Gunghir with me, I could slide onto his back for a better vantage, but he's safe at the old settlement of Wall. So, I rush to the closest tree, where they grow sporadically at the bottom of Barrow Hill. The birch trees are flimsy things, their barks all white and shiny, but I manage to haul myself up two of the spindly branches and gaze up the hill.

The scene that greets me is less worrying than I feared. Oswald's men are effectively stuck against our shield wall. More men will need to rush across the shields to attack us from the rear if they truly wish to win this battle. My men are advancing, slowly for sure, up the incline. That's good. It means that we'll still have our victory.

To either side, Cynddylan and Clydog and their warriors fight superbly against Eowa's warriors. But Eowa is making no move to come around Cynddylan and reinforce him from the rear. That's worrying. My brother needs to see more chance of a victory before he fully commits to our alliance.

I growl. This was supposed to be a hasty battle.

But I know this place. I have men in one more location to upset the tide of battle. They'll be less noticeable in their intentions than Oswald's in theirs.

"Signal them," I call to my warrior, Wulfnoð. He grunts an acknowledgement and goes to light the small fire already prepared the previous evening. The trail of smoke on the bright sunny day will tell my men, led by Æthelfrith, Aldfrith's oldest son, that they're to start attacking Oswald from the rear, to leave the dubious shelter of the ancient barrow.

These men volunteered for their task. I've not commanded any of them, for they have the most dangerous duty to accomplish. They must attack Oswald from the rear to try and find Oswald and kill him before his men can kill mine.

I shield my eyes against the bright daylight, taking another glance at the activity on top of Barrow Hill. A horse moves, a shining thing all white and shimmery in the heat haze. Oswald is watching me as closely as I watch him. He's trying to gauge his moment, just as I do.

I hope Oswald doesn't understand the importance of my smoke, although Eowa may. Not that Eowa would tell him? Or would he?

I look for my brother along the shield wall, hoping to see his telltale helm, gifted to him by our father, all beaten metal and almost black with age. But the fighting is too close. I can't see the actual front line of the shield wall as well as I can the top of the hill.

Where I commanded that the fire be lit, a thin trail of smoke is starting to lift into the sky. I know it's time for me to return to the fighting.

The two sides are more evenly matched than I predicted. But this attack should give me the edge I need to convince my brother that I'll win, and he should change sides immediately.

Jumping from the branches, I attack Oswald's warriors. They're fearsome creatures, no doubt from the old tribes in the North. I wonder if they're enslaved or if they fight freely for Oswald. If they fight freely, they should die, but I pity them for their plight if they're enslaved. They shouldn't be forced to die for a man who thinks he can rule through his religion alone.

Yet, as the first man dies on my blade, surprised to have been attacked from the rear when all around him every spare man's fighting, I find I feel no sympathy at all. An enslaved person or willing participant, these men have come here to fight for Oswald. So, like him, they must die.

Wulfnoð, Eoforwine and I cut down another ten men before we reach the back of the shield wall, festooning ourselves with the blood of our enemy. The deaths are important ones. They allow my men to concentrate on the attack at the shield wall, not on any from behind them. As I shoulder my way back to my original place, I feel our shield wall advance as though a great wave has hit the shore, spreading further and wider as the tide crawls back inland after its grudging retreat.

I cheer and scream my enjoyment. Then I hear a welcome noise. Oswald's warriors are bellowing for help from their rear. Aldfrith's son has accomplished his task.

✛CHAPTER 23✛

Oswald of Northumbria
AD641 Summer

Barrow Hill

My horse collapsing beneath me is the first sign that all isn't going as well as I hoped.

The poor beast simply buckles. I spring clear from it, my hand going for my sword and shield without thought. I believed I'd ensured no stray enemy warriors were hiding around Barrow Hill. I was wrong.

There are no more than a hundred foe-men. They're inflicting terrible damage on the rear of my shield wall, which I'd hoped to command from my horse rather than from the front line. I curse softly and then apologize to my Lord God and offer a quiet prayer instead.

I've brought a handful of monks with me on this journey. I watch in horror as Penda's warriors attack them first, leaving blood trailing from open wounds, before turning to the back of my shield wall.

I call for reinforcements, for Eowa to come and reinforce the shield wall, but at the same time, I hear, rather than see, that it's giving ground. For a moment, I know genuine fear and panic. I've never yet lost a battle, but this is beginning to look like it could be the first.

Eowa assured me this would be a good site from which to attack Penda. But he's done all the attacking so far, advancing uphill despite all the odds. The steep rise of the hill should have prevented his warriors from making too much headway. That hasn't happened, and for an ugly moment, I allow myself to think that Eowa knew of this, that he's actually trying to help Penda. But Eowa has converted to my religion and asked for my assistance against his brother. Why then would he put our side at a disadvantage?

My eyes roam the hill, looking for something, anything that could give me an advantage. I glance at the banners of the kings of the British who've come to assist Penda. Then I have an idea.

The men fight well, as do their warriors, but they're smaller forces. It would be easier to infiltrate one or other of the sides to enable my warriors to attack from the rear as well as from the front.

I shout for Eowa, but it's his commander who comes to my bidding. His name eludes me, but he understands my words quickly enough. In almost no time at all, he's running towards the rear of Cynddylan's force, using the natural curve of the hill to mask his actions. He's taken no more than thirty men with him. Hopefully, that'll be enough to disrupt their attack.

That done, I turn my attention to the men ravaging the rear of my force. My horse has died because of them. I vow to avenge him. He was an expensive animal, a gift to show my holiness and that God had ordained my right to rule from my wife.

I rush against the first man I see, shield tightly in my hand. He's happily hacking his way through the rear of my men. Some have turned, shields raised to meet the attack. But the men at the back of the shield wall are the weakest of all my warriors, young and untried in battle. Or too old and, while used to action, unable to respond quickly with slow-moving arms and hands.

A pile of bodies lies at this particular warrior's feet. His face is covered in blood. His byrnie slashed by an opportunistic strike. Still, he attacks without ceasing. I need to kill him before a hundred of my men lose their lives on the edge of his sword.

I step behind him, hoping to catch him unaware. He must hear my footstep, for he turns, an ugly smile on his blood-soaked face. He swings his shield, trying to knock my sword out of my hand. I wish I'd chosen a different weapon with less reach so that I could step closer to him and not rely on having a large arc to get the required amount of power to make the blow count.

"King Oswald." The foe-man growls, bowing just the once, before stepping too close to me, his axe soaked with the blood of dead men. He takes a wild swing at me. That's the only mistake he makes and one that costs him dearly. He should have taken his time and factored in my unreadiness before trying to kill me. But he doesn't, and that's the only reason I don't die there and then.

Instead, I reach out and pull on his axe arm, unbalancing him in the process. I step back. I slice his suddenly exposed neck as his head is flung back when he slips on the bloody ground. He grunts as my blow connects, and then he grins again.

"Enjoy your last kill," he utters. Then his eyes flutter in death, and my warriors are watching me with appreciation. It was a clean blow, a good strike that used the warrior's strength against him. It's a lesson I'm keen for my warriors to learn, but not now. Now, we need to stop more of the attacks and wait for the assault on Cynddylan to take effect.

I search for the next of Penda's warriors along the rear of my shield wall. I'm careless as I do so, and the slice of a blade on my ankle makes me look down in shock. The warrior I thought I'd killed is watching me with a blood-filled mouth, laughing and choking on his blood as he does so. He's not yet dead, and my leg is bleeding as profusely as his neck.

"Shit," I shout, only then remembering to bend down and ensure the warrior is genuinely dead.

"Fool," I think he growls as he dies. I know he's right. He could have killed me if his reach had only been that little bit longer.

To the left of the battlefield, where Eowa's man has gone to cause trouble amongst Cynddylan's force, I hear a rousing cheer.

I consider what it means, hoping it doesn't foretell that the men are dead with their task not yet accomplished. I need them to disturb Cynddylan to have any chance of success here.

I limp away from the dead man, knowing that if I face anyone else in hand to hand combat, I'll be distracted by the blood surging from my ankle, sapping my strength with every stroke of my sword.

Yet, the cheer did mean something as there's a significant surge to the left. Hastily, I command my men at the rear of the shield wall to rush and assist the attack on Cynddylan. If my God is answering my prayers, then Penda's attack has been severely weakened.

I hobble to the top of the hill, not caring who sees me or that I'm covered in the blood of another man. The view that greets me is a delight, and I smirk. Cynddylan's force is busy fighting itself or not fighting itself. I watch with interest as I try to decipher the meaning of the battle taking place between my men and Cynddylan's.

True to his word, Eowa's man has taken his warriors around the hill to its bottom and has then rushed the back of Cynddylan's warriors. All without them noticing, almost until my men are at the front of Cynddylan's shield wall. Something isn't right there, but in the heat of the battle, and through my pain, I can't decipher what's wrong with the images before me.

Instead, I hastily issue commands, having men hurry to assist my warriors to the left, to have them push through Cynddylan's forces, who quickly scatter when they realise they've been infiltrated by men who aren't their allies. I howl with delight as the entire shield wall crumbles away, men running for their lives. My warriors flood to the back of Penda's shield wall.

Once more, Penda has two fronts to fight on, the front and the rear. Those of his men who came to try and attack from our rear are dead or captured.

Eowa continues to battle against Clydog. I can see his dark helm in the bright daylight. But then even he rushes to the back of the shield wall, to see what's happening, and as he does so, he meets my gaze. It's a steady gaze, one that tells me more than I need to know.

Eowa's ability to be a false ally for his brother has just about won this battle.

Quickly now, for the fortunes on the battlefield are changing with each pound of my heart, I command my warriors to attack Penda from the left and to circle around to attack Clydog from the right. What few of Cynddylan's warriors remain alive are starting to run away long before any command is given to retreat.

Now it's my turn to use a smoking signal to my advantage. I order that the youth who's been minding the smouldering fire on the top of the hill removes the heavy hide that covers it. Smoke flickers into the deep blue sky.

It's a bright summer's day, and my warriors, hiding not on the hill but to the far east, where the land dips low as though there should be a river, but there isn't, will ride out on and attack those who try to escape back to the encampment at Wall.

All I need now is for Penda to give the command to retreat, and I know I'll have won the battle. All it will have taken is a great deal of deceit and a lack of brotherly love. And, of course, the support of my Lord God. I must never forget that, even though my monks are dead. It'll be their spilt blood that's angered my God and allowed me this victory.

CHAPTER 24

King Eowa of Mercia AD641 summer

Barrow Hill

I never expected either of my plans to come to fruition, but I'm to be rewarded for my Christian faith and for converting against my brother's wishes.

I was prepared to hedge my bets, to see which side was victorious, but I've finally bettered my brother, managing to act in such a way that his strength has become his failing.

I swallow thickly. Deceit and lying have never come easily to me. This has been particularly difficult. I said I'd only allow myself to follow whoever was the stronger man, and that's only just been made clear to me.

I didn't lie to Penda when I told him I'd support Oswald against him if he proved to be the more powerful. I believe Oswald is the more commanding man. This battle was almost at a standstill until something changed. I don't know what it was, but I harbour the thought that it has something to do with my commander, Glaeðwine, who's now missing from my side.

Not that any of it much matters. All I need do is face Penda in combat, kill him, and my position will be the most secure it's ever been.

Yet, the cry for retreat doesn't come when I think it should.

I curse my brother for his arrogance. If Penda doesn't retreat, his men will be cut down by Oswald's mounted warriors, men who've learnt their skills either in Dal Riata or fighting against the warriors of that kingdom. I could almost pity my brother his fate at their hands.

I find I'm willing him to retreat, but my brother isn't a man to give up, even when the odds are against him, as I think they are now.

Instead, a rallying cry soars through the air. I rush to Oswald's viewpoint to see what my brother's doing.

I watch in surprise and no little amazement as he manages to re-orientate his men so that the shield wall stretches further and further along the left side of the battlefield as well as across its middle. But all he's doing is delaying the inevitable and, perhaps worse, cutting off all chance of retreat.

Oswald's watching him with a glint of amusement in his eye, and for all that I've vowed to fight for him now, to be his ally, I feel a hard stone of unease in my stomach. What have I done? I want to rule without my brother's interfering hand, but to witness his death was never my intention.

Luckily. Oswald doesn't speak to me, so I don't have to muster a lie or speak words I don't want to voice. It's a small consolation.

I watch my brother rallying his men, calling to Clydog, getting reinforcements; it's a hive of activity. Deep in my traitorous heart, I feel half a hope that my brother will win through after all. He is, without doubt, the more able warrior, the better tactician.

Despite his bloody clothes and lack of a horse, Oswald continues to smirk. It's his smirk that drives me away from him. He looks so confident but also so assured of his victory. Oswald believes he's fulfilling his God's work, but I know better.

At that moment, I realised I couldn't tolerate Oswald as my overlord. Suddenly, I know the truth of who I am and what I am. But it's almost too late to do anything about it.

Without a word either to Oswald or from him, I rush from his presence, half expecting him to detain me, but all of his warriors are embroiled in the attack. Because he wasn't a part of it when the vital moves were taken, he can't find a way back into the battle with his injury. So Oswald watches and waits for what he believes will be an inevitable and preordained victory.

I sprint, my breath harsh in my mouth, down the back of Barrow Hill, towards where I hope my horse is waiting for me. I almost tumble because of the steepness of the slope, but somehow, arms flailing and sparking the memory of a childhood game, I manage to keep on my feet.

Only when I reach him, almost on my knees, is my fear wholly gone. He's strayed further than many of the other beasts who mill around their improvised enclosure, most probably because he doesn't like the smell of blood or battle, just like myself. My breath's ragged.

I look up to where Oswald continues to watch the battle. Just there, surrounded by no one, he's completely vulnerable. I understand that I've wasted the opportunity to kill him. In my haste to help my brother, I've let the moment pass.

I consider my options. I could go back and kill Oswald now, but if I do, I risk my brother and his allies being overrun by Oswald's mounted warriors.

Indecision wars inside me as I try to capture my breath and think clearly, in a way I've not been capable of ever since Cadwallon's unexpected death. I want to kill Oswald. I want that renown for myself, but I'll only gain it at my brother's death. That I don't want. Not yet.

So resolved, I urge my horse to move, rounding up as many of the other horses as I can. My brother and his warriors might not be skilled in fighting from horseback, but if I take horses to them, they'll at least have half a chance.

I manage only a few, five horses other than mine. Fearing that I'll be caught, I ride quickly to the right. I can hide my intentions behind the hill that stands tall there. I risk a glance at Oswald, but he's looking the other way, his gaze fixed on the battle. I wish I'd brought more men with me, but my decision was so impulsive that I've come alone and can now only take back a handful of horses to rescue my brother. But a few is better than none, or so I assure myself.

I urge my mount forward. He's unhappy at the other horses that follow him, tied together, nose to tail, but he's going to have to move, or my brother will be dead. As though he finally understands my urgency, my horse takes off at great speed. Finally, I think I might be able to do some good in supporting my brother instead of Oswald. I only hope I'm not too late.

The area I'm heading for, a small cut that runs through the surrounding hilly landscape seems to take forever to come into view. I'm despairing, worried that the horses will be too tired when I finally get there, exhausted by their sudden swift flight, but eventually and oh so slowly, the path I wish to take forms before me.

The cries of the battle, which had been so distant when I ran for my horse, materialise into a solid line of fighting men before me as I crest the hill. I'm on the correct side of the battle now. I can see my brother fighting with his men. Oswald's mounted warriors haven't yet arrived as luck would have it. I imagine the thin thread of smoke is barely visible in the too-bright sunshine, although it seems to pulse with intensity and threat whenever I gaze at it.

Penda's warriors see me before he does. They turn angry eyes my way. For a moment, I think they'll kill me for my betrayal, but something in them stops my death. Instead, Penda's attention is snagged by one of them, and he strides towards me in his war gear, every part of him moving with assurance, for all that he's nearly lost this battle. He looks how I've always imagined Woden would manifest in the flesh. His face is bloodied and beaten. A wound pulses fresh blood on his arm, and over his arm rings which now have an ugly copper tone to them.

Penda's smile beneath his black helm is all I need to see.

Whatever has happened is instantly forgotten as he sights me and sees the horses at my back.

"You must retreat. Oswald has mounted warriors. He's signalled them with that smoke. I brought all I could."

I expect Penda to laugh at my antics, demand to know if this is just another trap, but instead, he leaps into the saddle of one of the beasts, a huge black thing that could almost be a double of Gunghir. His sure voice rises above the battle cries of his warriors.

"Retreat," he bellows. The call is quickly taken up by the rest of his warriors, as well as by Cynddylan's beleaguered force, hounded by both my men and Oswald's and also by Clydog's. Yet, for all that I want to run from the battle site, take my horse and rush back to Wall, Penda doesn't. He sits on his horse. For a long moment, he's still, so very still, and then I see what he sees, and I understand why he doesn't yet move.

Oswald's watching. Even from here, I can see the horror on his face and hear my men realising what's happened. I think that Penda could have won the battle, as my men fight to get to my side, abandoning Oswald as they do so. But instead, Penda stands a guard, ensuring his men and mine retreat. I remain beside him, hacking at any of Oswald's warriors who try and attack men running from the shield wall, even as I allow my warriors to rush past me. Sometimes, it's a close call, and one man shrieks my name as I almost decapitate him. Then I remember he's one of my warriors, a good man, and I let him pass with a shouted apology.

My fear is gone, my uncertainty, my lack of faith in myself that I somehow managed to turn into a crisis of personal faith between Oswald's fake religion and my much deeper faith. And there lies the difference. I see it all clearly now. I have faith in my Gods, not in a religion that offers so little in return for subservience to its doctrines and creeds.

My blade, already bloodied that afternoon but in aid of the wrong cause, flashes brightly with men's blood. Only when I hear Oswald's warriors rushing toward Penda and myself do I cease my actions and urge Penda to galvanise his horse to action.

Some of his men fight on, ensuring the shield wall stands for as long as possible so that their comrades can escape. I worry he'll refuse to move, but as he yells "retreat" once more, the urgency in his voice permeates the men's senses. They turn and run as well, as fast and quickly as they can, as though pursued by Oswald's devil.

As the men run around us, Penda and I, without words or discussion, stand in the way of the advancing horsemen who've finally arrived. We trick them because they think we'll move aside, but we won't, not while our warriors are in danger.

I don't know how many horses face just the six of us, but I appreciate that we have the advantage.

The lead horse crashes against Penda. He smashes the man's face away with his shield, at the same time managing to kick the advancing horse in the face with his heavy, blood-stained boots. The animal shies away in pain. This time, Penda, without holding onto his horse's reins, but trusting him all the same, grabs his long black sword in one hand and uses it to impale the rider on the horse.

Beside him, another man tries to tempt his horse toward me, but I'm covered in blood and gore, streaked with filth and muck from the shield wall, and the noise that comes from my open mouth is enough to scare the Christian devil back to his Hell.

The animal baulks, throwing his rider to the ground. I allow my beast to stamp all over the man. He'll be dead before too long. The cracks and grunts of his breaking bones are a strange sound to hear above the roar of the battle, but I hear each and every one all the same and relish in the man's pain. I only wish it were Oswald beneath the horse.

The other men, all of them, and there's far more of them than just the two that Penda and I attack, and the other four behind us with Penda's warriors on them, stop at our savage attack. They're only prepared to fight when they have no opposition to stop them because their victory is assured. I agree with their decision. Such well-trained horses are too valuable to lose.

In that split second, Penda slaps my horse's rump, sending the beast rushing forward towards the safety of the old Roman settlement of Wall, and then he follows, his teeth red with blood, his grimace of battle joy almost a mask over his filthy face, as I watch over my shoulder.

I don't know what his first words to me will be, but one thing's for sure. He's far more trusting than I ever thought he was and forgives more easily than I ever have.

I've always been in awe of my younger brother, almost scared of his abilities. I should have been less fearful and more open.

My brother and I are a deadly force when we work together, as we must now do, to rid our island of the menace of Oswald.

We ride quickly. This hasn't been the victory that either of us envisaged when the sun first rose over the eastern horizon, but something monumental has occurred here, and even if it's only the firming of my resolve to support my brother, that's still worthy of note.

Now all I need to do is win my peace with Cynddylan and Clydog if they've even realised what's happened.

✤CHAPTER 25✤

Oswald of Northumbria
AD641 summer

Barrow Hill

I watch without truly seeing. Then I turn and watch once more, my head swivelling from where Eowa was just standing to where I can see him now, on his horse and beside his brother.

In what moment did he decide to abandon my alliance, turn against my men and me, and why take the horses?

I try to understand what I'm seeing, but it's the penetrating gaze of Penda that arrests me. He looks every inch the avenging God, blood-streaked and stained with gore, his helm covered with the remnants of another man's life, his confidence on his borrowed horse a testament to his belief in himself.

Penda watches me frankly. His expression is not difficult to understand. He hates me. He always has. He hungers for my death.

I try to meet his eyes, to defy the anger and the hatred, but as I'm questioning my beliefs, the work my God sent me to do at the same time, I find his gaze uncomfortable. I flinch away from its intensity.

When I dare to look at him once more, he's laughing. His

bloodied sword is raised high in one hand, his axe in the other, and the horse, an animal I recognise from my stables, is steady under the control of his legs.

What sort of man is he to turn this defeat into his victory? What kind of power does he have?

It's Penda that breaks our gaze, but not because he can't meet my eyes, only in order to kill more of my warriors. He strikes to arrest the mounted men from the northern lands attempting to clobber Penda's retreating men. Even in that regard, I watch with amazement as he imperils his life to save that of his warriors.

I'd not be as keen to ensure the survival of my warriors if a hundred enemy horsemen were bearing down on me.

Penda fights with calm, precise movements, never disturbed by his opponent's movements. It's almost as though he foretells their actions. Nothing surprises him. I almost wish he were my ally, not my enemy and that I'd chosen the other brother. Beside him, Eowa pales into insignificance, for all that he fights as well as my best warriors. I can understand Eowa's desire to ally with me. Eowa needed something, anything, to give him an edge over a man who can kill without conscious thought and yet who's clearly thinking all the time. Penda's face, the parts of it I can see through his warrior's helm, are a fixed grimace of delight.

Perhaps, Penda is Woden made flesh, just as Bishop Birinus warned. I'd put the bishop's hyperbolic words down to his priestly ways, but I was wrong. He truly saw Penda for the man he has become.

Before me, the battlefield has descended into chaos. I know I should be issuing instructions, telling the men what to do, ordering them to follow the retreating force of Penda and his allies, but I feel numb.

My God has abandoned me in the middle of enemy territory. Instead of protecting my warriors, he's allowed a beast to stalk my battlefield, taking lives as it will, feasting on my oath sworn warriors and my hopes and dreams.

I feel defeated for all that it's Penda who flees the battlefield.

I wish Oswiu were here. He'd never give up. He already doubts the power of the new God. Oswiu would have ordered the men to harry the retreating enemy. But I see no point. Penda was on the brink of collapse, my shield wall almost surrounding him, and yet he still lives, and worst, so do the majority of his men.

"My Lord King," Baldgar, my commander, rushes to my side. He's as blood-streaked as every other man here. His face shows his confusion and unease that he's not been ordered to pursue the enemy.

"Secure our position," I command instead. He looks at me, puzzled.

"They'll have defences at Wall. They'll not ride out again today, and they'll already be making plans to retreat deeper into Mercia. Secure our position. We need to recover and then follow them, but we need to trap them in the open, where they can't take advantage of our lack of knowledge of the area."

At last, my mind is beginning to thaw from my frozen shock. I'm relieved I can think clearly.

"Lord Eowa?" Baldgar asks. "What of his men?"

"Bring them to me," I command. Eowa has left at least half of his force behind. I can use them against him or kill them and make martyrs of them all.

"On second thoughts, round them up. Take them back to Tamworth and use them to imprison Eowa's family. We'll hold them hostage, or we'll kill them."

Baldgar thinks this is an excellent idea. I nod to show he has the command. Eowa has abandoned me in the heat of battle. I doubt he's considered the implications for his family. His young son is an impressionable thing. I might have him taken to my court in Northumbria, have the raising of him and turn him to the Northumbrian way of thinking. That would be the ultimate revenge against the man who deserted our alliance.

More and more of my commanders seek instructions. I list what must be done. A makeshift wall of wooden stakes must be raised, the horses must be protected, the wounded cared for, the dead buried, and then when all that's done, I must consider my next move.

Will I chase Penda deeper into Mercia? Will I take the risk? I think I must, but it will be a huge gamble. I'd welcome more time to amass extra men. I need to call on my allies, have Cenwahl of the South Saxons do more than infringe on Penda's borders, have my brother here instead of holding the ever-shifting battle line in the north.

But these allies are too far away. It'll take too many weeks to get a messenger to them and then have their warriors ready themselves for battle. I need to react more quickly, catch Penda off his guard, allow him no time to regroup and lick his wounds.

King Onna of the East Angles. I have no choice but to demand his attendance upon me and have him bring all of his warriors as well. Onna has no love at all for Penda. Onna will fight him until they're both dead. That's the resolve I need to win a victory that means more than this battle.

I watch my warriors pick their way through the dead, some crowing with delight when they find some particular treasure of worth. I also listen to other men's words as they dig trenches to house the dead.

The victor is always left to bury the dead or leave them for the carrion crows and wolves. I prefer to bury the dead, all of them, ally or enemy, to mourn their death. But perhaps not today.

"Leave Eowa's dead," I command harshly, my voice echoing around the battlefield and above the shouts of wounded men who are seeking help or an end to their lives. My warriors respect my instructions, but whether they approve or not is another matter entirely.

It's usual to leave the enemy dead in the open, but it's not something that I've ever done before. It's an act of petty revenge, but when we leave this place and march to attack Penda, if I choose to do so, it'll act as a warning to those who live nearby. Word should also reach Penda. I mean to be as ruthless as he is. I'll leave his brother's dead and more.

A flash of inspiration and more hasty commands. I demand that all the bodies are stripped, their treasures brought to me.

My men are hungry for the metals that accumulate before my

feet, for the odd flash of a well-crafted sword, complete with jewels and gems, with the short daggers, the axes, the mail coats. I have all of them brought to me, and then I sort through them, take the greatest trophies. I have plans for these. The rest I leave for the men to argue about.

I finally leave my post at the top of Barrow Hill. It could so easily have been a resounding victory, but instead, I've been left in limbo, and to the west, I know that Penda and his allies will be arguing about their future. I wonder if his brother's deceit will have been noted. If Cynddylan and Clydog will have realised what lies at the root of their near failure?

If not, I should ensure that they do know. Perhaps I'll spare one of the wounded enemy, allow him to be healed and then sent on his way, with stories of Eowa and his inability to stay loyal.

I call yet another warrior to me, tell him my orders and that he must ensure the warrior survives. Only then do I turn my back on the battle site.

This was the battle of Barrow Hill.

It wasn't the victory it should have been, but I have enough treasure to slake the thirst of even the unhappiest warrior. And my plan is simple. I'll hide that treasure. Bury it in the ground, and when Mercia is mine, I'll reclaim it all and gift it, in thanks and in the name of my God to a new church that I'll raise in his honour and glory.

I smirk.

Today has been a disappointment, but I remain confident of success.

✠ CHAPTER 26 ✠

Penda of the Hwicce AD641

Near Wall

My warriors rush from the battlefield. I follow them, albeit last of all. My thoughts are a riotous confusion. Yet I know one thing more than any other; my brother tried to betray me but couldn't bring himself to do it. If it hadn't been for his swift actions, I'd have been cut to pieces on that battlefield, and he'd be king in my place.

I'd like to know of his motivations and why he changed his mind but now isn't the time for such a discussion. I need to consider my options.

My brother rides beside me for now, but when I enter the camp, depending on what Clydog and Cynddylan know, or even suspect, I'll need to take action, be decisive, do what kings must do.

For all that, I know that my spur of the moment decision to fight with my brother, rather than against him, was the correct one. I simply need to ensure that my actions don't get muddled when faced with my allies.

This hasn't been the victory I promised them, and worse, my brother has been the cause of our undoing, but also perversely, our salvation. I'll need to tread carefully and act depending on events' current interpretation. I doubt that Cynddylan will be unaware of what happened amongst his warriors. It's Cynddylan who's most likely to walk away from our alliance. He was explicitly targeted by Oswald and by Eowa's men.

Clydog is probably completely unaware of what turned the tide of the battle. But I doubt he will be by the time I return to the encampment.

Depending on what my allies do now, I'll have to respond quickly to ensure my warriors' survival and bring bloody Oswald to battle again.

At my side, Eowa is silent. I don't attempt to converse with him. Even if I could breathe and talk simultaneously, something that I think is currently beyond me, I wouldn't want to speak with him. I imagine his thoughts are on his family and, most specifically, his son.

Oswald will have sent men to apprehend them. I can only hope that my brother had the forethought to guard them and guard them well. Otherwise, his focus will be centred only on getting to his stronghold and not on the next phase of this attack. This is only the ending of another part of the movement against Oswald. It's not the ending I hoped for, but it's not without its merits.

Within sight of Wall, I abruptly rein my horse in and turn to view the path we've just traversed. Squinting into the bright sunshine, I'm surprised to find no enemy following me, trying to strike me down before I can reach Wall. Is this some new ploy of Oswald's? Will he allow us to escape and not hunt us down? Surely in doing so, he's missing a huge opportunity.

Instead of the sound of horsemen coming from before me, I hear it coming from behind and turn in surprise to find Clydog already on his horse, his shield in one hand, his axe in the other. He's not even taken the time to slosh away the blood that mars his face. He and his men have come to ensure that everyone who can retreat manages to without further menace. I'm pleased to see he's so keen to ensure our warriors live to fight another battle.

Surprised to find me already on a horse, he stops and looks at me.

"Penda?" my name is all the question I'm going to get.

"Eowa brought the horses, fended off Oswald's mounted men."

Clydog grunts. I think he's disappointed he's not about to renew the attack.

"My men and I will ride on. Ensure that Oswald is staying put for the time being."

I nod, suddenly weary and pleased to know that Clydog, at least, shares my views on the battle. Neither of us speaks about the failure of the offensive.

"Brother," Eowa says as we continue riding toward Wall. I sigh deeply. I'm not ready to speak to him yet.

"Later," I command and kick my horse onward. Clydog's men can ensure that the warriors who're still limping back to Wall make it there safely. I need to seek out Cynddylan before any other gets to him.

My brother calls after me, but I ignore him. I'm not angry with him. I'm not even surprised by what happened in the battle, but I need to deal with the consequences before losing a much-needed ally.

Cynddylan greets me personally as I slow my horse before our hastily erected defences, a long strip of wooden stakes, levelled at just the right height to impale either a man or a horse.

"Penda. It's good you survived," he says, watching me slide from the back of the horse. His tone is welcoming. I brace myself for his inevitable anger, all the same.

"And you. Did you lose many men?"

"Some, more than I would have wanted. Oswald was better prepared than I thought he would be." His words are mild. No trace of his battle anger remains, but I think that's not a good sign. I tense myself for an outburst about my brother.

A long silence hangs between us, in which one of my warriors brings food and water to quench the hot day from my mouth. I could do with a bath, but I don't foresee that happening anytime soon.

"Will he counter-attack?" Cynddylan continues as he too eats and drinks. We walk amongst his warriors, ensuring they're well or that those with wounds that can be treated are offered clean water and fresh cloth to bind them. Cynddylan's actions are too routine. It's almost as though we've not just been embroiled in a battle for our lives.

I know then that he's aware of Eowa's betrayal. I'm curious to see how he intends to handle it.

"Not yet, or at least it seems that way. Clydog has ridden out to check."

"I know. We discussed it before he went."

Ah, that's a telling admission. I have my confirmation that Clydog does know of what's happened, after all. There's a commotion at the front of the encampment, and I turn to see that Eowa is being forced from his horse whilst his remaining warriors protest his treatment.

I should intervene, but I've made my peace with my brother. It's with Clydog and Cynddylan that he needs to reconcile. Then I reconsider. Clydog is gone. It's Cynddylan with whom Eowa needs to make his peace. Clydog has made his views on the matter clear by absenting himself.

I sigh deeply, rubbing my face with my bloodied glove, noticing for the first time that I'm neck-deep in other men's blood and shit. I'd prefer to take the time to get clean, to wipe the battle from my body, but I'm not to be given that time by Cynddylan.

Undeterred, I force my way through the camp. My warriors and Eowa's try to get to him, but Cynddylan holds him, knees folded on the ground. He looks so much like my son in that pose that I almost strike the men away from him, punishing them for daring to lay a hand on my child.

"Make way," I shout when Cynddylan's warriors go to block my path. Instead of doing so, they look to Cynddylan and my ire sparks. They should heed my words. I'm just as much their commander here. Angrily I reach for my sword and shield, determined to fight my way to my brother's side if I must, but at some signal from Cynddylan, his warriors move aside, all apart from the two who hold Eowa to the ground as Cynddylan steps away to face me.

In the brief time it's taken me to reach him, Eowa's helm has been batted from his head and lies discarded on the ground, being examined only by the horse he used to save my life. In its place, he's been gifted with a helm of darkening bruises and black eyes.

Rage once more takes control, and the two men are sent flying, their helms tumbling from heads as they both stumble to the ground under the weight of my punches.

"See how easy it is to beat a captive man," I spit into their faces. Only the steadying hand of Eowa on my arm prevents me from killing Cynddylan's men, there and then. Eowa's right to caution me, and although I've still not spoken with him of the battle, I nod my thanks and turn to meet the furious gaze of Cynddylan. I've always thought he was a good looking man, but at that moment, his face twisted with hatred and anger. He looks ugly, mean, beyond reasoning.

"He has no intention of turning aside from Oswald. He played you because you're his brother. He learnt our formations, and then he told Oswald of them."

Cynddylan is almost incoherent with rage. Warriors on both sides of the divide are yelling their furious insults at each other. I want to let the men have their heads and do what they feel they must, but we shouldn't do the work Oswald could not accomplish. We shouldn't kill each other.

I open my mouth to speak, but it's Eowa's voice that rises above the angry men. His words sound strange. He has a fat lip and a bleeding tongue to contend with, but all, even Cynddylan, heeds his calls for peace. I think he wants to be unconvinced of his opinion of what happened. Eowa's following words make that impossible.

"It was Oswald. He guessed my intentions and instead sent one of my commanders amongst Cynddylan's men. You thought they'd come to help you, but instead, they attacked his warriors.

Glaeðwine is dead. He can't be punished for his treasonous actions, but I apologise on his behalf and hope you'll forgive me."

It's not the truth. I know that, but it's just possible that Cynddylan might allow himself to be swayed by Eowa's words.

"Why didn't you stop him?" Cynddylan shouts angrily. It's a good question.

"I didn't know that Oswald had commanded him and that Glaeðwine had followed his instructions without recourse to me."

"Why didn't you bring your men to our side when you understood what was happening?"

Cynddylan's voice continues to hold a hard edge. His men are unhappy, but I think Eowa might be able to convince them of his innocence, even if it's not the truth.

"I was fighting in the shield wall. I was waiting for you to attack up the hill to make sure of the victory."

Eowa is turning his argument back on Cynddylan. He doesn't need to cast another insult to cover his actions. I caution him now with a light touch to his arm.

"I didn't think the time was right to turn. I thought that you had more ground to gain yet," Eowa tries again, his words less inflammatory.

"So why the horses?" Cynddylan presses.

"The battle confused me—the ebb and flow. I thought you'd won, and then I saw Oswald standing at the top of Barrow Hill, a great smirk on his face. I had to see why he was so pleased. It was only then that I understood your peril, and only then that I realised what had happened."

"You didn't warn Penda of the horses when you last met," Cynddylan continues to probe, but the threatening air is starting to subside. Cynddylan's allowing himself to be convinced publicly. What he says to me in private will be a matter for us to decide.

"I didn't know about the horses until before the battle."

Eowa's standing now, his warriors forming a protective horseshoe shape around him, through which Cynddylan can be glimpsed. Weariness consumes me, the after exertion of the battle taking effect. I want to sit or sleep or eat or both. But I don't want this debate to continue any longer.

Cynddylan looks as though he'll turn aside, only then a further commotion at the front of our encampment clears to show another man, bloodied and broken, being brought before us all. I hear Eowa swear under his breath.

It seems that this man is Glaeðwine, and to save his life, he's shouting that Eowa commanded him to follow Oswald's instructions. That he only acted as he was told.

This then is it. I'll be forced to choose between my brother and my ally, and right now, with Oswald less than a swift horse ride from the encampment, I need to keep both of them by my side. I should insist on helping Eowa rescue his family and concentrate on finding a more profitable site to meet Oswald in battle again.

I listen to the man, his voice rising and falling as Cynddylan's warriors prod him and force him to his knees before Eowa. His words are almost unintelligible because he's been badly beaten as well. If only he'd shut up, the situation could be saved. But Glaeðwine wants to live, which just doesn't fit with the future that I need to happen.

Tired and exhausted, I look at the man, noting his twisted face, his angry eyes, and then I step forward to finish the man. Before I can, Herebrod steps before me, his short sword out, and as he swipes it across the kneeling man's throat, having forced his head back so that his neck is exposed, I appreciate just how well Herebrod knows me. It should be my brother who understands my intentions before even I do, but instead, it's Herebrod, my warrior and my friend.

"Traitor," Herebrod roars as he pushes the bleeding corpse forward. "Traitor," he cries again, making himself heard over the angry voices within the encampment, bringing his seax high and allowing another's blood to flood down his chest.

"Look," Herebrod says once more, holding the gaze of Cynddylan, who looks shocked by this turn of events. Herebrod reaches into the man's byrnie, and he pulls out a great wooden cross with the Christian God lying against it. Cynddylan's eyes narrow. It's not enough evidence for him. After all, he believes in the same God, albeit in an older form. Cynddylan opens his mouth to argue, but once more, Herebrod understands that more is needed. He reaches further into the dead man's weapons belt and pulls loose a sack heavy with something.

Herebrod grins as he hefts the weight and spills his treasure to the ground. Gold and silver tumble to the ground, a few stray red flashing rubies and even a piece of rare amber.

"His pay off, from Oswald," Herebrod shouts triumphantly. Herebrod killed the man. Some of this treasure, I imagine, will belong to him, but there's enough of it to make even Cynddylan want to be able to claim some for himself.

The clamour of the men subsides. Herebrod finally allows Cynddylan to speak. He does so but only when he's standing beside Eowa and myself, facing his warriors and my own.

"It's agreed. This man here," and Cynddylan kicks the body of Glaeðwine that's finally stilled in death, "was the traitor. He allied with Oswald to kill us all."

Convinced or not, the warriors, just as weary as I am, cheer to see the problems of the failed battle resolved. They turn away to their tasks leaving Eowa, Cynddylan and I to speak. Herebrod is close but doesn't step any closer. He knows he doesn't have a part in this conversation.

Cynddylan is pensive for a long moment before meeting my eyes.

"You've woven a pretty tale, but that's all it is. My men and I will ride from here tomorrow morning. Our alliance is dead. Your brother is deceitful, but I'll tell the men that we've been threatened from the west and that we need to go home to protect our kingdom. Penda, you'll always be welcome at my court, but Eowa, you will not."

Cynddylan doesn't even give me time to try and sway his resolve. I watch him go, feeling helpless. He's assured my honour, and that of my brother's won't be imperilled, but he's refused to help me further. I need him to kill Oswald when we meet in battle again.

"Shit," I say and walk away towards my tent.

I need to pee and sleep and eat, in any order.

Eowa stays behind me. I don't know how he feels, but I'm sure that Herebrod is about to tell him just what he thinks of him.

I leave them to it.

I'm too exhausted to think.

⌘ CHAPTER 27 ⌘

King Eowa of Mercia AD641

Wall in the kingdom of Mercia

A rough hand on my arm wakes me when it's still dark outside. I reach for my weapons without even considering that it might be an ally.

The last day has taught me that nothing is as it seems, especially where I'm concerned. My brother accepted me, saved me, allowed Herebrod to kill the man who knew the truth, but then allowed Herebrod to exhibit his full wrath against me.

I've fought a battle, ridden faster than the wind, been beaten physically and had to beg for my life. I've told lies, heard lies and had lies told about me. I've had to grapple with the knowledge that my family might be in danger or might be safe if my warriors have reached them in time.

The uncertainty has exhausted me, but it seems I'm to get no rest.

"It's Penda," the words burst from his mouth in a loud exhalation, and I sit upright abruptly. I forget all about my weapons.

"Oswald will attack at dawn. We need to mount an attack or leave."

He's not whispering, but neither is he speaking overly loudly. I can hear other men talking, weapons rattling, and men busy about their business.

In the dull glow from a fire outside the tent we've shared for the night, I eye him quizzically.

"Cynddylan is leaving, as he said he would. He knows Oswald will attack with the dawn."

"Clydog?" I say, and he nods.

"He stays, but he doesn't want to. He thinks we should find a better site."

"Any news of my family?" I ask. Penda shakes his head regrettably. I hope my warriors have found them and escorted them to safety.

"Clydog is right. We should sneak away, leave Oswald with nothing but the smoking ruins of our fires. It'll frustrate him and give us time to recover."

I think Penda had already decided the same, but I respect him for seeking my opinion as well.

"Come on then. Rouse your men. We need to go. Not quietly but quickly. Leave anything you don't need behind."

He hardly needs to tell me that. I came with only the clothes on my back and the weapons I was reaching for when he woke me.

Penda has more to lose if he leaves his possessions behind, but even he'll have little of actual value. He doesn't carry his wealth with him. He's a warrior on this expedition, not a king.

The noise of the camp begins to fall into a pattern I understand. All too soon, I'm back on my stolen horse, Penda on Gunghir, and before the grey streak of dawn is even lighting the sky to the east, we're riding away from Wall. We head back towards Penda's kingdom, following the great road laid out by the Romans who also built the settlement in which I've been sheltering. We don't follow Cynddylan, but it's inevitable that the stragglers of his party soon mingle with our advance. Their conversation becomes ever louder the further they travel down the road, away from Oswald and the failure of Barrow Hill.

Not that we ride without care for another attack from Oswald. Penda covers the rear, and my warriors, who survived the initial battle, are shaping up around me. There are no angry words directed my way, but I think they fear it could happen. So they shelter me in the only way they know, by riding in a close formation, Clydog's men in front of us, and Penda's to the rear.

Some of my men have managed to borrow the horses of dead warriors, but just as many are running to keep up with the faster-moving horses. Those who have injuries are trading places, taking turns letting the horse do the walking for them. I'd offer my horse, but I know that no one would take it, more concerned with my safety than they should be.

As daylight finally floods the land behind us, I turn and look back at the way I've come. I feel as though I'm going the wrong way, as though others have taken my choices, but I also know that I'll be able to think more clearly in the future. This whole experience has allowed me to finally become a man who thinks, a man capable of leading, not just a scarred man hiding in the shadow of his younger brother.

I feel grief for who I let myself become and hope for who I can become.

At midday, a cry from the rear of our weary procession has me stopping my horse and turning in fear. Has Oswald followed us? Or has my family caught us up?

I turn and thread my way back toward Penda. He and Herebrod are sitting attentively on their horses, warriors surrounding them, ready to take whatever necessary action to keep our force safe from attack.

He sees my approach but keeps silent, and I can't still the hope that it's my son and my wife, my daughter as well, who ride toward us, surrounded by my warriors. Penda knows of my hopes and doesn't force me onward, even though I would be safer back amongst my warriors, than waiting with him at the rear of the force.

Not that Penda waits idly. No, he and his warriors form a defensive line with their horses, ready to stop whatever might be upon us.

Yet the small force to our rear stops, almost out of sight. My family wouldn't linger but would race toward us. My hope dies there and then.

"Oswald," Penda says. His men grunt that they agree, and I turn back to push my horseback to my original position.

I don't know where my family are, but I offer a small prayer to Woden, an offer of sacrifice and apology, that if they live, they'll be safe from Oswald and his anger.

We ride or walk all day, heading ever westward. Only as the long day draws to a close does Clydog call a cease to our journey and organize a semi-permanent camp. It's then that I truly appreciate the strength that Cynddylan had added to our force.

Penda has many men, as does Clydog, but with half of my men dead or prisoners and Cynddylan wending his way home, the careful alliance that Penda constructed to defeat Oswald is broken and fragmented.

I curse softly. This is my doing. I made my decisions too late, and it'll be up to me to bring Cynddylan back to the alliance if I can. I've little choice but to attempt a reconciliation with him. Either that or there's the genuine possibility that Oswald will still be my overlord, and I've already betrayed him once. Oswald won't allow me to keep my kingdom, not if he's the power on this island.

Although I want nothing more than to sleep, I make my way to the smoky fire where my brother speaks with Clydog. The men watch me with curious eyes but no malice. I'm surprised. I'd have expected them to harbour some anger toward me. Penda's following words again show me how well my brother knows me.

"He doesn't like you anyway," Penda confirms, as though we're in the middle of a conversation, not the start of one. "He never has. You share borders. It makes alliances complicated."

I fold my legs beneath me, resting on an empty campstool. It seems they were expecting me, for all that I think I've come of my volition.

"Is there no chance of rebuilding the alliance? You gained his agreement last time."

"I know, but it was difficult to do. Cynddylan made certain demands that I wasn't sure I'd be able to honour. I made them all the same."

Clydog listens intently, but this all seems to be known to him.

"Some of my kingdom?" I ask lightly, wondering how much of my kingdom my brother gave away without even asking me.

Once more, I see I'm caught between men who want what's mine; my brother and Oswald. I can only hope that because Penda also has a claim to my kingdom, he bartered away less than Oswald would.

"No, not your kingdom. Your future."

Ah, it seems he pledged one of my children in a marriage. Of that, I approve.

"What, he'd mix his blood with ours?"

This does surprise me for a man who Penda states hates me.

"Yes, because it gives him the distant possibility that in the future, his grandchildren will rule our lands again, as they did in the past."

I don't miss that Penda uses the word 'our' lands, but I choose to ignore it. He's decided to ignore my treachery. His assertion to the kingdom of Mercia is to be expected. Still, I hope I've not traded away one future for another that I'll find equally untenable.

"He'll not honour that agreement now, though?" I query. In choosing our allies, it was my responsibility to win over Oswald and Penda's to gain those he could from amongst the ancient British kingdoms. I've never really spoken with Cynddylan, which is why his hatred of me is such an irrational and unlooked-for issue. We've met when ceremony dictated it, but we've never spoken, not as I do now with Clydog and Penda, around an open campfire while we talk of the future.

"I'll win him back," I say, and both men nod as though this is precisely what they expected.

"Allies are valuable," Penda mutters. "We either buy their support or, and this is the rarest form, we share their wishes and desires. Cynddylan wants Oswald dead. Use that when you speak with him. Use that and offer him a marriage alliance and something else, something he won't be able to refuse."

Clydog watches me pensively as I absorb those words. I'm not sure what I have to offer that he won't be able to say no to, but I'm a clever man when my head is cleared from inconsequential worries. I must win back my brother's belief in me, a belief I didn't even know he had until we met on the battlefield at Barrow's Hill.

✢CHAPTER 28✢

Oswald, King of Northumbria
AD641 August

The unrelenting heat is driving the men to distraction, and so too myself. I'd far rather that Penda had been chasing me than the other way round. Instead, I find that we're forced to journey ever further inland, even further away from any sea breeze.

I curse Eowa for his betrayal. If he'd remained at my side, then the battle would have been won more than a month ago. I'd be home once more, where the cooling breeze of the sea would take the sting from the heat.

The men are weary and exhausted. This wasn't supposed to be a long, drawn-out campaign but rather a quick one that left Penda dead. I've had to delay to wait for the warriors that King Onna has promised me. Although I've been following Penda on his westward march, it's been done so slowly as to be almost derisory. Some days I've allowed the men to rest, to take advantage of the chill rivers and the respite they offer from the constant heat. It's as welcome to me as to them.

Oswiu has sent word that he'll be arriving soon as well, and so I know that I don't have to endure much more discomfort so far from home, but I'm impatient now. I should be at home, overseeing the latest projects that Bishop Aidan has started on Lindisfarne and ensuring the crops grow well and the animals fatten as they should. This campaign has lasted too long.

The summer is for campaigning, ensuring my warriors' skills are used, but it should have been a quick raid, nothing more. This has gone on for so long that our food supplies have long since run out, and we're eating the fruits of Eowa's Mercian farmers. They don't like it, not at all. Every day, a skirmish leaves men dead, both Mercian and Northumbrian alike. The whittling away of my force is affecting the morale of my force, as is the need to hunt for food.

We're warriors, not farmers. We should be feasting on the spoils of war, not scavenging amongst fruit bushes in the hedgerows.

I have many scouts scouring the countryside, and they all tell me news that thrills me. Penda's alliance has crumbled away. His brother's indecisiveness has cost them both dearly. Even now, Cynddylan sits and sulks in his stronghold while Clydog grows weary, and some of his warriors rush for home.

They have no one else's support upon which they can call. I'm tempted just to attack them now when they're weak and disorientated. When they're spread across the flat land to the west that stretches as far as the eyes can see before it begins to rise into the hilly region that serves as a natural boundary between the lands of Mercia and those of the British kingdoms. All apart from Cynddylan. Of them all, only his kingdom has any great extent this side of the mountains.

I think I could ally with him if only he hadn't been so close to Cadwallon. We have more traits in common than Penda does with him, our religion, for one, but I hear that he hates me for murdering Cadwallon. Perhaps if I managed to speak with him, I'd be able to convince him that I accomplished a great thing, made his kingdom more secure.

But no. Cynddylan sits and sulks, and between him and I, Penda and his warriors are waiting for me.

I only wish King Onna would hurry up and arrive.

If I had something to trade with Eowa, I could end this conflict without further bloodshed, that he'd perhaps consent to kill his brother in exchange for the safe return of his family. But his wife and children have gone into hiding. I don't know how they knew of the reverse in Eowa's fortune, but whoever protected them knew of it so that by the time my warriors reached Tamworth, a ride of less than half a day from Barrow Hill, they were gone from his stronghold. They haven't been seen since.

They could be dead, but I doubt it.

I think Penda knows where they are. I imagine he holds them against any further betrayal on Eowa's behalf, but it's only a hypothesis. For all I know, they might have rushed to the kingdom of Kent for protection, or even to Cenwahl of the South Saxons, or even to Penda's wife. She's a woman to be feared, a true princess of the Britons.

My scouts believe that the best position for the coming battle will be on the flatlands, and I agree with them. There's no landmark that'll offer us any significant advantage, but neither is there one for Penda to use. And as my scouts report, it's not for lack of looking. Every day Penda's warriors ride out on what appear to be foraging parties but are really attempts to find a better place to defend.

For every day they stay still, they're able to build defences. A great ditch already stands before their encampment, demarcated by a set of vicious-looking wooden spikes.

Penda is readying himself to defend the site. He must know that we'll meet on the plain and is trying to make his defences because the countryside lacks any. My scouts watch them from a distance, so nothing is a secret. It's a counter-productive move, a waste of his warriors' strength.

When the battle comes, I'll not allow it to reach his defences but will taunt the men and women until they abandon the ditch and the wooden stakes and fight in the open. And then we'll cut them down, like wheat on the edge of a scythe. And then Mercia will be mine to rule as well. Only then will I' be able to go home and get away from this damn heat. I think that I'm being tested, just as God's other martyrs have always been, but I know that I'm capable of achieving success. If this is the most significant test I must face, I welcome it.

I've considered my abandonment on Barrow Hill by Eowa. That was the beginning of the test set by my Lord God to ensure I'm worthy of being the instigator of the conversion of the Saxon people. It's a position that's been half-filled by other men, most notably King Edwin before me, but they didn't have Bishop Aidan or Bishop Birinus to assist them. So they failed. I won't. But I'll be tested before I obtain success.

Penda's men murdered my priests, and I've no one else to consult until King Onna arrives with his priests. All the same, I believe my interpretation to be the correct one. The true Lord was always taxed throughout his life, but he's remembered for surviving those difficulties and overcoming all who tried to stop him.

That's how I wish to be remembered as well.

When I defeat Penda, I'll gain more than just the reputation as his killer. Men and women will laud me. I'll also achieve acclaim for being a holy warrior against a pagan monster. Bishop Aidan will praise our God for my endeavours, and no doubt Bishop Birinus will demand a new church be built in the West Saxon lands, perhaps dedicated in my name.

Yet if I fail, I'll also gain notoriety as the Christian king killed by a pagan monster. Then, I'm sure to be the winner of the battle, no matter whether I live or die. Although obviously, I'd prefer to be the one who's alive at the end of it all.

A shout from one of my scouts, and I turn my horse to await his message. I detect joy in his voice and hope that it means one of my allies has been sighted. All this thinking about battle has wearied me. I wish to fight it, not consider it.

I'll have the numbers. I'll have my God ensuring that I win, and I'll have no one to compromise my victory this time, for Eowa is gone. Let him do what he wants, provided it's Penda's battle he ruins.

"We've found a trail, My Lord King," the messenger tells me as he breathes deeply. He's not been racing through the summer heat, but it sounds as though he has. He's wearing his byrnie, and it must be uncomfortable. Sweat beads his broad face and runs down his exposed arms. "We think it'll lead us to Eowa's family."

It's not quite the news I was hoping for, but I'll happily take it. I thank the man, ensuring all hear, and then I gift him with a token of my thanks, a small gold ring taken from my finger and incised with the Christian cross. It's a small gift, but it means much to the man as he turns and races away again.

If the trail is good, I might have something with which to force Eowa back to my alliance, not that I much want him, but I want Penda to have him even less. I could punish Eowa then for his treason.

But if the trail leads to nothing, I'll have simply rewarded a man for using his initiative. That, too, is worthwhile doing. Every man needs something to work toward, be it a place in Heaven or a handful of gold. At the moment, I work for a place in Heaven and Penda's head.

Soon, when my allies arrive, I'll move against him as he steadily retreats toward the British kingdoms. I doubt he's really running for his life. But when I beat him in the battle, I'll ensure that everyone knows that was what he was doing; that he was fearful for his life and knew that I'd be victorious when I had the opportunity and no one to undermine my attack.

It's good to have men of God at my command, such as Bishop Aidan. They'll record the history of my reign as I believe it should be recorded, ensuring that God is praised in one sentence, and myself in the next. I'll ensure that Aidan has a full accounting of the final battle and the lead up to it and that he shares it with his monks and other allies. And it will all have been accomplished in my God's name.

The thought of that renown is what drives me now, not my hatred for Penda. Or so I tell myself. It's wrong to hate him, as I do, and so I convince myself it's a concern for the souls of many that drives me, not my antipathy toward one man. I find it easier to reconcile such explanations with my religious convictions.

God teaches that it's wrong to hate, but Penda, the man who gave my brother's murderer the power to do so, is worthy of my hatred. So I must dress it up in some other form and give it a meaning that my apologists will accept without much thought.

It's easier to lie to myself as well as to them.

Another cry from in front of me, and another grinning man reaches me.

"My Lord King," he hails me. He's one of Eowa's warriors, a man who's long been loyal to me and who's infiltrated Penda's encampment to bring me the most up to date intelligence. I nod to show he can go ahead.

He looks like a typical Mercian, complete with his iron circle of Woden around his neck, yet he's long been a convert to Christianity. That's why I trusted him with such an essential task as watching Eowa. When Eowa deserted the alliance, Eafa decided to go with him, to learn all he could.

Now it seems he's come back, and for good this time as he carries all of his equipment with him, draped over the back of his horse and in saddlebags.

"The alliance is broken. Penda has lost Cynddylan's support, and even now, Clydog is gathering his men, ready to leave."

The news thrills me and also sparks my frustration. Where are my allies? This is just what I've been waiting for, but I know Penda's guile. Within a day or two, he'll have managed to coerce his allies back to their original agreement. I need to attack now before Penda's luck reverses once more.

Eafa senses my annoyance, and he shares it. He's turned his horse and looks back the way he just came.

"If we attack tomorrow morning, we should decimate his force," Eafa speaks in a rush. He's a small man, almost wiry, but he makes up for his lack of physical presence by never seeming to sit still and being everywhere at once.

"Find Ealdorman Alduini," I command, and Eafa rushes away, keen to put his intelligence into action.

It's early in the day. I sit on my horse, looking along the roadway that heads westwards. Eafa must have escaped under cover of nightfall. I assume he won't be missed, but even so, I command my warriors near the front of our encampment to double their watchfulness.

I feel as though, after Eowa's betrayal, I see only deceit and double-crossing before me. Yet for all that I linger, watching the roadway, no sound of a pursuit reaches my ears. When Alduini walks toward me, trailed by Eafa and more of my warriors as well, I know I can take the time to plan the attack for the morning, with or without my allies.

I hope that my allies arrive in time and also that Eowa's wife and children are found and brought before me, but all the time, I'm mindful that to take full advantage of Penda's disintegrating alliance, I need to preempt him, launch an attack.

Tomorrow.

Tomorrow I'll finally better him.

⌘ CHAPTER 29 ⌘

Penda of the Hwicce AD641 August

"I told you," I mutter as I find my brother carefully tending to his weapons on a campstool. It's a warm day, and all around me, the men have shrugged off their protective wear and instead, muscles and warmed brown skin flashes in the pleasant heat.

"What?" Eowa retorts, but he knows about what I'm talking.

"Did you not even suspect?" I ask, probing him to see how deep this wound of betrayal will run.

"I knew one of them would do it," Eowa confirms, focusing on his weapon, stance entirely calm. I believe he's speaking the truth. He did expect one of his men to betray him.

"You know you have spies amongst your household?" Eowa tries to repay my attempt to aggravate, but it's my turn to shrug off his words.

"The morning, then. You think he'll come then?"

"I know he will. He always attacks in the morning. It's almost as though he thinks his God holds more power at the birth of each new day." Eowa's tone is filled with disgust.

I find my brother's words strange to hear, so I ignore them. He knows Oswald better than I do. All I want to know is what tactics he'll use.

"He'll think there are few of us, so he'll attack the encampment, or will he try and draw us out?"

"Out, he'll want you on the flat land, not hiding behind any stakes and ditches."

"But he has nothing we want to draw us out?" I counter, trying to decide what he'll do based on what I'd do.

"He has my men, those who didn't come with me. He might have my wife or my children. If he tries to kill any of those before the battle commences, my warriors won't be able to stop themselves from confronting him."

I smirk now. I see what Eowa means. But what he doesn't know, because I haven't told him, and neither do I intend to just yet, is that his wife and children are safe with my wife. His two children, both too young to truly appreciate what's happening, are unharmed, but his wife only just managed to escape. She lies dangerously ill, or so my brother, Coenwahl, tells me. He brought me the news himself, but I've sent him back to guard my kingdom without Eowa even knowing he was here.

When the battle is won, and Eowa can ensure his reputation, I'll tell him of his children and wife. But until then, I need him to focus on the coming battle and tell me all he can. It's best that way.

"He'll expect you to lose your allies, to be retreating to the British kingdoms in the west. He'll assign his good fortune to his God."

"He's a bloody idiot," I growl. Eowa nods, but he's looking away from me, into the distance as though he can see Oswald from here. I take the time to look at him. The time we've spent outdoors during one of the hottest summers I've ever known has turned his skin a deep bronze shade, his hair almost so fair it's painful to look upon him. When he returns to his family and his kingdom, Eowa will genuinely look like one of our Gods made flesh.

"We should abandon the defences, fight as he wants, send word to Cynddylan that he needs to get behind Oswald and attack from the east."

My brother's words are said with consideration. I listen to

them carefully. He learnt the ways of war from our father, but I think he perhaps listened more carefully than I ever did."

"And Clydog?"

"He should come from the south. Oswald won't be expecting any of this."

"What if he brings King Onna and his brother, Oswiu?"

"It won't matter. They could bring two thousand men, and we'd still have the advantage."

It's not often that I've heard such confidence in Eowa's voice. He should have arranged this battle himself rather than gift me that part of the alliance. I think we'd have reached this position much sooner if he'd had responsibility for the coalition against Oswald instead of keeping Oswald as an ally. But then, Oswald and I could never have been allies. Our hatred for each other runs too deeply."

"As you say. I'll send messengers to Clydog and Cynddylan."

"Cynddylan will come, won't he?" Eowa suddenly asks, and I laugh.

"Of course, he will. You've made your agreement. He was angry. Now he's not. The rest is all a ruse."

"You trust too easily," Eowa mutters, but I laugh at that as well.

"I don't trust my allies," I say mildly, "I look for deceit everywhere and just hope it doesn't happen. I'm prepared to be proved wrong, but I hope I always have a clear understanding of what motivates the people I meet."

"Even me?" Eowa queries, but I don't answer. Certain words should never be spoken between brothers, and these are some of them.

"We should move the camp?" Eowa muses, and I look at him with new admiration. I'd not have considered that idea, but it has merit if he's now thinking what I'm thinking.

"What, back?"

"Yes, back," he says, looking alert as he stands and surveys the area, looking for an advantage I've not seen. First, Eowa wanted to abandon the camp. Now he wishes to use it to benefit us.

He looks behind him, where the field of canvass stretches outwards. It's neat and tidy, and it's been constructed to prevent our enemy from determining our actual strength. Battle is all about deceit, never more so than about the size of your force. Oswald might know that Cynddylan has left, but he won't know that we have other reinforcements hidden in plain sight inside the circular arrangements of temporary structures.

"See, where there's that slight dip. If we move behind it, the ditches will claim the lives of some of his men when they race to engage us. They won't realise that the trenches are there because the land's natural shape obscures them.

I look where he's pointing, buoyed by his enthusiasm and idea. I'd not wanted to sit and wait for Oswald to attack, but this is where Cynddylan has agreed to reinforce us, and so I can't move, not without risking losing his support or angering him by making decisions without first discussing them with him.

Eowa's correct in what he says. I thought we'd chosen the flattest piece of land to make our encampment on, keen not to have to fight another battle either up a hill or down one. But, in choosing this particular place and digging our ditches to the front of the tents, we've partially hidden ourselves down a small embankment. It means that, just as Eowa says, we could move back, and Oswald would be none the wiser.

If we do so, it means his men would fall into our ditches, thinking that they've not yet come close enough to encounter them.

I like the idea. It's cunning but also very simple and will show Oswald that the battle isn't going to be fought on his terms.

"We should do it under cover of darkness, ensure his scouts don't see us."

"We should, yes, but we're not going to do that. The nights are long at this end of the summer. We'd have to wait too long, and then the men would be too tired when the attack finally came with the sunrise. We'll send out our scouting party and have them apprehend anyone they can, and if not, then they'll have to kill them. We can't let Oswald discover this before it's done."

My brother stands and repeatedly turns from the front to the rear of our fortifications. He's seeing the battle play out before his eyes, and as he does so, they glisten with satisfaction or start a little with surprise when something unexpected occurs to him that might not be to our advantage.

I've stood and done this many times in the past. These battles between the kingdoms that seem to spring from nowhere are entirely the opposite. We Saxons let our resentments build before we lash out at our enemies, and only if the possibility of success presents itself do we carry out any attack. And my resentment has been building for years, not quite since Cadwallon's death, but since not long afterwards.

Oswald didn't fight at Hæðfeld. He did little but pretend to be an ally of Edwin's and then abandon him in the final attack. His brother, Lord Eanfrith, deserved his victory for all his efforts. I curse once more that Cadwallon killed him without considering the probable consequences.

Cadwallon was someone I admired greatly, but he was blinded by his anger and rage at Edwin. His brotherly love soured slowly. That's the worst way for it to go. If Cadwallon had simply lashed out at Edwin, then he might have gained some instant gratification. As it was, he allowed hatred to fester, to make him single-minded and determined to accomplish only one thing, Edwin's death, at his own hands.

I have many enemies, and the majority of them hate me. My brother isn't one of those men. And neither is my other brother, Coenwahl, guarding my wife and now Eowa's as well. He assures their safety whilst Eowa and I battle against Oswald. I'm grateful for Coenwahl support. I hope my sons have the same luck with each other.

But Eowa and I have a far more complicated and not easily defined relationship. I know he resents me and is jealous of my reputation and skills. Yet he's not alone in that. I wish I could enjoy peace and stillness as he does. I wish I could allow events to unfold around me without directing them myself.

Eowa will wait and react. I can only ever instigate. The

thought of being idle irritates my skin, leaving a red mark in its wake for all to see.

"Fine, I'll send Herebrod again. I think he likes killing Oswald's men. It makes him feel as though he gains a tiny seed of revenge each time."

"It's true then?" Eowa asks as I look at him blankly.

"Oswald allowed Cadwallon to kill Lord Eanfrith?"

"He didn't allow it, no. But neither did he stop it, even though he knew it was likely to happen. He was close enough that he could both have warned his brother or gone with him and interceded on his behalf with Cadwallon. The two weren't close."

"Oswald gained much from Lord Eanfrith's death."

"He did. He occupied a kingdom that wasn't his to hold. At the same time, it enabled him to say Cadwallon was the aggressor and that he had to kill him to gain revenge for his brother's killing."

"I thought as much," Eowa muses as our camp moves around us. The men, stationary for the best part of a week now, are keen to do anything, especially if it's to cause a blow for Oswald when he attacks. They're eager to face him in battle once more. The battle of Barrow Hill isn't one about which the skalds will sing. The men know that they can do better and reclaim the warcraft items stolen from their friends and warrior brothers who died in the battle.

I'm allowing them to build their hatred and resentment. In the past, I always thought that men with a personal grudge against their enemy made poor warriors. Now I disagree. I've seen my warriors speak of their fallen comrades. They know they'll have been accorded no respect; their bodies will have been stripped; their weapons and byrnies taken from them, perhaps even their boots, and then their bodies will have been left in the open, to fester and stagnate, for crows and wolves to chew.

Oswald won't have adhered to the ways of the Old Gods. I doubt he'll even have considered interring them in the already constructed barrow that gives Barrow Hill its name. Once this battle is fought and Oswald is dead, we'll return to that first battlefield and set all to right.

Until then, my men allow their anger and rage to build; their hatred for Oswald is almost as manifest as mine and for similar but different reasons. Oswald killed their friends and allies while he stole my rightful place as leader of the Saxon kingdoms. In doing so, he murdered Cadwallon and many more of my allies.

Such things can't be allowed to happen without retribution. I know that Oswald knows all about retribution, only in the guise of his new God.

My retribution is colder and more thorough; a slice of a seax or a sword through the heart will have the same effect. Iron and blood speak more to me than words and pandering to the needs of men too scared to face their own death.

I don't long for my death, but neither do I fear it.

Time will come full circle. There's no other truth to be had. Life and death. Death and life. The same but different, contrasting and yet always the same for in our lives we think continually of our deaths, fearing what will come afterwards, while at the same time desperate to know as well.

I know that Oswald will find out the truth of his God's heaven long before I will.

"In the morning then?" I repeat. It's a question and also a statement.

"In the morning," Eowa echoes, his voice solid and hard. He's more ready for this battle than he's ever before in his life.

"Tomorrow we'll win, and then, well, then we'll decide what we'll do next."

I grip him firmly in my arms, allowing the men to see how close we stand, that we now act as one with the same purpose in mind.

The men cheer.

The thought of battle should always cheer a man.

✢CHAPTER 30✢

King Oswald of Northumbria
AD641 August✢

Long before the thin haze that presages morning has coloured the sky to the east, I'm awake and readying my men.

For much of yesterday, when I knew that battle would come today, I offered my prayers and petitions to my God, hoping for success but knowing that only his goodwill could bring it to fruition. At some point, I realised that I wasn't alone in my prayers and that many of my warriors had joined me on the grassy rise where I'd chosen to offer my obsequies. It was a wondrous spectacle, the sight of so many men all united in one purpose. It almost distracted me from my fervent entreaties to my Lord God.

My warriors are keen to strike at the heart of the threat of the Old Gods that Penda represents. They're assured of their victory because our Lord is a victorious deity whose sole aim is to spread his enlightenment to all and sundry. It fills me with righteousness.

Now though, as I prepare myself for the battle, aware that as of yet neither my brother, Oswiu nor King Onna of the East Angles, have arrived to fortify me, I feel a slight quiver of alarm.

Penda is a warrior. I know that. If he weren't, he wouldn't have managed to so neatly evade me at Barrow's Hill even when

I turned men he thought loyal against him.

That failure still smarts, but I'm trying to be forgiving for now. If I should meet Eowa again, I'll demand his total conversion. I'll have my priests speak with him at length and show him the might of my God. I'm sure that Aidan, my holy bishop of Lindisfarne, so used to speaking with myself and the kings and great men of the kingdom of Dal Riata, won't fail to encourage him to the correct religion.

But that's only if I should meet him again. I know I pray more for his death than his survival in my heart. I'd rather never re-encounter Eowa, and then I'll never need to learn to practice the forgiveness that my Lord God demands, with his understanding that men are sinful creatures.

My scouts tell me that Penda looks weak. He's been abandoned by his allies, left with only half of Eowa's force. More, he seems unable to retreat any further into the British kingdoms, and so he's stuck on the open lands between here and the hills to the far west. He has nowhere else to go because Cynddylan is preventing his retreat.

Or so it seems, yet I'm wary. Eowa and Penda have shown me that they have no compunction in offering misinformation.

I lick my lips, dry and in need of water, that I don't allow myself, not yet. My righteousness from the day before remains firmly in place. Still, I worry it all looks too simple and that in my religious fervour, I forget hard-won lessons from my youth, when I fought for my Dal Riatan host, the men who kept me safe during my exile.

I wish my brother were here. He'd offer his thoughts freely.

Yet, if the scout is correct and Penda plans on attacking today, I need to meet his attack. I can't miss the opportunity.

I offer yet more prayers for my Lord God, hoping for guidance. As the soft rays of the early morning sun finally turn the sky from grey to a hint of purple and pink, I know that I must move or risk losing the advantage.

Outside my tent, my warriors are ready to attack. They look resplendent in the early morning chill, a true force to fight in both my name and for our religion. I feel the sureness of yesterday's prayers infecting me again. I know that I'm ready for the challenge of leading the men to victory.

Eohart, a man raised with me in exile, is ready with my horse, and so are the other men who have horses. We'll ride so far, and then the horses will be rounded up. We'll fight on foot without those warriors who can attack from horseback, in a pitched battle, on flat ground. I fear that the horses will be more of a hindrance than a help.

No, we'll ride to battle, a conquering force, with my holy cross before me, the one I raised before my battle with Cadwallon. It will fly before my banner of the cross and my white sword, a testament to my faith and military reputation both. Penda will be unaware of our approach until we near him. He expects to attack us, not vice versa.

I turn to my warriors. Now is the time for a powerful speech to commemorate our expedition and assured victory. I mount my white horse in the early morning calm. I feel the eyes of a thousand men on me. They're deferential but fired up as well. They know what I expect of them.

I meet the eyes of a few of them, those close enough for me to make out who they are beneath their helms and their war equipment. Those men stand a little taller, a little prouder, at being singled out by their king, and my confidence rises even more.

Brictfrith, a colossal warrior, almost dwarfing his horse beneath his massive legs, slaps his arm across his mighty chest when my eyes meet his. He wears an elaborate helm decorated with the art of the northern lands, with rich swirls and figurines that catch the sun and reflect in the growing light. Others who see his action repeat it.

I glance to Ælfmon, who hails from the northern lands. He told me of his longing to support my family even when I was in exile. He laboured to undermine King Edwin's power. He wears a small helm, much beaten and battered. He's fought in too many battles, and yet he still hungers for more. I don't think he'll stop until he knows that all claimants to my kingdom have been quashed. He's keen to fight in my name, die in my name, anything provided it secures my family's claim on the kingdom. I offer him a nod of my head, my helm, a legacy from Eochaid Buide of the kingdom of Dal Riata, stays firm because it fits so snuggly.

Further back, a youth, no more than half my age, watches me intently. He should be terrified of his first battle, but he smirks joyfully, his ill-fitted helm covering his eyes. He'd do better to discard it, but his uncle gave it to him, retrieved from his father's corpse when he died at Hæðfeld. His father might have been fighting for my despised uncle, but he earned an excellent death all the same.

So many men and I know all their stories and respect them all the more for their desire to support me. I'm their king, and they should fear me, but they don't. They wish to serve me. They want nothing more than to earn acclaim fighting as my warriors. If they die here, and I hope that few of them will, they'll do so knowing that their families will be proud of them. As am I.

They'll earn a proud Christian burial, and then they'll go to heaven.

I think all of this and still words fail me. I want the men to be inspired, but how can I better the inspiration they already feel, fuelled by our prayers the day before?

Instead, I lovingly pull my white blade from its sheath on my back, mindful of the effect the sunlight has on it, reflecting the bright light and allowing it to splinter off in strange directions. At the sight of it, the entire host, even those who used to be Eowa's men, join their voices in a massive roar of approval.

"To victory!" I simply shout, bellowing it along with my men. The roar intensifies, and I think that it might have woken my Lord God from his slumbers.

I turn my horse without even looking back toward the distant safety of Northumbria.

No, this will be a great victory, and tonight my men and I can think of home. For now, a battle must be fought and victory gained.

Bebba, my new horse, steps smartly before her warriors, as though she knows the importance of what we're about to accomplish. She's a worthy mount for Northumbria's holiest king.

⌘ CHAPTER 31 ⌘

King Eowa of Mercia AD641 August

Maserfeld

I've barely slept, but I feel more alert than if I'd rested for a week.

My ruse has worked. Even in the gloom of the morning, I've ridden in front of our new encampment and realised that the initial defensive ditches are no longer visible.

Men will die in those ditches. It'll be a nasty death, as those above them, too intent on their attack to realise that they're killing their allies, crush them.

Perhaps as many as a hundred men will die there, weighed down by their equipment, for the warriors at the front of the attacking line will be the ones who've trained for this since old enough to hold seax and spear. They'll have the best equipment and the most silver arm rings to recognise their services to their king or kings.

I hope we are lucky today in the wake of Penda's sacrifice of Oswald's scouts yesterday. All five of them were killed without weapons in their hands so that their blood-soaked the battlefield in preparation for today's sacrifice. They were unwilling participants in our ancient ceremony enacted to ensure men would perish in that ditch. Then, there'll only be the less experienced and the least well-armed warriors to pick off, individually or as part of a hastily formed shield wall.

I always thought I had no taste for such bloodshed, but it seems I was wrong. I hunger for it now. My men are keen to battle. I'm more than willing. I crave the feel of my weapons beneath my hands, knowing that my strength is intensified by the presence of iron and wood at the end of those hands. My sword was my father's, bequeathed to me on his death for all that a warrior and almost king as mighty as he should have taken it with him to Valhalla.

My father begged me to take it with his dying breaths. He said its song wasn't yet sung and that more men needed to slake its thirst for blood.

I slide it into its sheath down my back, caressing the metalwork that graces its handle. It's a frivolous addition for a weapon of death, but my prideful father wasn't to be dissuaded. He told me that Woden's own blacksmith had forged the weapon. Even as a child, I knew he lied with such a tale, but now, I can believe almost anything in the semi-haze of dawn.

A fine mist has formed during the night. From it, I think any great beast from the ancient tales could step, come to do our bidding, to ensure our victory, with great gnashing teeth and a fearsome tail. That's what we'll be today, that beast made of men. We'll crash our mighty teeth together and flick our monstrous tail and tackle all who stand in our way.

Neither is the sword the only gift from my father. In his barrow burial, he took with him little more than his byrnie and his small gifts of food for Woden. He was assured that Woden would make good any deficit when he entered Valhalla. He was keen that his sons should carry on in his place, aware that Woden would be observing us, ensuring we were victorious in his name and brought no shame to our ancestry.

No, I also have my father's seax, a small deadly thing, with a blade sharper than ice after the winter freeze. It, too, carries a small adornment but is a weapon of death and blood, not a fine thing to show others. It breaks my skin if I forget and mishandle it, and my blood gushes over its smooth surface.

It's a hungry little bastard.

My shield is old and well used but freshly painted, with Woden's symbol and a splash of the dead scouts' blood. It speaks to me of its wishes to defend me and its desire to hammer our enemy's heads, smash fingers, and crush exposed feet.

I feel like I'm just the puppet by which these items intend to kill men. I'm just the man who'll hold them while they fight their war against my enemy. I feel as though Woden walks beside me, his spirit flaring in me time and time again.

Neither am I alone. My warriors share my resolve and conviction. I can see it in their small and tidy movements as they tie their boots tight and ensure weapons belts contain all they might need to kill the Northumbrians, the bloody Christians who swarm across Mercia as though ants come to feast on rotten fruit.

But Mercia is not rotten, and its warriors are keen to prove their worth and bravery, their adherence to the ways of Woden.

This began as a battle for supremacy, to be the greatest king on the whole of our island, but it'll end as a battle of the old versus the new. Like the British, in the form of Cynddylan and Clydog, have made it clear from their histories against my far distance ancestors, what is new is not always right or more potent than what went before. How else can they account for their tenacious hold on their kingdoms in the wake of the savagery of the Saxons?

They're mighty warriors, and although they might share some of Oswald's views on their God, they don't fight in their Gods name but rather against Oswald's might and his presumptuous ways. His actions cast even their slightly different take on Christian observance together with our worship of the Old God, the rightful God, the God of war and blood. Woden and his fellow inhabitants of Valhalla.

Penda walks toward me. I smirk to myself, for just as I thought, he stands as though he is Woden, the God of war, and so I *will* fight this battle with Woden at my side. He has his spear with him, gifted to him by our father in honour of naming his horse in the same likeness. But he too carries a family sword, a great black beast wrought of twisting iron and angry looking spikes along the haft. It's a wicked looking sword, far more deadly than mine, and in place of jewels and elaborate decoration, its blackness attests to its purely fatal intent.

Penda's shield is smeared with the blood of dead men, almost entirely masking his symbol of Woden's raven, come to feast on the entrails of the deceased. His byrnie is dark with the blood of dead foes. Penda never cleans it, would injure any who tried to, aware that the power of men he's already killed adds to his own.

Penda's helm is a nasty looking piece of metal, as twisted as his deadly sword. Its blackness absorbs the light. He's the vision of the blackness of hell that Oswald's converted followers try so hard to avoid with their good deeds. Penda truly is their worst nightmare, and he revels in it, as do his followers.

Penda's a vision from the tales of the early days when the Gods roamed our lands with their petty jealousies and spite.

Not only that, but Penda is a huge man, built of sinew and muscle. When he walks, it feels as though the ground should quake beneath his feet, as though each step should send ripples spiralling through the rivers and seas. Penda should cause tremors with his every breath, sucking the air from the sky and returning it in a maelstrom of twisted branches and hurled rocks.

He's as mythical as any man I've ever met. Today, I'm glad to be associated with his reputation and renown for the first time.

We're the sons of Pybba, and we'll fight together against this Christian horde who threaten to steal what's ours and who offer to justify it in that self-same Lord's name.

"Brother," Penda calls, his voice resounding so that all around can hear it. He smirks at my smile of greeting, his head on one side, lifting his helm away so he can see me more clearly.

"I amuse you?" he whispers for my ears only, and I shrug.

"I was thinking of the Gods, and then you appeared and made them seem flesh."

I don't think he's expecting my words. For a moment, he's speechless, absorbing the implication in them. His weather-stained face creases and he smacks my back hard, and yet I stay upright.

"We're brothers. We fight with the might of Woden on our side, and so he paints us in his image. That's as it should be."

Penda's voice is raised once more. He wants our warriors to hear our discussion, and I understand why. To fight in the name of Woden is one thing, but to battle with Woden made flesh is quite another. He's not above using the same tricks that the Christian God employs and that Oswald will be offering his warriors with his white cloak, white horse and even whiter blade.

Those close to us raise a fist at his words or growl deeply in agreement. These men are warriors. They know the taste of another man's blood on their tongue, and they know when their own time has come to an end. But not today.

No, today, the sons of Pybba, descendants of Woden, will beat back Oswald and lay claim to the land and people we should always have ruled.

"Come, we should be ready when Oswald arrives." And with those words, our force is effectively divided, some to the east, others to the west, ready to assist Clydog or Cynddylan when they come. The rest of us make ready to defend our encampment, the shield wall already loosely in place, the horses far to the rear, stabled away from the coming blades and axes, but saddled and ready to be called into play when the time comes to attack any who try and retreat.

As if conjured by my thoughts, I hear the outraged cry of Gunghir, his shrill neigh reverberating around the encampment in the chill morning air. I pity the poor man who tries to calm his rage and spite. He's not happy at his enforced removal from Penda.

Penda grins at the noise.

"Bloody beast," he says as though Gunghir is a test for him. But I know he loves that horse, and that's why I let him have him. I could only wish that Sleipnir had lived such a long and full life, but now isn't the time to think of him, long dead and gone. I made my choice back on that fateful day, and I've never regretted it.

It falls to Penda to reach for me again and hold me in his embrace, his body heat almost a comfort in the cool air.

"Be safe," Penda warns me savagely and lets me go as abruptly as he's grabbed me. I'm left off-balance and struggling to reorientate myself to this sudden show of affection from my brother. I watch him walk away, surprised once more by his capacity to forgive and love.

Perhaps, I don't know him after all, for all I think I do.

I'd spend the day considering what's just happened, but Penda is readying his men, calling them into order, his words greeted with high voices raised in excitement and fear. He responds with his gruff words and sarcastic comments. I can see why warriors flock to do his bidding. I almost wish I could rush forward and be commanded by him as well, but I have my part to play in this battle, and I need to be about my duties.

My force, almost half of Penda's alongside those of my men who managed to escape from Barrow Hill, have witnessed the display between Penda and me. For those of Penda's men who thought they'd been given the worst of two options when they were assigned to my shield wall, I see renewed respect on their faces.

I turn to watch my brother once more, doubting the sincerity of his display toward me, although perhaps I shouldn't. Whether he did it to imbibe his men with the desire to fight for me as they would for him, or whether it was just a spontaneous display of affection, it's worked on both counts.

I feel as invincible as he looks. His warriors are now keen to fight under my command, readying themselves with almost no words or instructions, and happy to jostle with my men who all want the honour of fighting beside me.

I watch with pride as the men make themselves ready. They come in all shapes and sizes, those warriors who do nothing but train all day, with axe and shield and sword in hand, somehow dwarfing those for whom this is a pastime they take up only when commanded by their king. There are young men for whom this will be their first battle, come to reinforce Penda from his heartlands, and there are others, long in the tooth and stained by previous battles and kings. They're either the lucky ones or the wily ones, who've managed to fight and never die or incur an injury that makes it impossible for them to continue.

They're the men who can read a battle better than any Christian priest can read from one of their great books. They understand how war craft works and where the ebbs and flows will occur. They're worth their weight in gold, and they fairly drip with the spoils of their previous successes.

The young, untried youths desire to be like the older men. If they fight with the power of Woden, they'll survive this attack and tomorrow, they too will be adorned with the talismans of their kills and with the appreciation of their kings.

From beyond the thin misty drizzle, I hear the sound of men running. I turn, surprised by the noise, but it's merely the scouts, returning as quickly as they can, grins on the parts of their faces that can be seen beneath their helms.

"They're coming," they shout, and now the shield wall is made whole, shields slapping into place, one over another, as they form a moving and living wall of wood and iron. I wish I were watching from the other side to see how well the men bond and cooperate.

Through the haze, the sky turned to pink and purple, while the dampness still hugs the grassy ground, and through squinting eyes, I begin to think I can make out the dark shapes of our enemy, black in the gloom but a solid wall just like ours. It takes long moments for the impression of the men to become more than just that. Abruptly, the sun peeks through the cloud cover overhead, and the entire area is bathed in the soft glow of a warming summer's day.

Oswald's warriors are a magnificent force to behold, with their banners flapping overhead. Oswald's personal banner and his cross from his victory against Cadwallon are held proudly forward. His men come, not with the joy of battle in their movements, but instead with purposefulness, their demeanour quiet, as though waiting for their priests to bless them and offer words of comfort before the battle.

Penda's half of the battlefield greet the sight with derision, his voice booming loudly in place of the silent approach of our enemy. I join my voice to his, raising it high, jeering, hurling obscenities, anything to turn the cold commitment to anger. Angry men are easier to kill.

At the heart of their shield wall, where it stands, ready to attack on the whim of their king, I see the white of King Oswald. The flash of his long blond hair, the glint of his white blade, and the dazzle from his shield, daubed in the same white and missing the dark hue of blood that marks all the shields of our shield wall.

I estimate he has nearly a thousand men, all told, a number that, for now at least, looks to be far more than ours. His shield wall is a thick thing, built of layers and layers of men, stretching not quite as far to the sides of ours, although it might change when the charge comes, just another ploy on Oswald's part to try and lull us into making a mistake.

Battles are about strength, blood and stamina, but more than that, they're about sleight of hand, guile and undermining the enemy before they can demoralise you. They're as much a test of the mind as they are a test of the endurance of a body or a body of men. Should one breakaway, more are likely to follow.

Great men, warriors such as Penda, can inspire men with the courage to endure even when the odds are patently stacked against them.

Oswald, though, already thinks he's won the battle. That means he's at a disadvantage. While Penda and I speak of our victory, and our men cheer to hear our words, we both know that the outcome is never decided until the last sword stroke against the last shield, until the last of the enemy is dead or fled, Oswald doesn't think in the same way.

Oswald thinks his Lord God will protect him, as he once did

against Cadwallon. He's a man swollen on his exploits and pride. He's already made his most fatal error, surety in his victory.

I hold my shield firmly in my hand, but I take the time to consider with which weapon I'm going to start the battle. Many of these men at the front, the seasoned warriors with their battle scared faces and faith in their God, and their king both will flounder in our concealed ditch, the men with whom I'd use a seax. Those who follow them will be less skilled and won't expect to face a savage attack from the beginning of their campaign. I think using my axe will fill them with fear, for it's a lethal weapon when used correctly.

It can snag on men's clothing, skin, hair, necks and rip open the softest of flesh and the hardest dried and treated leather.

Yes, the axe.

I heft it in my hand, ensuring the balance is correct and the edge sharp as I touch it with my gloved hand. Along the shield wall, warriors do the same, ensuring they have what they need in the places they need them. Some men will fight only with one weapon, but others will have a vast array at their command, held in their weapons belt. They'll be the true warriors; the men bred only for death and destruction and with a fierce loyalty to their true king, their ring giver.

I count myself one of these men. My father and Aldfrith taught me to fight with every weapon I could command. Spears, swords, daggers, deadly seaxes, and my shield, an item that looks as though it's to protect me but which can be employed to grind the heads of unprotected warriors to little more than dented cups from which the contents will spill with devastating consequences.

Today men will die at the end of my axe.

I can already taste the tang of their dying breath on my lips.

⌘ CHAPTER 32 ⌘

Penda of the Hwicce
AD641 August 5th

Maserfeld

The holiest king, Oswald, first of his name, brother to a dead king, son of another dead king, stands before me, his white blade flashing in the bright sunlight that suddenly floods from its place high above my head.

His cloak is white, his helm almost, and his hair, long and blond, hangs around his elaborate helm.

I could almost laugh at him, but I know the risks involved in scorning an enemy before a battle has begun.

I'm his polar opposite, a thing of blackness and night, infused with the very things he detests and strives to eradicate.

What right does he have to condemn me for my thoughts and beliefs? What makes him believe he's a better man than I?

I suppose it's the same things that make me believe the same, only I know I offer more than he ever can. I'm a fairer man, as skilled in warcraft as he is, but I offer something he's incapable of understanding because of his religious fervour.

I offer choice and freedom to the warriors who stand with me, for me and by my side. I care little what men think will happen to them after their death. I know my place in Valhalla is assured.

What other men believe is a matter for their hearts and heads, not their king, and certainly not a king from another kingdom.

Oswald is presumptuous and thinks too much of himself, buoyed by the stories his priests and bishops shovel into his ears. He listens and notes everything they say, twisting it to his ends. I believe that if they told him he could fly, he'd attempt to do so, his faith blinding him to the reality of what's tangible and doable and not a mere whim.

Yet, I'm the one who's cast into the darkest light. I know what his priests say of me. I know how they try to scare good followers of the Old Gods to their new ones. How they try to offer comfort by amalgamating the familiar and comfort of the Old Gods to the new one. I curse those who listen to them, but I also understand. For some, the idea of heaven, as opposed to a Valhalla, is appealing. The belief that you can make your own choices and that the great Spinners don't choose them for you is a beguiling thought.

A ridiculous one, but I understand it all the same.

Yet today, I'll endeavour to reveal the uselessness of his new God. Woden walks within me, and we'll spill blood and turn the battlefield mauve in our worship of him. Then, Woden's beasts will come and feast on the proceeds of that battle, taking men to Valhalla if they've died well and leaving behind those who no longer worship him.

Even my banner flaps blackly in the anon-existent breeze, stained with the blood of so many men that it can no longer hold its red tone. It's a message of my intent, a signal to Woden to come and join the fray.

His monsters and warriors will smell the iron of blood and know what it means. A great slaughter is coming, and they'll not want to miss it.

Oswald stands silently, his whiteness against his sea of warriors a stark contrast, just as the lack of all sound highlights the differences between his force and mine.

I've taken the time to consider that we're simply the opposite sides of the same coin, one cast in lightness and the other in the heat of the forge, where the flames lick and drip along the edges of the heavy metal, disfiguring as they go but with the use of enough rough sand, revealing the shinier image, the clearer view.

I don't think it can be a true comparison. Oswald is a coin in his own right. He was forged not in the heat of his hell but rather in the light of his heaven and weaker for all that. He's not been exposed to the true hell of the fire, its stifling heat, its liquid embrace.

I was forged by Woden's blacksmith, in Woden's very image, and I spread his heat and his fire wherever I go.

I growl. I'm so ready to kill the bastard.

But I must wait. I can't start the attack because if I do, my men will have to cross our ditches, and then our temporary retreat accomplished yesterday will have been for nothing. I need not have slaughtered Oswald's scouts who spied our deceit if that happens. I could have let them live to tell Oswald of my plans and not offered them as a blood sacrifice to Woden, as a bargain for my success and a promise of more blood to come.

Instead, I look toward Oswald, hoping the fire of my eyes will burn him. I want him to look my way so we can size each other up one more time. I want him to see my intent to kill him here.

Oswald will not see the sunrise tomorrow. His death must be the outcome of this laboriously staged ruse. No matter what.

I bang my shield and sword together, adding to the cacophony of noise. My men follow my example, the thump of wood and metal against one another adding to the roars of rage that emanate from their mouths.

Against the silence of Oswald and his warriors, our actions are even more striking, more deadly. Yet, he doesn't turn my way. I know he's dismissing me as something lesser than him because of my beliefs. He thinks his God is so great that those who don't follow him are weaker by their lack. I know the opposite to be true, and yet still, I must wait for him to make the first move.

I signal to the men behind me. They run to my spear throwers, telling them to offer a faint threat to Oswald's force, to throw a few spears into the no-man's land that divides us. But not too many. We might yet require all the spears, especially when his warriors begin to desert their king when he lies dead or dying. When Oswald is surrounded not by his followers but by his blood, surging from many injuries and turning him even whiter. It will match his sword and his reputation, bleached, blank, devoid of all life apart from that which he steals from his inner beliefs and masks in the crazed words of his priests and monks.

The spears land with wet thuds into the damp ground. Oswald and his men watch them without reacting.

I think they're waiting for us to attack. Only we can't. Not yet.

Will Oswald mistake our hesitation for fear? It would be good if he did. Just another psychological blow for his warriors who'll meet my mine, men hardened to this task and ready to kill as many as they must to ensure our victory.

They have no fear of taking the breath from other men, of severing their limbs or t necks from the rest of their bodies.

Just as my father and Aldfrith taught my brother and me, I've trained the majority of these men myself, ensuring they know the rules of a battlefield as well as the rules of single combat. There are, of course, few rules, but strength, speed, and guile must be utilised. The way a warrior uses his body is a sure way of knowing where the next strike will fall, and my warriors, all of them, have learnt to do just this.

Even now, as we holler obscenities at the Northumbrians, I can tell those who are standing and coolly waiting for the order to attack and those for whom our taunts are having an effect. If Oswald doesn't give his command to attack soon, some of his men will break his shield wall and rush forward. That will hobble his attack before it's even begun and before our hidden ditch has had any effect.

Should it happen, my spear throwers have orders to aim at the men, ensure that they die before they give away our ruse.

Yet, the impatience of our enemy is starting to infect me as well. I want Oswald to attack, and soon.

I glare as though my thoughts can influence his, but his gaze is fixed before him, on my brother. I wish Eowa had chosen not to fight in the front line of the shield wall. I know he wishes to redeem himself in the eyes of his warriors and mine, but if Oswald hates me, he detests Eowa for his duplicitous ways. Oswald must hunger for his blood, for his white blade to cut through the skin of a man who played him for nearly a decade.

I understand his hatred, and I know a moment of profound fear for my brother.

"Herebrod?"

"My Lord?" he says. His voice is muffled behind his helm, a gift from myself for his services to me, and which I must now call upon once more.

"Protect my brother for me," I ask, and I hear, even behind his helm, the sharp inhale of his breath. He would do anything for me, anything at all, but he doesn't respect my brother and never has, even now. Herebrod doesn't even offer an argument but steps smartly from his place beside me, taking with him a few of his chosen warriors. He leaves just as many behind to guard me. I feel the ripple of the shield wall as it reforms around the gap his departure has left.

The knowledge that Herebrod will protect my brother calms my fears. I once more concentrate on Oswald without his scrutiny of my brother concerning me more than it should.

When will the bastard attack?

Only then he does. As one, his shield wall begins their advance, hesitantly at first, those who've allowed their rage to temper their icy attitude the first to step forward, to encourage the less eager beside them or behind them.

A shield wall is only as strong as its supporting parts. It must move as one, or it'll disintegrate and become nothing more than a collection of small battles taking place amongst a bigger one.

Some men won't want to move as fear will finally have infiltrated their religious fervour and turned their bowels to water and their stomachs to little more than mush. But as one, they must come forward or risk being known as a coward, a man not worthy of fighting in his lord's shield wall.

This is it. My rage has dampened. My purpose is before me. This is why I've trained all my life, every morning, every night, with a sword in one hand, an axe in another, and a shield strapped down my back.

This is what my father foresaw for me before he died.

This is what he foretold for me when he gifted me Gunghir. He knew who I'd become. He knew I was more than other men.

I growl with delight. This is battle, and I delight in it.

Oswald's men walk forward slowly, each step giving them added resolve. Each step is coming a little more quickly than the one before.

The lay of the land looks flat. It's deceitful, just as I am. Just when the men decide the time to run has come because we're standing still, not moving or even twitching other than to beat our weapons against our shield and to shout angrily, they run up the slight rise in the land, and some amongst them must realise the peril they're in, but it's too late.

I watch coolly as the first warrior steps into the concealed ditch. It's no huge thing, just enough to make it difficult for any who wanted to attack the encampment to accomplish that end without having to unbalance by raising a foot. It's deadly all the same.

Instead of continuing their attack across the stretch of unclaimed land that lies between our two forces, men stumble, and then they tumble. Some cry out in shock and warning, others in horror as their feet or their hands encounter the sticky remains of Oswald's scouts, the men sacrificed to Woden yesterday and now guarding us instead of them.

I watch, and I savour the moment. This won't give me the victory, but it's enjoyable to see the speed with which the seeds of fear begin to infiltrate Oswald's warriors. They thought themselves touched by their God. They thought themselves almost as immortal as my Gods.

"Wait," I shout, the command echoing down the line. My warriors are growing impatient. They can see the disintegration of Oswald's shield wall being accomplished almost without their input. If there's one thing that warriors prepared for battle hate, it's to be denied that battle.

"Wait," I bellow again as a stray spear flies overhead. I wish I knew who'd wasted the spear on men who're already dying. I'd kill the damn fool.

I see the spark of Oswald's white. I know that somehow his warriors have prevented him from tumbling into our ditch, that his clothing will still be the purest white and not steeped in the blood of his warriors. But although Oswald might not have fallen prey to my trap, I estimate that as many as a hundred and fifty men are floundering as their comrades do all they can to step over them or avoid them. Only it's impossible.

The men are laden with their weapons of war, their swords heavy, and their shields even more so.

Already, I see the staring eyes of men who'll never see again, of warriors who've died in the stampede. They might have had a sword in their hand when they died, but they didn't die to beautify their God's name or in honour of Woden.

I wonder where they'll go after death, for surely no God would want them in their afterlife.

Oswald attempts to rearrange his shield wall, but even he must know that the death of his first line of warriors has been accomplished. They're gone, or nearly so, and as the men before me stumble and try to reform, I give the command to attack. It reverberates through my shield wall with the grumble of a summer storm filling the sky with its angry roar. I laugh, high and loud. I don't care if it's the last battle I ever fight in. If Oswald manages to overturn my advantages by some chance, this will be a battle that men sing about, just as they do the men of the kingdom of the Gododdin from my father's time.

As one, the shield wall moves forward at a brisk trot. The ditch has worked its damage, and now it's the time of shields and swords, axes and seaxes. If that doesn't prove to be enough, my allies, Cynddylan and Clydog, will enter the fray, coming to reinforce my side against Oswald and drive home our overwhelming victory.

I've much in reserve, and I understand that none of Oswald's reinforcements has arrived. I'm not sure if I believe that. I think they might be hiding somewhere, just as mine are, but I also have men hoarded against a sudden reverse in my fortunes. For now, it little matters.

My sword and axe, seax and shield have bloody work to do, and so my force finally meets Oswald's reconstituted shield wall. I feel the thud of near enough two thousand men meeting each other as a swirl of wind ruffles my hair, where it shows beneath my helm.

It's an excellent portent, the greatest honour of which I could ever ask.

Woden is come to watch and observe, lend his support, where and if he can.

I laugh and laugh, the sound rumbling from my chest and erupting from my mouth as though through a geezer, spurting high and higher into the clear blue sky and covering everyone in its frenzy. This is battle.

This is death.

And I'll deliver it freely.

✣CHAPTER 33✣

King Oswald of Northumbria AD641
August 5th The Battle of Maserfeld✣

I realise the error of my judgment immediately, but too intent on my prayers the day before, I've failed to account for my missing scouts. I simply assumed that they'd deserted in the face of the coming battle, too scared to face Penda, the warrior sheathed in black. I even prayed to forgive them for their cowardice. I should have been praying for the hideous deaths they must have endured from Penda, the living embodiment of his God, Woden.

I should have known better.

Penda is a warrior with more tactics and tricks to deploy than any man I've ever encountered. Penda deserves his reputation, but he's gained it by utilising strategies I've never encountered before. I almost think he was toying with me at Barrow Hill, assessing my strengths and weaknesses before making his move. Only the happy incidence of Eowa's commander's movements weakened his ability to win there before bringing into play whatever else he had planned. I imagine there was more than just hiding some of his men in the ancient barrow and letting them erupt forth as though dead men returned from whatever hell they'd been inhabiting at his fingertips.

When they emerged from within its enclosure, I knew I

was dealing with someone otherworldly, preternatural. But this. This I didn't expect.

I'm only glad that I pulled back from the front rank of the shield wall, too intent on lining myself up opposite Eowa to stand and watch the howling men who were my enemy. If I'd stayed where I was, I'd be dead as well or crushed against the remains of men who used to be my warriors, my friends and my allies.

I should have realised it was unlikely that five scouts would disappear in the same day.

I allowed the belief in my God to guide my steps and failed to account for more malevolent forces.

Now I must attempt to repair the damage.

Much of the first rank of my shield wall are floundering in Penda's ditch or already dead. Those who stand behind have been ordered to raise their shields before them, not in front of the dead men. But I already know that in the panic that's occurred, some of them will have been skewered with the spears of Penda's warriors. There's little I can do now but promise to pray for them when the battle is won, and I've taken my vengeance against Penda.

I feel, rather than see, the shield wall reforming itself, the lines of men quickly recovering from their shock, to slide their shields into new positions.

I had a thousand men, I imagine I stand with a hundred or a hundred and fifty less now, but still, I have more than Penda. Once the shield wall has correctly reformed, and I'm stood in the second row of men, almost opposite Eowa, and able to direct the men in the brief lull before Penda's men attack, I order the two sides of my shield wall to encircle Penda. Penda's shield wall is too short, mine far longer, and as at Barrow Hill, it'll allow me to wrap around them. Then, we can attack from the rear as well as the front.

Too soon and before I can be assured that everything is as it should be, I feel the force of my enemy against the man in front of me.

I've fought many battles, some more skirmishes than full-blown attacks, but the weight of Penda and Eowa's men against mine feels monumental. It's as though a Northumbrian winter storm has suddenly blown into the great curving bay near Bamburgh, sending sea spray and foam high into the air to batter the sandy dunes that my force represents.

In attacking as they do, the Mercians risk leaving some behind above the high tide mark, or rather, alone against the shield wall.

"Resist," I bellow, the cry taken up by men all around me. So far, we've been silent in our attack, content to let the sight of so vast an army speak of our wrath, nothing more. Now we need to put words to our resolve and intent.

"For our Lord God," I add, my voice somehow rising above the mass of everyone else so that it rings out clear, a genuine cry from the heavens above.

I could almost stop and listen to its effect, but there's no time. The scrum at the front of the shield wall has started, and men shove against others, trying to use their strength, and sometimes their lack of it, to gain an advantage over their enemy.

The man in front of me, Eafa, grunts at the effort he makes as I press my shoulder against his, offering my support, planting my feet wide and ensuring I have the requisite balance to support him.

My shield rises above his head, its whiteness reflecting the bright sunlight and making my eyes swim when I inadvertently glance at it. Eafa has a seax in his hand, a favourite weapon for the front of the shield wall, and beneath my legs, I feel the reaching glance of a spear from the warrior behind me. He's trying to hobble the Mercian that Eafa faces.

Behind us, I can hear the shouts of other warriors as they realise the horror that faced the front line of the shield wall, for the leading edge has made it past the ditch, filled with the dead and dying. We're now able to fight on the slight incline that restricted my view and made me believe that the Mercians were defending their encampment

But another noise also penetrates my hearing as I labour in

the shield wall. For a moment, I worry that Penda has encircled my force, but soon I hear the rough voice of other men from the north and understand that Oswiu has arrived and just in time to take his place in the shield wall.

I don't know how many men he commands, but I hope it's enough to tip the balance firmly in my favour.

A significant surge of support bolsters the fledgling shield wall. I watch men weave their way to the front of the wall. These are Oswiu's men. They're as warlike as Penda and just as used to attacking the British as they are other Saxons.

With Oswiu's arrival, all of Penda's efforts to hamper the attack have been undone. I imagine that the men who died in the ditch have been replaced, and more besides. These men are true warriors, just as Penda and Eowa are.

"The King," that cry resounds loudly as my brother tries to locate me. I realise that my bannerman must have fallen, and whisper harshly to the man behind me to locate it and find it. He nods but grabs my shield, a move I'm not expecting.

"Take it, My Lord King," he says, shoving his shield at me. Only then do I understand his intent. He means to use my shield as a banner, to attract Oswiu to my side.

We've fought a few battles together, but Oswiu's reputation is that of a warrior's.

In the space of time it takes for Oswiu's warriors to find me, the man before me, Eafa, is gutted by a slashing movement from a wicked looking axe. I see it grab the man's shield and force it down. Although I try and jab with my sword, I can't prevent the inevitable. I'm forced to step into the breach caused by his death, aware as I do so that Eafa chokes on his blood, clawing at his throat, his eyes wide with fear and pain both.

I offer a brief prayer to our Lord, hoping the boy's suffering will be short, but I need to move quickly, stopper the breach and prevent it from growing wider. I wish I could see how the edges of my shield wall fare and if they're making any progress against the Mercians. But the battle is too tight, and I dare not disturb the careful layering of the reformed shield wall.

"Lord Oswald," a voice behind me. I turn and grin, for Oswiu has sent his greatest asset to reinforce me. Willyn was built only for wielding his war axe and shield. His baulk is great enough to take the place of three men. Now he stands behind me. His shield is almost as broad as two regular shields and protects my head, blocking even the sunlight that's burning down my back and causing sweat to pool down my face.

It's going to be a warm, windless day. Not a good day for a battle to the death.

"Willyn," I respond through gritted teeth.

"Let me," he urges, and all I hear is a thud. The pressure against my shield subsides as the warrior who was testing me falls to his knees and dies there and then, his helm doing more to damage than protect because of the force of the blow.

It gives me the time I need, and Willyn and I manage to shuffle places. If I stand behind him, no man will come anywhere near me.

His following words fill me with greater hope yet.

"Our scouts have spotted King Onna. He should make it before the day is done."

More reinforcements. This is just what I need. It appears as though the timing of the battle has been precipitous.

Willyn speaks levelly, unaware of the weight he has against his shield. He could almost be standing, talking in my hall, for all the attention he's paying to the man trying to kill him.

"Oswiu is directing from his horse. The shield wall has overlapped with the Mercian one. The battle will be swift and quick now that we're here."

I allow Willyn the arrogance in his voice because there's no denying that his arrival has turned the flow of the battle back in my favour. I'll have to pay my brother a considerable price for his assistance, but then, I have gold and jewels to spare, taken from the dead Mercians at Barrow Hill and buried deep within the ground, in a place of which only I know the whereabouts. It wouldn't do if other men knew where I left my greatest treasures. But when I return home, I'll swell my coffers, and my men will be eager to ride to war with me again.

"That's excellent news," I huff, stooping to catch my breath, trying not to trample on the lifeless body of Eafa. War is a messy business, and blood already scours my boots and legs.

"Here," Willyn speaks, and he hands me the torn pieces of my banner. They're streaked with blood and gore, but they still flash white. In turn, I hand them back to the man behind me, the man with the spear. He looks at me blankly and then understands my intent and wraps the tattered piece of cloth around the end of his spear before raising it high above his head.

My warriors need to know that I live. The warrior also hands me my shield. I try and raise it above Willyn's head, but it's no good. He's a full two heads taller than I am, and I can't reach him. For that reason, he has a massive helm, graced with splintered pieces of metal, affixed by my blacksmith, a man who knows beauty in creating deadly pieces of warcraft.

As my banner is once more lofted high in the air, I hear my brother's voice shouting my name, assuring the men that I yet live. I also hear an angry eruption from amongst the Mercian line. The Mercians know I live now as well, and they direct the focus of their attack against me, making it felt in the renewed vigour of the men in the shield wall before Willyn

They're furious now, determined to get to me. I imagine that Penda has promised riches to the man who kills me, or at least who takes me to him so that he can kill me. But that won't be happening today because Oswiu has seen the danger and has sent yet more of his men to assist me in holding the frontline steady.

With them at my back, I begin to feel the first stirrings of success. I can taste it in the air, as, tiny movement by tiny movement, we manage to force the Mercian force to take backwards steps, not forward ones.

This is all that's needed. A break in the line, caused by a man stumbling or by another meeting their death unexpectedly, and we'll be able to rush our way through into the Mercian shield wall, turning the attack upon itself.

I've been silent for too long, but this slight advantage has my voice swelling to encourage my men to ever greater and greater efforts.

And finally, as sweat beads my face and my shoulders burn with the effort of trying to hold my shield, I manage to take an entire step forward as the Mercian line visibly falters.

This is it.

I can hear frantic voices from behind their shields, trying to force men to greater action. But they must be spent, overwhelmed by my reinforcements and with nothing more to give, first Willyn and then I step directly into the Mercian shield wall.

The men to either side of me quickly turn to meet my attack, raising their shields to their sides, their half-hidden faces masking any fear they might feel at having me suddenly enter their private world. All of them make ready to defend the two halves of the shield wall, cleaved through by Willyn, with more of Oswiu's warriors following him inside. I think they'll all stand aside, wait for us to renew the attack, but then one warrior alone steps forward to meet my attack, and I instantly recognise Eowa.

His shield and axe show signs of the ferocity of the attack, but it's his face, sheeted in sweat, that shows both his exhaustion and determination to counter my advantage.

Out of the corner of my eye, I notice that Penda's men aren't without thought. They've turned their shields to defend themselves from our attack, and those near the rear have formed a new shield wall, ensuring their shields clasp tightly to each other, the colours overlapping so that it's an eternal rainbow of bloody reds and mauves.

My men's success, achieved with such a roar of appreciation, isn't complete yet.

"Oswald," Eowa's voice is rich and robust. Clearly, clothing himself in his brother's reputation has imbibed him with a ferocity I've not seen before. And a serenity. He swings his axe with expertise. I watch it swirl through the air as though we're stood on a training ground and not in the middle of a bloody battle. The shapes he makes with his blade are hypnotising. He's not without great skill. I've not realised before.

"Eowa," I acknowledge, aware that neither of us has honoured the other with their correct title.

Eowa's intent is clear. He wishes to fight, man to man, to once and for all settle the dispute that's arisen between us. I can't help it. I laugh at his determination. I have no desire to fight him. Instead, Willyn steps between us while more of my men form a shield wall within a shield wall to stop the Mercians from interfering.

I see not so much shock as disappointment in Eowa's eyes at my movements. For a moment, I reconsider. In resigning my position to Willyn, I've belittled myself even in the eyes of a Mercian of the Old Gods. What would my own Christians think of me?

Yet I dismiss the notion. I'm not here to die but to live and win a great victory.

Willyn grins in delight as Eowa finally tears his gaze from mine to look at him. Eowa shows no fear at the man's size he must battle, which surprises me again.

I've always thought there was no substance to Eowa and marvelled at how he managed to gain a kingdom at Penda's expense. If this isn't a new character trait for Eowa, I might have finally glimpsed what makes him a worthy king.

I think that if I could see his face, he'd be rolling his eyes in derision at Willyn's size and baulk. But Willyn is an agile warrior, despite his size, and soon Eowa will learn to fear him. I look forward to it.

Willyn makes the first move, using his vast shield to try and swipe the axe from Eowa's hand. Willyn moves too slowly, and Eowa is long gone from his standing position before the shield can connect. Eowa turns the movement to his advantage, casting a swipe down Willyn's exposed underarm.

The axe thuds on impact, but Willyn doesn't notice it. Instead, he moves his shield aside quickly, a contrast to his first move, and uses his sword to try and tear through the thick leather byrnie that Eowa wears.

Eowa's warriors are offering him encouragement where they can while still being aware that only a hands span away, the Northumbrian force is waiting to break through their shield wall. So many men now fill the gap that if the Mercians manage to mirror our actions, at least forty or fifty men will be unable to retreat.

It's not the wisest of moves, but as Eowa and Willyn size each other's strengths and weaknesses, there's little I can do to recall the men to their senses.

My attention is quickly snatched back to the personal battle within the larger one. Eowa moves closer and closer to Willyn, using his lighter steps to work his way inside Willyn's reach once more. I can't see how this is anything other than a bad decision by Eowa, but as he manages to slice his axe cleanly across Willyn's exposed neck, I reconsider. He exactly knows what he's doing, using Willyn's strength against him.

Riled and fearful for Willyn, I ensure my blade is steady in my hands, and as Eowa steps backwards, I raise my blade to slice down his back.

He laughs at the impact, for all that a spray of bright red darkens his byrnie. I can't help feeling that he's directing the fight, not me.

Willyn grunts at me annoyed that I'm interfering. Eowa's blow, while it impacted his neck, hasn't made more than a superficial cut. Eowa was simply trying to entice me to fight, not kill Willyn, which angers me. I need to think more before I act. Now Eowa is unleashing the force of his blows against me. I stumble as I force my shield in place.

I've made a move that I'd chastise any other man for, and I'm going to be made to pay for it.

Eowa moves quickly, his axe striking my shield. He tries to force it down and away from my body, regardless of Willyn at his back. Eowa shows no fear and simply grunts with his exertions, intent only on wounding me.

I hold steady, my shield in hand and my sword ready for when it's needed. I might do as well to let him exhaust himself before I do anything else. Eowa's blows on my shield intensify, moving almost so fast that I can't believe it's only one man who attacks. Left, right, centre, high, low, the blows are thundering on my shield, and despite my strength and my reputation, I feel my arm begin to tremble from the barrage it's taking.

Eowa plans to wear me down, and not vice versa.

Willyn attempts to bedevil Eowa with blows down his back. Eowa takes no steps to defend himself, his focus exclusively on me. I'm unsurprised when one of his warriors forces their way through the shield wall and wedges themselves between the two men. Eowa takes no notice, but it leaves me facing his cold rage alone. I feel a bite of trepidation.

I'm not used to Eowa in his warrior guise. To me, he's always been a man intent only on reconciliation, on making himself amenable to me. Eowa, in his battle garb, is a man worthy of killing me if his Gods serve him and mine fails to protect me.

I focus my thoughts. No matter what I face, warrior or Old God made flesh, I'm Oswald Whiteblade. I can kill any who encounter me. I earned that reputation in battles and skirmishes far dirtier than this. I just need to roll back the passage of years and become that man once more.

My blade flashes starkly, menacingly, as I take a quick swipe at Eowa. As he hammers against my shield, I need to distract him so his ferocity is interrupted and I can move my sword more freely.

My initial blow falters. Although his eyes never leave my face, he must read my movement before I make it. As his shield meets my sword, the force of the blow upsets his grip on his shield. But he never falters. His clouts on my shield continue to rain down. Against an axe, my shield will only last so long. The axe has the power to bite into the wood, wrench the carefully worked pieces of wood free from each other and leave me holding nothing more than the strap to the rear.

I keep my eye on the battle between Willyn and the Mercian. As little as I like to admit it, it may be that I only stand a chance when Eowa is facing two attackers, not one.

Against the Mercian, Willyn can use his weight and speed to

better effect. Eowa's man is well trained, yet he lacks the foresight with which Eowa battles. He can't read the battle dance as well as his king, and it won't be long until Willyn is free to assist me once more.

I decide to bide my time, swinging my sword with less force but with enough inconsistency that Eowa never quite knows where I'll strike next. Not that it unduly worries him. Eowa continues to attack with ferociousness. If Willyn takes too long, Eowa will gain an advantage against me.

I hear the wood crack and know that my shield's time is limited. It'll break sooner rather than later. I could do one of two things. I can hold on and wait for the damn thing to disintegrate, or I can discard it now and use both of my hands to attack with my sword and my axe, or my seax. Both weapons would sing in my hands.

I catch a glimpse of Willyn out of the corner of my eye, and he meets my gaze, his expression tortured. He can see what's happening to me but can get no nearer.

I step away from Eowa, narrowly avoiding his lunge and use the slight respite to cast aside my shield. It falls to the ground between us, its metal rim complete but little else to show that it used to be a shield.

Eowa's stance shows nothing at my change of tactic. Neither does he seem surprised when I begin to stalk him, with my seax firmly nestled in my hand.

Eowa's clothing is stained with men's blood. He laughs so that I notice he might have lost a front tooth at some point in the shield wall. He steps out of my reach then, and in the interests of fairness, he throws his own complete shield to the floor. This might just be his downfall.

I'm skilled with both my right and left hand and can injure at will with either. I doubt he possesses the same skill. He already holds his axe, but from behind his back, he pulls out another axe, this one bigger and far heavier than the one with which he's been hounding me. It's worthy of Willyn's frame, not his.

It scythes through the air in his hand as though it weighs no more than a newborn babe. The whistle of air reaches my ears even over the noise of battle and dying men. I swallow against my fear.

Eowa cackles then, and the noise makes the hairs on the back of my neck, even matted as they are with sweat, rise. I've never encountered Eowa in this guise. Never.

The axe misses me, but I don't think it was supposed to connect, just distract and that it's done. I feel a blow on my left arm, the one that holds my seax. The impact hits just below the elbow and forces my hand to open so that my dagger drops, landing so that it's embedded in the ground, my hand flailing to catch it and failing utterly.

While I struggle to comprehend what's happened, Eowa's larger axe bites close to my head, missing by no more than a finger's width as my eyes follow my seax down, forcing my head down as well.

The sudden flood of panic at my unintentional survival adds weight to my arms. I can barely lift them, the effort draining all my remaining stamina.

I could die here, like this, bereft of any means to defend myself because of my terror at the man Eowa has become.

My heart thumps in my chest, the movement almost painful as it knocks against my byrnie. The sound of the battle rushes back into my consciousness, alerting me to the peril my men are facing while I batter away against an unstoppable Eowa.

The space open to us has radically shrunk. My warriors are spending most of their time trying to escape back to our side of the shield wall. Willyn continues to labour against Eowa's warrior. Although he should have won long ago, his body is riddled with bloody cuts, the worst of which must be under his helm as blood drips down his face, mixing with his sweat and pooling in his light-coloured beard, rimming him in a pink to rival the early sunrise.

I can hear the joyous cries of previously beleaguered Mercian warriors, and the small space is shifting ever forward. For some reason, the Mercians are starting to gain, and it can only be because Penda has received reinforcements as well as I have.

I need to escape from my captivity, and the only way to do that, and do it well, so that the Mercians fail to take full advantage of their increased number, is by killing Eowa. If I could cut him down, it would turn the tide of a battle I was hoping was already more than half won.

I will strength back into my limbs, flexing my fingers around my sword, offering a prayer to my Lord God that he'll allow me to be victorious here. And then I lunge, sidestepping the sweep of the huge axe and dancing out of its reach. I need to move lightly, quickly, but my body is slow and cumbersome. I wish I didn't wear a byrnie and helm. I feel as though the weight of their constituent metals forces my head to wobble under the strain of keeping it upright. My eyes lose focus and then cloud.

Still, Eowa laughs. I don't think he's even paused for breath, and his axe swings from side to side, getting ever closer to my body and head. It sounds as though angel wings have come to shepherd me to my death. It's that which finally returns my senses to me.

I'm not dying here and not at Eowa's hands.

I know what I need to do.

Eowa is getting nearer and nearer to me, his axe itching to take a bite from my neck. My options are limited with only my sword in my hand, my shield long since discarded, and my seax embedded in the thirsty ground. My sword is no match for such a heavy weapon. I need to neutralise it before it impacts my body.

There's no other choice.

Just as I'm considering allowing the axe to strike me so that I reel Eowa in by tipping the heavy weight against him, the axe crashes to the floor, missing my body by a mere hand span, and inspiration flashes.

Eowa wasn't expecting the axe to embed itself in the ground. As he labours to free it from the grasping turf, I rush forward, stepping on the axe, and using it to launch myself into the air, my sword already held high and climbing higher all the time.

It's a reckless move, a stupid manoeuvre, but as I leap upwards, I take the time to meet Eowa's eyes. He's stunned into inaction. At that moment, my sword arm completes its arch. I use all of my strength to drive the sword downwards, ever downwards, forcing it past Eowa's helm, which cleaves in two under the force of the attack, and further down, down until I know the blade has sliced through the top of his head and buried deep inside the top of his body, coming clean through his chin, in a splatter of bloody matter.

I land heavily on the ground, the air whooshing from my lungs, my breath stunted and painful.

Eowa still stands, his eyes disbelieving as blood dribbles from his chin. But he can't even open his mouth to utter a cry of pain. I've pinned his mouth together with my sword, and it's only a matter of time until his body catches up with what's happened to him. Dispassionately I watch him, waiting for that moment so I can retrieve my sword and celebrate his death.

I'm astounded that I've been able to execute the action without falling myself, but I have, and now my one-time ally is dead. The power of Penda's warrior force will be broken.

I wait, impatiently, for him to succumb to the inevitable but instead, he raises his hand above his head and possessed by something otherworldly, something God-like, his hand snakes around the bloodied blade of my once white sword, its sharpened sides digging into Eowa's hand. Blood gushes freely down them to join the stream that already rushes to exit his body as he begins to wrench it free. The grey of the gore inside his head contrasts sharply with the pulsing maroon of his fatal wound.

Fascinated, I can do nothing but watch the dying man remove my blade from inside him, the effort surely too much for him, but somehow he manages it. His eyes are focused, his desire to kill me paramount as he stumbles forward, looking to turn my white blade against me. Amazed by what I'm seeing, I almost fail to move out of the way of the one mighty swing he directs towards me. It nicks my lower chin, the shock of the blood spurting free spurring me to action.

Only, finally, his wounds catch up with Eowa. Although he

tries to raise my sword against me once more, his arms flail and his knees collapse beneath him. First the right, and then the left. Still, Eowa clasps my sword, taking it with him wherever he goes after his death, his intentions clear. He's using my blade for his traditions, subverting its Christian birth to his ends. With his last breath, he mutters one thing.

"Bastard," and then he dies. Willyn, noticing my success, bellows the news far and wide, my warriors heeding his voice and cheering, whereas angry howls reach me from the Mercian force.

Their king is dead.

Now I just have bloody Penda with whom to contend.

⌘ CHAPTER 34 ⌘

Penda of the Hwicce
AD641 August 5th

Maserfeld

I'm equally streaked with sweat and the iron of dead men. My concealed face itches, as does down my protected back. When I'm finally able to remove my byrnie after the battle, I know I'll have welts where my clothing has rubbed my body raw.

It's a small price to pay for the success we're having. There was a moment of concern when Oswald received reinforcement. The additional men were felt not so much in an increase in the pressure against the shield wall but rather as a swell in the noise of their warriors. Our enemy had been mostly quiet, but Oswiu, for I've caught a glimpse of him directing the battle from the back of his horse, knows the importance of giving voice to fear and pride, grief and joy, no matter that it might not be Oswald's way of waging war.

I also felt the slight pinch in the shield wall and knew that Oswiu's warriors had allowed the Northumbrians to punch through a small part of the shield wall. But I was also content. I knew Eowa to be close to the gaping wound with Herebrod, and they'd ensure the shield wall restored. And then came the most significant moment of all, when I felt Clydog's warriors joining our shield wall from the south. I knew the battle was open for our success once more.

Yet as I raise my axe, shield and head above the melee around me, it's not triumph that I hear. The noise increases the hair on the back of my neck and more, turns my stomach to lead, my arms to stone, my weapons useless at the end of fingers that can no longer feel anything. By some means, a considerable swathe opens up between my line of fighting men and the very thing I've been hoping not to see.

Speechless and thankful that around me, Herebrod's men have taken up the spirit of the attack that I'm suddenly standing outside of, protected by some invisible force that prevents any blows from reaching my unguarded body, I watch with disbelief as Oswald faces my brother in battle. Oswald's desperation is clear to see in his stance and actions. My brother's sure axe strokes make it seem impossible that he'll not slice Oswald's head from his neck. However, in the very next moment, the unthinkable has happened. I'm stunned to see my brother, still standing, but with Oswald's white blade embedded in his head. There's no chance that he'll ever recover from such a wound, although he's not yet fallen.

My howl of anguish joins that of other men, closer men, who see the death as I do, through the strange corridor that's enabled my clear view while men war to either side. I want to rush against Oswald, take his life from him there and then. But just as abruptly as I'm able to see the end of their battle, when Eowa, his body acting out his dying wishes of trying to strike Oswald, by moving towards him, the two split groups of men merge once more. It's impossible to make my way to Eowa's cooling body.

As understanding spreads through the Mercian men, our attack stalls and momentarily, the Northumbrians take more precious steps against us. My already leaden stomach fills with the bile of loss. I can't let this happen. I can't let my brother's death be in vain. I can't even process that my brother is dead, but no man can survive such a wound. Never.

I'm conscious that whatever protected me from the attack is

gone. Herebrod's warrior desperately calls my name, demanding my attention and assistance. Without thought, my actions conditioned by long years of practice and by battles I've fought in before this day, I go to his aid, fearful once more.

The Northumbrians are howling for the death of my men, the death of myself. I can feel their strength against the shield wall. Eowa's death might have undone all the good that having Clydog attack so late in the battle and so suddenly from the south has produced.

Eowa's sudden death, so unexpected and so damn unneeded, has unsettled my men and his own. Who do they fight for now? His son or his son's uncle; myself? I'd hoped that I'd not have to address this situation anytime soon, and certainly not in the heat of a battle that's already been long and bloody and which must continue. We must prevent the Northumbrians from gaining a victory and taking all of Eowa's kingdom under their protection.

"Penda," A hoarse shriek cuts into my musing. I raise my axe, effectively preventing the reaching blade aiming for my chin from gaining any purchase.

I need to concentrate to think beyond my brother's death and its implications for the future. All that matters is now—and winning. And killing that bastard, Oswald.

"Cynddylan should be here by now," I growl when I've regained my position in the shield wall and added my strength to its length. I've had my banner raised behind me. My father's line hasn't ended. Men need to know that my brother is dead but that I still live.

"Yes, he should," is all the response I get from Herebrod's warrior, Caedgard. Caedgard briefly turns toward me, having braced himself firmly in position against the raving Northumbrian he faces.

"Fight on for him," Caedgard urges me. There's grief in his words and also resolve. He might not have liked my brother because Herebrod never did, but Caedgard respected him as a warrior, perhaps more so in the last week than ever before.

Caedgard's words echo inside my helm, making sense as they percolate ever deeper and deeper to whatever it is that makes a man who he is.

I could stumble here, allow Oswald to have his victory, but I can't. Caedgard is correct when he says I must fight for Eowa. Eowa fought for me. I need to accomplish my side of that bargain.

It would be easier if Cynddylan were here, but that shouldn't stop me from thinking and using my men as I should.

"Take my place," I utter to Eni, the nearest warrior behind me. He slides into position with no trace of interest on his face. He's been fighting in the front line almost since the beginning of the battle. He's since had some respite, fighting in the third line, and springs to follow my orders with an elasticity I admire and envy.

Caedgard is right in his urgings, but to direct this battle, I need to understand its nuances and the upsurges of men that crash against the shield. I need to decipher the intentions of Oswiu and Oswald.

As I force myself to the back of my men, I curse softly. The flat landscape makes it hard to determine how the two forces fare. I simply can't get a good enough perspective. I understand why Oswiu has stayed on his horse. He'll have a much better understanding.

Annoyed and acting through my training so my grief can no longer guide my actions, I shout for a horse, amazed when one appears before me. Not at all surprised to discover it's Gunghir.

The damn beast must have escaped from his enclosure.

I could be angry with him for risking his life, but instead, I slap him hard, for I need to show my displeasure in some small way. I slide onto his back, forgetting I hold weapons in my hand that nick my exposed wrists and his back as I do so. His black cloak glows faintly mauve, but the wounds aren't deep. I take them as a small sacrifice to Woden from his spear made flesh. I need Woden to stalk my warriors, endow them with his strength and artifice.

When the battle slides into view before me from Gunghir's

back, I can understand Gunghir's fear. It seems that we're destined to lose, even with Clydog's support.

The once straight shield wall is shaped like the back leg of a hound. To the north, where Caedgard stands, the men are in danger of collapse, pushed almost back to the wooden stakes of our encampment. To the south, the Mercians have forced the Northumbrians back into the ditch where so many of their warriors initially floundered.

But it's the area in the centre, where Eowa lost his battle with Oswald, that stands wide open and enticing to the Northumbrians. It's there that Herebrod commands. The number of men has lessened, going to either side to join their brothers in blood, perhaps when Oswald initially punctured the shield wall. Although the shield walls have reformed, the warriors haven't resumed their places.

I swallow quickly. I need to send men there, but to do so, I'll need to divert either my warriors or Clydog's. Ideally, Cynddylan's men could enter the battle there, but despite my assurances to Eowa, Cynddylan would rather see us falter. He'd rather have Oswald as his overking than Eowa or me. It's a crushing loss and one I must quickly counter.

Opposite, I see Oswiu sizing up the battle, taking the same notes in his head as I do. It's as though two thousand men don't separate us, as we both reach for and brandish our weapons, each to the other. If all the men melted away, as though snow in the thaw, Oswiu and I would be upon each other with no more thought. I'd avenge my brother's death. Only it's not Oswiu whose death I crave, but Oswald's. I wish to kill the man who slaughtered my brother.

But I'm not to be given a chance, as behind Oswiu, perhaps unknown to him, I can see more men rushing to the battle line. A blood-red banner is held aloft. King Onna has decided to undertake his overlord's command and come to take part in the battle.

"Fuck," I shout, the word conveying all my anger, grief, and need to make this battle the one I was told about so long ago, the one that informed me I'd achieve greatness. That prophesied the loss of a brother to gain a kingdom.

I've never liked to think of those words. Not once in the intervening years have I given them any credence, convinced that Eowa would never die before me, for his ways were always more suited to debate and compromise than war. But now that Eowa is gone, I can think of those words, know that in my brother's death, I don't risk mine. That was made clear to me. Only on my brother's death would I achieve all that I could.

Cold certainty fills me. I beckon to one of the youths standing to the rear of the attack. This is his first battle, and fear holds him back. That's fine. I need someone like him to carry a message for me.

"Boy, come here." He looks fearful. I try to grin through my frozen mask of pain, tears, sweat and dust, but it must make me look more frightful, for he jerks away as though struck.

"King Penda," he says, trying to stand tall and clutch the weapons he's too scared to use. I admire him that he can even open his mouth to speak with me.

"I'm missing an ally. Go, rush straight to King Cynddylan and tell him these words for me. Tell no one but King Cynddylan."

"My Lord King?" the boy says again. I wish there were the time to soothe his fears and tell him that tomorrow the world would be as it should be. But time is something of which I'm woefully short. I neither miss the fear on his face at standing before his king and his king's spiteful horse nor decry it. It's fitting he should be scared, but he'll never gain the reputation of being a Mercian warrior unless he overcomes those fears.

"Go to King Cynddylan. He'll be close by with his warriors, but he's not yet decided whether to come to my aid or not, so tell him this. King Eowa is dead, slain by King Oswald; King Clydog has come but so too have Lord Oswiu and King Onna. Tell him to come, and come now, and tell him I'll gift him the greatest treasure a lord has ever received if he heeds my words and rushes here, now, and attacks from the north."

The boy swallows thickly and moves his mouth as he tries to remember the words I'm telling him.

"Go quickly." I slide from Gunghir and hand him up to my restless mount.

"My Lord King?" he all but squeaks, fearful of Gunghir, but I slap Gunghir's arse, a sign he's to run as fast and as straight as he can.

Cynddylan will heed the message, or he won't, but sending Gunghir shows my intent, my desire to be his equal. If Cynddylan doesn't come, at least Gunghir will survive the battle, although I pity any who must tend to his needs in my place, should I fall here.

Without the view from Gunghir's back, I move through the men, trusting my memory and instinct, forcing men to move, pushing those who still hover at the back to join the fray. I know where I'm going.

Oswald fights beneath his banner, even though blood has long since stained it and turned it into a mucky piece of stringy cloth that I'd not want to fight beneath.

He's back on the Northumbrian side of the shield wall, once more trying to force his way through to the Mercians and kill more men. Only this time, he has adequate protection to hold the cleft he wants to drive through the shield wall.

My plan is simple. Let Oswald come. Then he'll face me, as he did my brother. I'll not be falling before his blade. Rather, I intend to claim that blade as my mine and give it into my brother's care in Valhalla. I'll send him Oswald along with it, to be tormented by my brother for eternity. Eowa will deny him the entry to the heaven he craves so much.

If Cynddylan refuses to come to my assistance, I must still ensure that Oswald dies.

As I stride through the messy battle line, I note men stand a little taller, take the time to think about their next movement, work their weapons free from their belts. They appreciate that something monumental will happen soon and that I'll be the one to enact it.

I should have done this from the beginning, made a bold move to ensure my victory. Perhaps then Eowa would still live.

In position and sidestepping the place where my brother died, although his body has been moved as befits his status as a king, I ensure my banner is nowhere near me, but rather to the right. Any moment now, I'm hoping Cynddylan will launch his attack. I'm not above tricking the Northumbrians once more.

At my silent command, the shield wall before me, primed and filled with warriors that I've personally trained, allow the Northumbrians to know a taste of success once more. The shield wall doesn't disintegrate but instead relaxes in places.

The Northumbrians quickly realise what's happening. Men shout to each other, demanding warriors stand at their back, ready to make the most of the collapse of the shield wall. I ready myself. I know that Oswald battles opposite my warriors, who still hold the shield wall firmly in place, allowing either side to weaken just enough to give them hope.

Once the Northumbrians have gained the initiative, they'll rush from the shield wall, allowing a huge gap to open up. And it's into that gap that I'll step, my axe ready in one hand, my sword in the other. I'll use my axe as a shield and have the advantage of the clawed weapon.

A stir of breath at my side and Herebrod is suddenly there. I look at him in surprise, but he just grunts. We've always fought side by side, and at this moment, he's not prepared to let me fight alone, even if it is to avenge my brother, a man he little liked and who I sent him to protect, albeit it was impossible.

I acknowledge Herebrod's arrival by hitting the front of his shield with my axe. He growls and turns to face the shield wall. I want him to know my brother's death wasn't his responsibility. I asked too much of him. He did what he could. Undoubtedly, stories will be told of his legendary attempt to save my brother.

Any moment now, the Northumbrians will flood through the gap, and I'll face Oswald. Or at least that's what I hope.

When our foe-men break through the Mercian line, I look for Oswald, hoping to catch sight of his white beard and cloak, but there are too many men. All of them are vibrant and reinvigorated by their success. They manifest as flashes of blood and flesh, hair and teeth, angry men with deadly weapons, ready to strike down my Mercians.

"Attack," rips from my mouth, the cry resounding up and down the line. As one, my warriors move forward, the shield wall holds to the north and the south, but here, at the centre, it's collapsed on itself, and the Northumbrians think they're winning. They could be correct, but I think not.

One on one, at last, my warriors, frustrated by the long time the shield wall has held in place, attack their enemy with asperity. They're keen to kill men they can see instead of those who hide behind shields.

I wait, trying to find Oswald, but amongst the surge of men, I must miss him and instead face another warrior, with dirty grey hair showing beneath his helm and a wicked-looking scar on his chin. He's known many battles. His legs are long and planted in such a way that he can move freely and quickly. He rushes toward me, keen to land the first strike.

His movements catch me by surprise. Before I can even move my axe, I feel the thud of an impact on my shoulder. I glance at it in surprise and then move aside. My response is too laboured and too long in coming. As I turn, he already has another blow lined up to hammer across my exposed chest.

I feel the air huff from my mouth. I struggle to regain it, almost going down on one knee in surprise at the ease of his success. Herebrod is engaged in his own battle. I need to stand quickly and regain the upper hand.

Not that I'm alone in my floundering. Oswiu has anticipated my move and flooded the line with fresher men, probably King Onna's men, who've not been stood in the shield wall as the morning passes into the afternoon.

I curse as I fight, my axe finally coming into play and opening a wound on my enemy's exposed right arm. It's the summer, and he's decided that he doesn't need to protect himself as well as I do. It gives me ample places to rain down my blows and draw blood, the axe ripping skin without great effort.

My foe-man howls in pain and rage, and I wonder what sort

of fool fights without protecting himself as well as he can. Despite the heat and the discomfort, I'd never lay aside my helm and byrnie. They're just as effective as I am at dodging blows that would otherwise kill me.

In a short space of time, the man is on his knees before me, his arms useless at his sides. His death is only a moment away. Worried that my warriors aren't having the same success, I quickly slice across the man's throat and look for the next enemy. As I search, I note how my warriors are doing, and the truth of the situation worries me.

This is not going as well as it should be. Not at all.

This has been in the planning for too many years for it all to go wrong now, at the last possible moment. I can hope that Cynddylan finally arrives. If not, this could all go Oswald's way, and that'll really piss me off.

Two men rush to attack me next, one to the left and one to the right. They intend to confuse me and make me try and defend myself from both sides. But that never works. Instead, I allow the man to the left of me, the smaller man, to attack where he will so that I can concentrate all my attention on the warrior to my right. It's not so much his stance that alerts me to his greater fighting skills, but the weapons he carries. The seax is jagged. Its pommel curled around his hand so that he can't drop it and his axe is almost as huge as my brother's. If he can lift the thing, he'll be able to knock me out with a blow to my head.

Either of the weapons could end my fight today, but I wish to avoid the seax most. I know of men who fight with such things, and they leave terrible gaping wounds that never heal.

From behind, I feel a blow slice down my back, but it doesn't cleave through the protective material, rather ripping open the top layer of the thick padded leather. More concerning, it must also nick the harness that holds my weapons in place, and the weight lurches uncomfortably to the side. I hope it hasn't cut all the way through the thin ribbons of leather that holds them in place.

Annoyed, I turn quickly and slice my axe menacingly in front of him. The man doesn't even falter but aims his blade at my chest instead. I lash out at his arm, pleased when my axe hits home and his hand inadvertently opens, dropping his blade to the ground. As he bends to pick it up, his desire to have the weapon back in his hand overrides his battle sense, and I flick my axe across his neck. Blood flows freely across my hand. I allow a slight grin to cross my face.

With the warrior twitching in his death throes, I turn once more to the older warrior. He's been watching me and failing to take advantage of my distraction—the fool. By now, I should be bleeding from numerous wounds or twitching in my death throes.

This could be an easy fight, but I'm aware that my men are faltering, that the Northumbrians, with their reinforcements from Oswiu and Onna, are too many for us to overcome.

Where's bloody Cynddylan?

I fight through my frustration and anger, dancing close to my enemy and then out of reach again, toying with him and bartering with Woden. I promise Woden a giant ox as an offering, or more men, like last night, or even a temple raised in his honour. But more, I offer him the blood from the man I fight if he'll only bring Cynddylan to my aid.

I kill the man easily. No sound reaches my ears to let me know that Cynddylan has arrived. In fact, worse than that, the Northumbrians are gaining once more.

Herebrod has killed his man and is looking for the next victim while I worry about Cynddylan's non-appearance. Herebrod has the right of it, though, as he skips into another Northumbrian. It's sheer determination and stamina that will win this attack if Cynddylan doesn't arrive.

I follow his example, my ears still straining for the arrival of new blood but intent on doing all I can to turn the tide of the battle without him.

I hunt for Oswald in the mass of Northumbrian men, but there are still too many of them. So I stalk him, hunting through the men, looking for that flash of white.

Men groan and grunt around me. It's a hot day. All of us are thirsty and salty, drained by the sun and the length of the battle, but none of us will give in until the battle has become our victory to claim.

I'm no king as I fight, but a warrior, just like my men. I use all the skills I've been taught by my father, by Aldfrith and by every battle in which I've ever engaged. Warriors are made in the shield wall, not on the training ground. My father taught me that, and I've extended the same to my warriors, ensuring each year they had the opportunity to fight for their lord, to learn that their life hangs only in their hands.

I'm sheeted in sweat, and the smells of the battlefield have changed from that of a pleasant summer's day to the shit, puke and piss that prevail in the camp latrine. I'd wrinkle my nose, but it would encourage the sweat to dribble into my mouth, and I'm thirsty enough as it is.

Men fall before me. I barely see them, only noting that they're dead at my hand. I've cleaved a path through to the still-standing shield wall, but I've not encountered Oswald.

Men shuffle and shove. I wish I could be everywhere at once as I feel the tide of the battle settling against me.

This can't be my failure, not here.

I refuse to accept it.

The voice of Oswiu reaches me above all other noise, encouraging his men, telling them that their victory is almost assured. Such words spur the men on, as does the sudden resurgence of Oswald's banner just before me.

I swipe my arm across the bloody lower half of my face, wishing I could clear my eyes as well, but I can only do that if I remove my helm, and I'm not about to do that. Sweat drips painfully into my eye. As I blink it away, I finally catch the gleam of Oswald's helm and byrnie. But I'm too late, another faces him, Herebrod, and he has just as much desire to kill Oswald as I do. I'm not about to deny him the opportunity.

Only then, as Herebrod raises his sword to attack Oswald, do I hear the noise I've been bartering with Woden for, the sound of British voices flooding into the back of the shield wall. Cynddylan has finally, and almost when it's too late, arrived.

This is it. My men and I can take advantage of this expected but long-delayed addition to our force, or we'll lose the battle.

Cynddylan's voice can be heard urging his men onwards. I join my voice to his, faintly hearing Clydog's as well from the south.

My force is finally assembled, missing only my dead brother. I have the men to hammer home a victory, and if Herebrod manages to kill Oswald, it'll be a complete victory.

I want to stand and watch Herebrod at work, but instead, I order those of my men who are sensible to my words to reform the shield wall, to cut off the Northumbrians from any possibility of retreat, Oswald amongst them.

The men fiercely fight as they understand our intent, taking chances they shouldn't and making it easier for those who protect my back to kill them. In the Northumbrian line, the men, realizing the danger their king is in, are trying to fight their way through the shield wall to get him. But their movements are uncoordinated. Oswiu is as yet unaware of the imminent danger his brother faces. The terror and fear of the Northumbrians is making them careless, and better, easier to kill.

This is what I needed.

The battle has turned.

My sword slashes and crashes against shields and exposed flesh. My axe bites deep into hastily jabbed wooden defences. With each step, I can taste the victory of which I've been so fearful.

When I hear the voices of the British warriors mingling with my warriors, I know two things.

The Northumbrian men caught on this side of the shield wall are dead, and Oswald is isolated.

The berserker laugh takes me, my movements becoming conditioned not by my thoughts but by Woden, who guides each slash and crack of my weapons on the men who die before me.

He's the god of war and death and my ancestor as well. He's possessed my body to bring his trail of destruction to walk the dark green grass on this fateful day, and I mind not one bit.

✢CHAPTER 35✢

Oswald of Northumbria
AD641 August 5th✢

I ache from shoulder to ankle, each part of my body worn away by the extreme actions of the day.

I can only hazard a guess at how many men have fallen beneath my sword, although none a greater prize than that perfidious Eowa.

The battle has flowed to the advantage of the Mercians and then the Northumbrians with a frequency that's been difficult to grasp until now. Now that Penda has received the support of all of his followers, the battle is firmly to his advantage, and I've made a terrible mistake.

I search around me, desperate to find any of my warriors, but I've been cut off, and the only way to reach my men is to cleave a path through the throng of Mercians who're battling my men with the savagery that comes before a great victory.

I recognise it because I've laboured in enough victories to have experienced it. But it couldn't be worse for my current position. I'm alone, cut off, and no one will be able to come to my rescue.

My only hope is to fight as though I'm a Mercian, attempt to convince these men that I'm not their enemy and somehow slide back through the shield wall.

Only, well, I wear my white byrnie, streaked now with the rust of dead men. It'll only take one of the Mercians to realise who I truly am, and they'll all attack me.

For the first time since I began my kingship, dread almost stops my heart from beating. Men labour around me, but it's the sight of two men close by who stop me dead.

Herebrod and Penda.

Both men have a valid blood claim upon me. Both would be keen to win the honour of my death. All this I see in the blink of an eye, and then Herebrod fells his final opponent and turns his gaze my way. He knows me without even having to rake his eyes along my body. His face, that which is visible, shows his obvious pleasure at finding me alone and him in a position to bring about my death.

I no longer have my sword. Eowa stole it from me in his death throes. I was torn away from his body before I could reclaim it. I've been warring with the blade of another dead man, but it's an inferior weapon to mine. The weight is wrong, too heavy near the haft and too blunt near the blade. I think it's more of a hindrance than not having a blade, yet I feel reassured with it in my hand. Or I have until now.

Herebrod utters a triumphant cry and takes his time stepping toward me. Somehow, he's between the shield wall and me. I'm more alone than I've ever been before. I could risk running away, back into the midst of the Mercian force, but I wouldn't survive more than a few more moments.

No, I need to take my chances with Herebrod, but I already see my death in his eyes, and that spurs me to anger.

I'm a king, a warrior, Oswald Whiteblade. I shouldn't die on the blade of a man who hates me simply for not rescuing my brother from Cadwallon's blades. It little matters that Cadwallon was his ally, not mine.

Herebrod swings his weapons. In one hand, an axe, in the other a long sweeping blade from which a strip of cloth from the man he's just killed hangs. I swallow thickly. The reminder of the damage the weapon can cause is unwelcome as I try to find my bearings and decide how I can live through the attack.

While I weigh up my options, the glare of another man penetrates my thoughts. Penda. He's breathing heavily but victorious. I think he might push Herebrod aside, but I've forgotten how long they've been friends and allies. He simply makes a sweeping motion my way, indicating that Herebrod has the honour of the fight, but his stance is cautionary. He'll not interfere unless Herebrod should fail.

I need to kill not one man but two, and then I need to fight my way back through a horde of Mercian men.

I doubt I'll live through this, but it makes me no less determined in my efforts to do so.

Herebrod wastes no time, keen to show his strength as he moves his sword through an elaborate set of jabbing and slashing movements. It's as though he plays out his battle with me before reaching me. I watch him, as does Penda. Herebrod surprises me by attacking with his axe, not his sword. I raise my borrowed sword to try and counter his movement.

The pain of my sword encountering his axe sends a shiver of agony burning up my arm. I grunt loudly, only for him to follow the attack with a slash of his sword that shouldn't hit me, the space between us being too small, but it seems the entire length of the blade is sharper than ice. It nicks my exposed chin.

The sight of my blood pleases Herebrod. He wrenches his axe away from my sword and begins to slash against me once more.

His movements are frenzied, while mine are laboured and sluggish. I can only assume that I have another injury that I'm unaware of, and it's draining my ability to think and counter his strokes. Every time I move as though to deflect a blow, it's already hit its target. It's no longer just my chin that bleeds.

Herebrod means to kill me. I no longer have the strength to counter his attack. Each time I raise my sword or my seax, he sees my intent and flicks it effortlessly to one side or another. I can't get a single blow to land on his body while he swirls around me, almost faster than my eyes can move. Every blow strikes a fresh wound, and my head is starting to eddy, and I can no longer focus.

Through my pain and my fuzziness, I hear a howl of outrage. I perceive that Oswiu finally sees my peril and cannot do anything about it. This is it. I can either have a good death, thinking of my Heaven, or I can accept it begrudgingly and fight for every last breath.

My thoughts outrage me and stir me to action, but it seems I'm too weak, too riddled with Mercian cuts and bruises. As I try to raise my sword to connect a blow against Herebrod finally, I manage nothing but to knock myself off balance, tumbling to the ground without so much as a hand out to stop myself.

The breath whooshes from my mouth, but first, I feel Herebrod's blade slice effortlessly into my back. What remains of my blood must warm his hand, and then I can no longer snatch a breath, my body devoid of all sustenance.

Yet, I hear one final thing as I feel my blood leaking away, draining me, and leaving me nothing but a jumble of bones and war equipment.

I hear Herebrod's gentle voice against my ear.

"For your brother, My Lord King," and I almost think that the last seven years have all been for nought.

If my brother had lived, I might just have done.

But not now.

⌘ CHAPTER 36 ⌘

Penda, King of Mercia
AD641 August 5th

Maserfeld

Blood covers my face, sweat mingling with it and making the stinging cuts that cover my cheeks burn.

Overhead the sun is warm, too warm. No hint of a breeze stirs the ground. I'm exhausted, and also more. I'm victorious.

Before me, I watch the dead body of King Oswald of Northumbria with contempt. It seems that Oswald Whiteblade is, after all, and despite all the evidence to the contrary, a man made of bone and blood, his breath scoured from his body.

I only wish I'd killed him, but that honour goes to Herebrod. He pants beside me, exuberant because he's dragged the dead body to me and offered me his axe. He knows how I wish to treat the body of the man who tried to take everything from me.

Only in my moment of glory comes pain, intense pain.

My brother and I have been rivals for too many years. Our love for each other has so often mingled with hatred that it's become the same thing. I've always wanted what he had, and tried not to think of the prophecy, told me so long ago that I'd only gain what I wanted with his death.

I know Eowa dreamt of my death and hoped that this battle would give him the reputation of a warrior, and it has, but this. Not this.

Eowa told me he'd stand by the victor, and I should have been the victor. Only I wasn't. Not until today.

Now I'm the victor, but at what cost? Was it truly worth the death of my brother? I've laboured to keep him alive, to undo the harm of that long ago prophesy, but I've failed, and all has come full circle as my father cautioned me it would.

Before me are two bodies; my brother's and my enemy's. My brother died fighting for our alliance, something he resented and craved all simultaneously.

Sadness, rage and an intense feeling of loss mingle with exuberance. I don't know how to feel. I don't know what to say.

My men are joyful. We've snatched victory from the jaws of defeat, from Oswiu's careful manoeuvring.

My allies are congratulating each other. Cynddylan and Clydog, just as blood-streaked as I am, and with the death of their warriors on their hands, rummage through the bodies of our dead enemy. They take every item of worth they come across, appeasing their losses through the gain of silver and iron.

Our enemy is gone, long fled, as soon as they realised their king was dead. Not even Lord Oswiu could entice the men to continue their struggle.

I'm the King of Mercia now, and more, King of Northumbria if I take my fight through my new lands and further on. But I'd give anything to have my brother at my side. Anything.

Numb with my bleeding injuries and frozen heart, I stumble to my knees before my brother.

Eowa's eyes stare at me, so much like my son's, that I turn away in shock. I might not have plunged the weapons into his inert body that killed him, but it was my hand that brought us to this moment, made it possible.

My hand touches his eyes, my blood smearing his face as I force them closed. I gasp in surprise as I feel a gust of air on my gloved hand, mistaking it for my brother's breath, but it's nothing. His chest doesn't rise and fall anymore, and I know he's dead, for all his face is warmed by the sun. If it weren't for the flashes of blood that cover his chest and his legs, the ragged hole through his chin, I'd think he was only sleeping, not dead.

Tears fill my eyes, and I let them fall. I'm a warrior king, but I can grieve for my fallen men and my dead brother. My dead brother. I can't think the words, let alone say them out loud.

My brother.

My eyes cloud in grief, and on that warm ground, my memories swirl and take me back to that first day that I realised my brother was my enemy as well as my ally.

We were children, nothing more, and my father gifted us both with horses, my beloved Gunghir and Eowa's Sleipnir. The moment I laid eyes on Gunghir, I knew I wanted him.

My father, with old Aldfrith, held the reins of the two horses, both sleek in the bright daylight, Gunghir as restless then as he is now. I'd sucked in a tight breath, fear touching my heart. I'd wanted Gunghir. He was mine, but I could tell my brother wanted him too.

My father, a wise man who always knew my intentions before I did, had grinned at me delightfully, seeing the torment in my heart and mind. I wanted that horse, but I'd always been the younger brother. I knew my place. I'd have to wait and see what my brother chose first.

My brother, longer limbed than I, with his first moustache growing above his top lip, had looked between the two horses and then at our father before turning to me quizzically.

I think he wanted to taunt me, but Eowa hadn't done so. He knew me as well, just as well as my father, and at that moment I'd known that I'd never get my wish, that Gunghir, as I'd already named him in my mind, would go to my brother and I'd be left with the other animal.

Gunghir had glared at me, stamping angrily, snapping at my father as though daring me to lay claim to him. I'd opened my mouth to speak, to put forward my prior claim to him, but I'd held my tongue.

My brother had walked around Sleipnir, his hands roaming the horse's head and legs, feeling the strength in him. Sleipnir had tugged on his rein, keen to have his head caressed by my brother. I'd watched it all with held breath, my legs leaden in fear and a half-realised hope.

Gunghir had kicked angrily, my father laughing in delight at his unhappiness. Yet Gunghir had done nothing else because at that moment, Sleipnir had turned his head to look at him, and Gunghir had stilled. I'd appreciated, with that action, that the horses were brothers too, sharing a father, if not a mother. They knew of their family link, somehow.

Gunghir had quieted as though words had been spoken between them. My brother's hands had gone from Sleipnir's back to Gunghir's.

I'd felt as though I couldn't breathe as I'd watched my brother assess the horse I wanted so fiercely I could only keep from crying out by stuffing one of my hands into my mouth. And still, my father laughed.

My father had been a mighty warrior, hardened and toughened by his wars against fellow Saxons and the Britons both. He'd tell me of the early days of our tribe, when his father fought for his family's position and when everyone hated the pretensions of my grandfather and the continual success he had against any enemy he encountered.

My grandfather had made a name for himself, and my father had grown that reputation until he was a great warrior, with a huge band of men, and more, with two sons to follow in his footsteps. Two sons, both as different from each other as possible and both born as natural enemies, one to the other, for only one son could rule in his place on his death.

It had been my father's test, and I'd known it, even then. I was ten years old, and I was being marked for the rest of my life.

Yet, my brother and I loved each other, as no other could, our younger brother yet to make his appearance in the world. We were brothers, even then, and allies or enemies second. My brother had grinned at me, his young face showing me he understood and that he'd known of my desire. It was then that he turned to Sleipnir and surged onto his back. At last, I could run toward Gunghir, embrace his head, endure his nip on my ear and then slither onto his back, sidestepping his aggravated movements at being forced to stand still for so long.

Still, my father had continued to laugh, his good cheer bringing the eyes of others in his household to watch. I'd been aware that his warriors watched this moment as closely as he did. I'd thought I'd had choices when I was young, but that moment had shown me that I was only ever going to be one thing, a warrior of great renown, and forever indebted to my father and my brother, for allowing their son and their brother to have what he wanted.

I should have felt triumph at having my prize. I had felt some small victory, but it had been tinged with remorse.

My brother had given me my victory, just as he had now.

With my eyes still closed, I turn them upwards to feel the heat of the sun on my broken and damaged face, my grief leaking from my eyes and pooling into my mouth and down my neck.

My brother has given me what I've always wanted with his life, but I never wanted it to be like this, denying my father's whispered words for over a decade.

I roar my anger and grief at my God, and slowly others join my voice with their own. First Herebrod, and then my warriors, and as our cry fills the sky, turning the sun to a deep orange with our rage, strength fills my tired and broken limbs.

I stand, my mouth still open, my breath fractious and ragged. Herebrod stands beside me, his axe in his hand and then in mine.

I have more to do here today.

He signals that my brother's body should be moved, and men rush to do his bidding, carefully holding all that remains of the great light that was once my brother. I turn to finish the dirty work of this battle.

Oswald was my enemy, responsible for my brother's death.

I swing the axe high, feeling the strain in my tired muscles and across my back. First, I aim for his lower left leg, severing it with one blow, and then the right leg, the left arm, and the right leg. Blood gushes up to strike me in my savagery, and then I take a moment to pause, to look at his eyes one last time, the open eyes of a man who thought his religion would always keep him safe.

A fucking fool.

And the reason my brother is dead.

I rage at the sky above me, tears mingling with my sweat, my blood, Oswald's blood. Then I swing, a loud cracking noise filling my ears as I sever Oswald's head from his neck.

I'm reminded of the end of Hæðfeld when I held a man's head in my hand and praised Woden for my victory.

Today, I drop the axe on the ground, where it lands with a soft thud, the ground wet from the rain of blood we've just endured, and I reach down, with my gore-soaked hand and pull Oswald's head into my hand by the long hair that's come loose from behind the back of his head.

Oswald wore it in the style of a warrior, for all that he thought himself a Christian king.

With his head level with mine, my arm raised high and steady to keep it in place, I turn to gaze at my warriors, my followers, my allies and those few enemy that I can see in the distance, watching me uneasily, no doubt Oswiu amongst them.

I spit twice, in each of Oswald's eyes, watching with satisfaction as his clear eyes finally cloud with the sight of the dead.

Oswald will be seeing nothing else. Not in this life and not in the next. Wherever he ends up.

Ragged cheers greet my actions. I drop the head to the ground and kick it as far as I can, the dull wet sound of my boot impacting his head, giving me some small satisfaction.

The head rolls away, far across the battlefield, and inspiration strikes me.

"Have his limbs, his head and his torso staked out for the birds to pick clean," I speak roughly to Herebrod. I feel weaker than a newborn babe as my limbs shake and grief threatens to leave me on my knees. The exertion of the day is catching up with me.

"Have them guarded, day and night, until his bones are picked clean and then have them brought to me, wherever I am. The bones of these Christian men have great power for their followers, and I'd deny Oswald that admiration."

Herebrod simply nods once, his eyes light with an appreciation for my decision.

Still, my men cheer, and I turn to them and swallow thickly.

This isn't how I planned my victory, but it is just that, a victory. I must put my grief aside and accept their acclaim.

My brother is dead.

I am King of Mercia. And of Northumbria, if I want it and can take it before Oswiu claims it.

I am the King of Mercia.

I am the king.

ANGLO-SAXON CHRONICLE

(taken from the readily available version on the internet)

A.D. 633. This year King Edwin was slain by Cadwalla and Penda, on Hatfield moor, on the fourteenth of October. He reigned seventeen years. His son Osfrid was also slain with him. After this Cadwalla and Penda went and ravaged all the land of the Northumbrians; which when Paulinus saw, he took Ethelburga, the relict of Edwin, and went by ship to Kent. Eadbald and Honorius received him very honourably, and gave him the bishopric of Rochester, where he continued to his death.

A.D. 634. This year Osric, whom Paulinus baptized, succeeded to the government of Deira. He was the son of Elfric, the uncle of Edwin. And to Bernicia succeeded Eanfrith, son of Ethelfrith. This year also Bishop Birinus first preached baptism to the West-Saxons, under King Cynegils. The said Birinus went thither by the command of Pope Honorius; and he was bishop there to the end of his life. Oswald also this year succeeded to the government of the Northumbrians, and reigned nine winters. The ninth year was assigned to him on account of the heathenism in which those lived who reigned that one year betwixt him and Edwin.

A.D. 635. This year King Cynegils was baptized by Bishop Birinus at Dorchester; and Oswald, king of the Northumbrians, was his sponsor.

A.D. 636. This year King Cwichelm was baptized at Dorchester, and died the same year. Bishop Felix also preached to the East-Angles the belief of Christ.

A.D. 639. This year Birinus baptized King Cuthred at Dorchester, and received him as his son.

A.D. 640. This year died Eadbald, King of Kent, after a reign of twenty-five winters. He had two sons, Ermenred and Erkenbert; and Erkenbert reigned there after his father. He overturned all the idols in the kingdom, and first of English kings appointed a fast before Easter. His daughter was called Ercongota – holy damsel of an illustrious sire! whose mother was Sexburga, the daughter of Anna, king of the East-Angles. Ermenred also begat two sons, who were afterwards martyred by Thunnor.

A.D. 642. This year Oswald, king of the Northumbrians, was slain by Penda, king of the Southumbrians, at Mirfield, on the fifth day of August; and his body was buried at Bardney. His holiness and miracles were afterwards displayed on manifold occasions throughout this island; and his hands remain still uncorrupted at Barnburgh. The same year in which Oswald was slain, Oswy his brother succeeded to the government of the Northumbrians, and reigned two less than thirty years.

CAST OF CHARACTERS

<u>Penda King of the Hwicce</u>
<u>Cynewise</u> his wife
<u>Paeda</u> his young son
<u>Herebrod</u> his warrior (married to a Pictish woman)
<u>Caedgard</u> Herebrod's warrior
<u>Ohthere</u> Penda's blacksmith
<u>Brunfrid</u> Penda's warrior
<u>Aldfrith</u> Penda's father's friend
<u>Æthelfrith</u> Aldfrith's son
<u>Cudberct</u> Penda's warrior
<u>Wulfnoð</u> Penda's warrior
<u>Eoforwine</u> Penda's warrior
<u>Eni</u> Penda's warrior
<u>Coenwahl</u> Penda and Eowa's brother

<u>Eowa King of Mercia</u> (Penda's brother)
<u>Artair</u> Eowa's warrior
<u>Glaeðwine</u> Eowa's commander
<u>Eafa</u> Eowa's warrior

<u>Penda's allies</u>
<u>Cynddylan King of Gwynedd</u> (Welsh kingdom) Cadwallon's successor
<u>Clydog King of Ceredigion</u> (Welsh kingdom)
<u>Petroc Baladrddellt King of Dumnonia</u> (Modern day Cornwall), his father was Clemen
<u>Domnall Brecc King of Dal Riata</u> (Part of western Scotland and Ireland), his father was <u>Eochaid Buide</u>

Oswald King of Northumbria
Æthelwald Oswald's son (from a previous union)
Eohart Oswald's warrior
Brictfrith Oswald's warrior
Baldgar Oswald's commander
Ælfmon Oswald's warrior
Ealdorman Alduini Oswald's ealdorman
Bebba Oswald's horse
Oslac and Oswudu Oswald and Oswiu's brothers
Bishop Aidan of Lindisfarne from the monastery on Iona
Hereric one of Aidan's monks
Oswald's allies
Oswiu of Northumbria, Oswald's brother
Willyn Oswiu's warrior
Cynegils King of the West Saxons (Wessex) (dies in 640)
Cyniburh, Cynegils daughter married to Oswald
Cwichelm Son of Cynegils (dies sometime between 635 and 640)
Cenwahl Son of Cynegils, becomes King of Wessex after Cynegils
Bishop Birinus – from the continent, tasked with converting the West Saxons
Onna, King of the East Angles

Misc who appear in name only
Rædwald of the East Anglians bretwalda (wide-ruler) over Britain before Edwin, and his ally until his death
Æthelfrith of Northumbria (Edwin of Northumbria's brother in law – married to his sister Acha and father of Eanfrith of Bernicia and Oswald of Bernicia) dies at Battle of the River Idle in 616 and Edwin becomes King)
Edwin of Northumbria (killed at Hæðfeld). Oswald's uncle and enemy, his mother's brother.
Osric (Edwin's uncle) ruled Deira briefly after the Battle of Hæðfeld.

Misc
Gunghir Penda's horse

Sleipnir Eowa's horse

HISTORICAL NOTES

This period in time is often known as the Golden Age of Northumbria. The study of Saxon England is, generally, done in swathes, gradually moving to the south – first Northumbria, then Mercia, then Wessex, and eventually, from Wessex back north to encompass all of 'England' under one ruler. It allows historians to 'box' events and attempt to make sense of a seemingly endless string of unrelated events. Yet there were always more kingdoms than just the one that receives the most historical focus, and as such, writing this novel has allowed me to highlight the other kingdoms at that time, to show that, as with everything in the past, nothing happened in a dry vacuum. External factors were just as important as internal ones. Saxon England was surrounded by the British, the Picts, the men of Dal Riata, Gododdin, Strathclyde (Alt Clut) and Dumnonia (Cornwall).

Many books have been written about the Golden Age of Northumbria – and its kings, Edwin and Oswald, fewer about Mercia and Penda in particular because of the lack of insular Mercian sources. It's been postulated by historians that a Mercian Chronicle did exist and that it was destroyed by the marauding Vikings a few centuries later. Whether this is true or not, to discover information about Mercia, it's necessary to look elsewhere, in the Anglo-Saxon Chronicle, in the Welsh Annals, the words of Bede and stray references in the Irish Chronicles. This lack perhaps masks just how powerful Mercia was during this period. This story attempts to reassert its claim to greatness, a task started by Bede when he wrote of Northumbria and not Mercia in his Ecclesiastical History of the English People. The bias started within less than a hundred years of events depicted in this novel.

That said, the battle of Shifnal and Barrow Hill are entirely fictional but also quite possible. The site of Maserfeld, so far west, almost in modern-day Wales itself, speaks volumes either of Oswald's ability and arrogance that he'd march far across Mercia in pursuit of his enemy or of a ruse, orchestrated by Penda and his allies to effectively cut off his options to retreat. But something must have preceded Maserfeld (Oswestry) to make Oswald believe he could triumph, whichever option is correct – as such, Barrow Hill is his first attempt at victory and is a success, of sorts. D P Kirby has offered the view that Oswald was acting to assist his sworn man, i.e. Eowa. I've taken this possibility and expanded on it in many ways that aren't provable either way. In so doing, I've been able to continue the uneasy dynamic between Eowa and his younger brother, Penda. It's been argued that Eowa died fighting against Penda. This is just as likely as my interpretation.

As to any alliance between Eowa and Oswald, in Hæðfeld I formed one between Edwin and Eowa, where Eowa is hedging his bets to ensure he gets the best out of any battle. It's Penda's name that has resounded through the ages, and I think the relationship between the brothers might have been strained because it was Penda who accomplished so much more than his brother. This might have been because of Eowa's untimely death and not because of Penda's reputation, but it's impossible to tell from such a distance in time. So I've allowed the brothers to fight and argue, as all brothers do, and allowed jealousy to guide many of Eowa's steps, and yet I believe that their family loyalty to each other would have won out in the end.

Oswald is known as Oswald Whiteblade, and he was raised in exile in Dal Riata. Rumour has it that he might have been the blueprint for Aragorn. I've not read Lord of the Rings for over twenty-five years, so I can't offer an opinion either way, and I've subverted many of the aspects of his life that have been lauded. I've done this because I think it's about time Saxon England is studied with a broader understanding of what Christianisation meant for the minority of kings who inflicted it on their kingdoms and the wider population. Bede's Ecclesiastical History of the English people is just that, and we need to interpret events with that in mind. When writing a work of fiction, it's possible to play around with the main characters and see just what might have happened instead of what we're told happened.

The Gododdin descended from the Votadini tribe and held land to the north of Northumbria and Edinburgh. A famous poem, Y Gododdin, tells of their warriors in a famous battle, possibly in around AD600. There are conflicting reports about when the kingdom ceased to exist. Some cite the fact that Oswiu seems to have personal control there during his reign as indicative of its subversion into Northumbria. I need to do more research, but I don't think the answer is quite as simple as this implies.

Rheged, Strathclyde (Alt Clut) and Dal Riata are kingdoms that have faded from memory through the mists of time. Even their borders are hazy.

Yes, there is a hazy and unsubstantiated nod to the Staffordshire Horde. Why wouldn't I?

(On a personal note – I was raised in the Midlands, but now enjoy the more hospitable climate of coastal Northern England and have done for many long years. If I happen to visit my childhood home in the summer, the lack of wind is immediately noticeable. For my children, living in the north for almost all their lives, the change is virtually intolerable. I thought I should write it into the story to highlight the genuine climate differences between Northumbria and Mercia, the coastal ravaged Northumbria and land-locked Mercia. The growing season is always slightly delayed the further north you travel in the British Isles.)

MEET THE AUTHOR

I'm an author of fantasy (viking age/dragon themed) and historical fiction (Early English, Vikings and the British Isles as a whole before the Norman Conquest, as well as three 20th century mysteries), born in the old Mercian kingdom at some point since AD1066. I like to write. You've been warned!

Find me at mjporterauthor.com and @coloursofunison on twitter. I have a newsletter, which can be joined via my website.

Books by M J Porter (in chronological order, not publishing order)

Early English Historical Fiction

Gods and Kings Series (seventh century Britain)
Pagan Warrior
Pagan King
Warrior King

The Eagle of Mercia Chronicles (from Boldwood Books)
Son of Mercia (
Wolf of Mercia

The Ninth Century
The Last King (audio book now available)
The Last Warrior (audio book coming soon)
The Last Horse
The Last Enemy

The Last Sword
The Last Shield

<u>The Tenth Century</u>
The Lady of Mercia's Daughter
A Conspiracy of Kings (the sequel to The Lady of Mercia's Daughter)
Kingmaker
The King's Daughter

<u>Chronicles of the English (tenth century Britain)</u>
Brunanburh
Of Kings and Half-Kings
The Second English King

<u>The Mercian Brexit (can be read as a prequel to The First Queen of England)</u>

<u>The First Queen of England (The story of Lady Elfrida) (tenth century England)</u>
The First Queen of England Part 2
The First Queen of England Part 3

<u>The King's Mother (The continuing story of Lady Elfrida)</u>
The Queen Dowager
Once A Queen

<u>The Earls of Mercia</u>
The Earl of Mercia's Father
The Danish King's Enemy
Swein: The Danish King (side story)
Northman Part 1
Northman Part 2
Cnut: The Conqueror (full length side story)
Wulfstan: An Anglo-Saxon Thegn (side story)
The King's Earl
The Earl of Mercia
The English Earl

The Earl's King
Viking King
The English King

Lady Estrid (a novel of eleventh century Denmark)

Fantasy

<u>The Dragon of Unison</u>
Hidden Dragon
Dragon Gone
Dragon Alone
Dragon Ally
Dragon Lost
Dragon Bond

<u>As JE Porter</u>
The Innkeeper

20th Century Mysteries

The Custard Corpses – a delicious 1940s mystery (audiobook now available)

The Automobile Assassinations (sequel to The Custard Corpses)

Cragside – a 1930s murder mystery

Printed in Great Britain
by Amazon